who
i
kissed

janet gurtler

sourcebooks
fire

Published by Sourcebooks Fire, an imprint of Sourcebooks, Inc.

P.O. Box 4410, Naperville, Illinois 60567-4410

(630) 961-3900

Fax: (630) 961-2168

teenfire.sourcebooks.com

Library of Congress Cataloging-in-Publication data is on file with the publisher.

Printed and bound in Canada.

WC 10 9 8 7 6 5 4 3 2 1

For Max.

And for everyone with a severe food allergy.

Be safe.

before

chapter one

A loud thunk from the viewing area startles me as I flip-flop from the locker room to the pool deck. I glance over to see a boy dropping to the ground from the high top of the bleachers. He's staring at me, not even trying to hide it by sneaking in little peeks the way most boys do when they see girls in bathing suits. As he straightens himself up, he grins, and it's mischievous and cute but makes me *très* uncomfortable. Boys didn't show off or stare at me at my old school or swim club. They had no reason to. But things are different now, and this guy doesn't take his eyes off me.

The attention makes me feel naked, and not because the only thing covering my body is a thin layer of high-performance microfiber. His gaze is intense, as if my thoughts are appearing over my head in cartoon-like bubbles. I certainly hope they aren't, because the thought that he has a nice butt may have recently passed through my mind.

He lifts his hand, but I pretend not to see and tug my suit down over my own butt. Then in one big movement, I kick off my flip flops, throw down my swim bag, pull on my swim cap, and dive into the pool. After a couple of laps, I hear my name when my head comes up on a stroke.

"Sammy!" Zee's calling.

I stop and tread water and pretend the fluttering in my chest is from swimming too hard.

He points to the end of the pool and performs a little dance movement on the deck. "Let's get it started, huh," he sings, like he's doing a karaoke version of the Black Eyed Peas. "Let's get it started in here!"

I grin, swim to the end, grab my water bottle, and take a sip, glancing off to the viewing area. The boy is still watching. I recognize him from my new school, but it's suddenly less important and less irritating. Still, I bite back an urge to make a face at him.

"Okay. Enough fooling around." Zee grins, and my insides perform a dance similar to the one he just did for me poolside. It's weird having him fill in for my private lesson with Coach Clair while she's away for her sister's wedding. He's only a few months older than me. And hot. But since he's the only guy on the Titans faster than me and Clair's assistants are busy she asked him to do it.

I tell myself I only want to impress him because he's great in the water. But even I know it's a lie. He's yummier than a peppermint mocha with whipped cream and chocolate sprinkles.

"Okay. Let's see how you can fly, baby," he calls. "Go for two hundred at eighty-five percent."

After the butterfly set, Zee instructs me to get on the block for a freestyle distance swim. As soon as I'm in position he yells, "Go."

I dive in and streamline through the water, trying to blank out my mind and concentrate on kicking and pulling my arms, but the boy's face pops up as though he's connected to me by some invisible bond. My body drags a little, my concentration thrown off. I struggle to fight off the image and find my zone. Push through. Push. Push. Push.

When my hands touch the end of the pool, Zee is leaning over me with a stopwatch. I stare up, waiting. I've got just over a month before the state meet. And I really want a record in free. Zee understands, the same way I understand his drive in the water. We've got goals and times to beat. It takes hard work.

"Eight seconds off," he says.

Panting, I tug off my cap and throw it at the ledge of the pool. Zee puts out his hand to help pull me out of the water. He lifts me up by the arm like it's nothing.

"Don't look so bummed. You're close. Your kick is strong. And your breathing was good."

"Thanks." Our eyes lock, and I can't help a silly smile. I glance toward the viewing area to hide it. The boy is gone, but my dad is in his place. He catches my eye and points at his watch. It's exactly 5:00. When he picks me up, he's rarely late.

Zee follows my glance. "Sergeant is here, right on time."

I roll my shoulder back and lift my arm to cover my smile. The nickname is fitting, but admitting it would make me kind of a traitor.

"Make sure you stretch out. I'd do it with you, but your dad would probably jump over the railing to take me down." Zee grins and then turns and walks away. "Work on those streamlines, Miss Waxman," he calls loud enough for my dad to hear. As he strides to the coach's poolside locker, the muscles ripple across his bare back. No wonder girls go crazy for him.

Ignoring my dad's impatience, I pull my hamstrings out and extend my arms in the air to stretch out my sides. After a few more stretches, I slip on my flip flops and watch Zee take something from the locker, close the door, and walk back to me. I'm stowing my goggles and swim cap in my bag as he approaches.

"Hold out your hand," he says in a deep, rich voice that sounds like he gargles daily with sexy juice. I glance at my dad, but he's frowning at his BlackBerry. Zee reaches over and tucks a lumpy package into my hand. A bag of Jelly Bellys. My heart does a tiny dance of happiness. Yesterday he'd been messing with me that I had no vices, and I'd admitted an addiction to the jelly beans.

"You deserve them," Zee says. His cheeks redden a little under his dark skin. "You're the most disciplined girl I know."

"Thanks." My belly continues to twirl with delight. From the corner of my eye, I see my dad look up from his phone, frowning.

"Kind of cute too. Like a pit bull puppy." His teasing words make my insides feel like I've been sipping a cup of hot chocolate. Warm and comforted.

"Aww. You just compared me to a vicious dog."

I don't tell him I'll be analyzing the significance of the jelly beans and his comment for the next week. I don't tell him it's pretty much the first present I've ever gotten from a boy. Well, except in tenth grade, when a new boy at school who hadn't heard the gay rumors about me asked me out.

When I was thirteen, a girl on another swim team told everyone she saw me making out with a girl in the locker room. She was mad because I'd beaten her record for Washington state. It was a total lie, but it got around my school and the boys embellished it. Since I was shy around boys, everyone chose to believe it.

But this boy hadn't heard yet. His name was Pete, and he was sweet and had dark skin, beautiful teeth, and a flirty personality. I'd tripped over him at my locker on his first day. He asked me on a date and brought me a flower. I still have it pressed into a book.

He'd been so cool, handling my scowling dad with a couple of well-played jokes. He took me for pizza and laser tag. While we were hiding out in the dark from vicious five-year-olds on laser-shooting missions, he'd kissed me.

The next day, when kids from school heard we went out, he'd been teased relentlessly for trying to convert the lesbian. He never asked me out again. Soon after that he started hanging out with Emma Henderson. Far as I knew, they were still together.

"Pit bulls are actually really cute and sweet when bred properly." Zee's eyes stay on me as I grab my swim bag, slide the jelly beans into a pouch, and sling the bag over my shoulder.

"I'm not even going to try to figure out if you actually thought that was a compliment," I say.

"It was." His grin disarms me, and I look down at the chipping blue polish on my toes.

"So. Clair's back tomorrow," he adds.

I glance up, but before I can mask any tell-tale signs of disappointment, his eyes twinkle knowingly. My insides melt faster than a Slurpee on a sunny day.

"Aw. You will miss our private time together," he says with the ease of someone who medaled in teasing.

I hide a smile and start toward the locker rooms. "I doubt that," I call over my shoulder, aware that he's probably checking out my glutes. Thank goodness for dry land training. I faux-glare at him, and he lifts his shoulder innocently and grins, even though he's clearly busted.

I waggle a finger in the air. "You're one of the first things I was warned about."

"I'm not nearly as bad as Clair makes me out to be," he protests.

"Clair didn't say a word about you. I got my warnings from writing on the girls' locker room walls." Too bad my heart and my hormones are ignoring the warnings, real or not.

It both horrifies and amuses me that I turn into an amateur flirt around him. But he's so easy to talk to. He opens his mouth and looks a little panicked until a snorty laugh bursts out of me. God. Can I be any less sexy?

"I'm only kidding, Zee."

From the deck, Dad waves and points at his watch again, subtle as a two-foot shark fin, so I hurry to the locker room. After a quick shower, I sit for a moment on the bench outside my locker with my towel wrapped around me. Public swimming doesn't start for another hour, so I'm all alone with empty lockers. I slide out the package of jelly beans Zee gave me, rip the plastic off the corner with my teeth, and down a handful, enjoying the explosion of flavors. It's hard to wipe a smile off my face, even though it's silly. Girls swarm Zee. Candy doesn't mean he's going to ask me to be his girlfriend. We have a special connection because of water.

Finally I drop my towel, along with thoughts of him, and pull on clothes, tugging my team hoodie over my head. I step over to the mirror, brush out my hair, and pull it back into an elastic, all except the thin, long braid knotted into my grown-out bangs. The thin braid I dyed almost white with a home hair color kit usually dangles down in my eyes. It's held at the end by tiny colored elastics. The braid is the only thing on me that isn't completely boring. Dad doesn't love it, but it's less permanent than the shoulder tattoo of the American flag I keep begging for. He says I can get that when I make it to the Olympics. Ha ha. Chlorine and winning are what my dad sees for me and my future.

When I head out the doors, Dad's pacing outside the locker room. He's on the phone and so immersed in the call, he doesn't hear me approach. My cell makes a cheering sound, my setting for an incoming text, but I ignore it for a moment.

"She doesn't need to know, and that's final," he barks into the phone. The hair on my arms stands up, and he looks up and clears his throat. "Sam is done in the locker room," he says to the cell phone. "I'll talk to you later." He clicks the phone off and puts it in his pocket, watching me the entire time.

The only person he usually talks to that way is his sister. My Aunt Allie.

"Who was that?" I ask.

"No one." He waves a hand in the air, dismissing my question. "Let's go."

It's obvious he's keeping something from me. As usual. "Whatever," I mumble, but he ignores me.

"How was practice?"

"Good."

It's obvious he's not listening, and I'm tempted to say something rude to see if he notices. But of course I don't. As we head to the exit, I glance at the text that came in. A flock of nervous butterflies takes flight in my belly.

My night may have just got a lot more interesting.

during

chapter two

Dad is cranky and uncommunicative in the car, but instead of asking what Aunt Allie was calling about, I decide to let his mood improve before springing my news on him. At home I throw my swimsuit over the shower stall in my bathroom. Dad's room has an awesome master bath. Our new house in Tadita is a bungalow, but the bedrooms are big and it has a finished basement. It's nicer than the house we left behind in Orlie.

I'm broiling chicken and boiling brown rice when Dad walks into the kitchen and sits on a stool in front of the marble-top island.

"Thanks for making dinner." Neither of us are good cooks, but we've taken turns since I was old enough to use the stove. Tonight was supposed to be his night to cook, but I had an ulterior motive. Besides, even though it's not fancy, food usually tastes better when it's made by me.

"So there's a party tonight." I open the microwave door, stick my finger in the bowl to see if the frozen peas are hot, and pull my hand back quickly. "Taylor Landy texted me. It's at her house. My swim team will be there."

"Taylor the breaststroker?" Dad walks to the fridge but reaches over the top of it to the cupboard where he keeps his liquor. He pulls out a bottle of red wine. "Kind of short notice."

"It's a last-minute thing." I scoot around him as he searches the drawer in front of me for the corkscrew and reach around him to take the plastic veggie steamer from the microwave, carrying it to the kitchen table and removing the lid. Steam bursts up and warms my face. "And Taylor's a person with a brain and an identity. She's not just a stroke."

"You know what I mean," he says. Sometimes he forgets that inside my head is a normal seventeen-year-old girl. Not just a swimmer. He doesn't know that in my daydreams I have an imaginary boyfriend who has a face that looks a lot like Zee's.

"She's nice." In fact, Taylor is everything I'm not outside of the pool, which is probably why Clair made us travel buddies. On road trips we room together. She's peppy and happy and blurts out almost every thought that crosses her mind. She's gorgeous, with thick, long blond hair most girls would kill for. She's also hot and heavy with Justin Spritz, the second hottest swimmer on the Titans. Second to Zee.

My life would be so much easier if I were more like her.

Dad raises an eyebrow as he pulls the cork from his wine bottle and grabs a glass. "Her parents going to be there?" he asks, watching me closely as he pours out the wine.

"No," I say honestly and wrinkle my nose at the bitter smell he loves so much. "Her dad is in Europe on business and her mom went with him." There's no point in lying. At my age, parents are rarely home for parties and we both know it. "She has an older brother. But he's in Arizona. Playing hockey."

Dad shakes his head. "That makes as much sense as an outdoor swim team in Alaska." He sips at his wine and taps his fingers on the counter. "You won't be drinking? You don't have a practice tomorrow, but liquor would throw you off your game." He takes another sip. "Plus, there's the whole illegal thing."

"I know, Dad. It's not like I'm a big drinker." I stare at his glass, wondering if the irony is lost on him, but he just nods with a slight smile as if he's proud he's done something right with me.

Most of the time, I'm so responsible that I'm an embarrassment to my age group. Eating healthy, swimming, and working out. On a wild night I might go see a movie. My idea of rebelling is to not shower the chlorine out of my hair after a practice but hanging out with Dad every weekend has lost its charm. Even he knows I need diversions besides my fourteen hours of training a week. Gillian, my best friend from Orlie, is never around to Skype with anymore. She's hanging out with new friends. I guess it's hard to have a virtual BFF for too long when you have other options. My weekends in Tadita have been so lonely, I almost convinced Dad to get us a dog. And he's secretly afraid of them.

Honestly, the idea of going to a party alone makes me feel nauseous, and I have a strong pang of longing for my old swim team. At least when people thought I was gay, I never had to worry about boys. They weren't interested in me.

"All right," Dad says. "Go to the party. Just be responsible."

* * *

I take a deep breath on the front porch, fighting the voices in my head telling me to turn and flee to safety. The wind gusts up and lifts my skirt, and I shiver at the sudden change in temperature. If I don't go in, Taylor might take it the wrong way and give up asking. As if she's psychic, Taylor opens the front door. She's holding a beer, and as I shift from foot to foot her eyes focus on me and she squeals loudly and pulls me inside with her free hand.

"OhMYGODIcan'tbelieveyoucameIdidn'tthinkyouwouldcome I'msogladyou'rehere." She doesn't even take a breath. Her amazing hair is piled into a messy but cute ponytail with strands pointing out in every direction. She throws both arms around me and squeezes tightly. I've gotten used to her hugging addiction. Usually there's something about the intimacy of touching other people so closely that makes me uncomfortable.

"You look freaking hot!" From the smell of her breath, she's clearly already started drinking. She wiggles her finger and pokes it right in my face. "Are you really gay?"

I've heard liquor is a truth serum, and it appears to be true in Taylor's case. "No," I tell her. "A rumor from my old team. It was never true."

"I KNEW IT! ORLIE SWIMMERS ARE TOTAL LIARS!" she yells. "Look out, boys!" She lifts her arm and performs an invisible lasso twirl over her head. And just like that—boom—I'm straight.

"Um. You have a mirror, right?" I say to her and smile, even though having my fake lesbian shield ripped off is a little unnerving.

She stumbles a little and giggles, pulling up her strapless mini dress that is so tight and short I'm a little afraid for its safety.

In comparison to Taylor, my black skirt and white tank top are boring and desperately in need of accessorizing. I suck at putting outfits together. I'm too broad in the shoulders and too tall to pull off a look like Taylor's anyhow. The fact that Taylor rocks at swimming but has a tiny and narrow build makes me hate her. Just a little.

Taylor shouts again and pushes me past an enormous and very formal front hallway. She throws her hands out like a game show hostess and jokes, "Welcome to my mother's perfect house. Please do not break any of her china!"

I flinch a little at her volume, wondering why drinking makes some people hard of hearing, but Taylor giggles and propels me into the open area with the living room, dining room, and kitchen all attached. Everything looks expensive, even with the rooms vibrating with loud music. Other kids lounge around, sipping from plastic cups. They're draped over chairs in the living room and lean against counters in the kitchen, chatting and laughing and confident. They look fashionable and sophisticated, and my dorkiness seems to flourish and multiply.

I spot most of the senior swim team around and recognize a few other kids from school too. Mostly I don't know anyone's name. Eyes pass over me, and I imagine they're judging me and my outfit. My lame hair. Even the braid that I love so much. Suddenly everything about me feels awkward.

Taylor giggles and throws an arm around my shoulder. "Don't tell Clair I was drinking." I open my mouth to promise when Justin comes along, waves to me, and swoops her away.

I close my mouth. A rope of panic knots my insides. I glance around, feeling stupid, and think maybe staying home with my dad wasn't such a bad idea after all. I'm about to set off to find a washroom to hide in when a hand touches my back. It's Zee. I jump and barely hold in a scream of happiness.

Yeah. I'm cool like that.

He towers above me, playfully nudging me in the side with his elbow. "Not often I see you in clothes, Sammy W."

"True," I manage, and my puppy-dog enthusiasm evaporates as I try to think of something else to say and come up with exactly nothing. Clearly I'm not good at bantering while clothed.

"I was hoping you'd come," he says, and I notice that he's wearing more clothes than usual too, a black T-shirt and plaid shorts. He's got a shark tooth strung around his neck, and normally that might look lame, but with his dark, tousled beach hair, it works. He's completely and utterly gorgeous.

Zee puts his hand on my arm, and my skin tingles under his fingers. Suddenly my tongue gets too big for my mouth and I'm incapable of speech. My cheeks warm.

"You want a drink?" Zee asks, smiling at me and flipping his hair back from his eyes.

"Straight Jack? Scotch on the rocks? Shot of tequila from my belly?" A good-looking boy with whitish-blond curls pops his head over Zee's shoulder. He smiles at me and says something in Zee's ear, and the two of them laugh.

"I don't drink," I mumble, wincing inwardly at my party fail. Why can't I do the sexy banter thing here?

Zee points to the boy hanging over his shoulder. "Have you met Casper?"

Casper smiles the lazy grin of the self-assured. With his perfect hair and lean, tanned face, he reminds me of a Disney kid. "You're in Advanced English with me," he says. "And you beat me on the first exam." He narrows his eyes playfully. "I hope you're not planning to steal away my spot for valedictorian. There's a trophy, you know." He lifts my hand and presses his lips against my palm. Shivers go up my spine. "I love trophies."

Zee knocks his hand away. "Stay away from this guy. He's smart, but he's a horn dog."

"You up for a challenge?" His mouth turns into a lopsided grin, and his voice cracks and rises a little at the end of his sentence. "I could use some fresh competition." Casper winks at me and I can't help grinning. I may suck in social situations, but I'm pretty confident about my grades.

Embracing my inner nerd, I'm warmed by the delicious anticipation of getting better grades than the smartest kid in the class. But I'm not the type to brag about it.

"Dude," Zee says. "Party. This is a party. We don't talk about grades here." He slugs Casper on the shoulder. "Casper thinks having the highest GPA is something we admire about him. That and his big allowance."

"What can you do? When you got it, you got it," Casper pleads.

"Don't worry, we all know it." He smiles at me. "Even the new girl."

A girl crashes into Zee from behind him then, and he turns to steady her. She giggles and whispers in his ear and keeps touching his arm. He glances at me and makes a face she can't see, but he can't shake her. I have an urge to push her to the ground. Hard.

Casper is diverted by a beautiful girl in a short black dress who slides up into his side, wobbling a little on her heels. She looks kind of pissed off about something.

"Longest bathroom break ever," he says to her, and the two of them walk away, their heads together, whispering.

I'm kind of abandoned and feel myself disappearing. I'm about to slip away from Zee and the flirty girl when fingers touch my elbow. Zee spins me around and lightly pushes me along.

"Come on." I note the open mouth on the flirty girl but feign innocence as he directs me through the kitchen. He bends down and expertly opens a cooler without stopping, swooping up a bottle in his hand and presenting it to me. It's water. I smile, relieved to have something to do with my hands as he leads me past a dark wooden kitchen table to a patio door and slides it open. We step outside. Instantly the humid, claustrophobic air disappears and I breathe a little easier. He stumbles but corrects himself right away.

"You don't go to many parties?" he says, as he slides the door closed, but it's not so much a question as a statement. The night air is cold, but the deck is covered and the temperature is tolerable.

"Not really."

"They didn't have them at your old school?"

"We had parties. They just weren't so…"

"Fun?" he says with a grin.

"Grown up," I say and glance down. "We didn't drink. My friends back home. Swim people. Who can afford hangovers?" In the distance the wind howls.

"True. But this is a swim-free weekend." Zee takes a sip from the beer bottle as if to make his point, studying me as if I'm an exotic or weird beast. "All swimming and no fun makes Sammy a dull girl."

I tug at my braid. He thinks I'm dull. And of course he's completely right. I'm a lump of fun-suck. Sucking the fun out of everything is my specialty.

"Hey," he says. "Don't look so down. I'm kidding. You don't have to drink to be cool." He lifts his bottle and grins. "But I do. Seriously, how often do we get a Saturday night with no swim meet? What Clair doesn't know won't hurt her." His expression changes to a conspiring smile as if we share a naughty secret. His eyes are shiny, and I realize he's probably drunker than he seems. "I bet you're probably still sugar buzzed on Jelly Bellys."

"I have a high tolerance for the Bellys," I tell him. "Thanks." I try to stop my smile, but it stretches over my face.

"Yeah." He takes a swig of beer. "Swimmers see-food diet. I know a lot of girls would kill to eat like you and still be in shape."

He's right. Swimming builds an appetite. Despite a big supper, I'd wolfed down a sandwich right before the party.

Zee takes a step closer. I hold my breath, waiting. For what? Something. My heart trips, not quite believing I'm alone outside with Zee. At a party. And he's standing so close to me I can smell his skin. Even the beer on his breath. It's so much more intimate than standing beside him on the pool deck, even though at the pool both of us are nearly naked. Here, I'm a girl. Not just a swimmer.

He reaches over and tucks my braid behind my ear.

"You're sexy," he says.

I struggle to breathe. "I am not."

"Yes. You are." His voice is soft. "All the guys think so. You're different. Not all fake like some girls."

I shake my head with a little too much force, trying to cover how much I want to throw myself at him. His words thrill me. It's so foreign having a boy's interest, and yet here I am, wondering if his lips will taste like chlorine.

He leans even closer and strokes the skin on my bicep. Goose bumps cover my arm. "Strong but soft inside." His slow, easy smile has so much promise. I press my lips tight and suck in my breath, waiting for his mouth to move closer to mine, wanting him to so bad it makes me dizzy.

And then, behind us, the patio door slides open.

Sounds from the house fill the air, laughter and music. The door closes. My back stiffens as a gorgeous creature steps into our space. She's Tyra Banks tall, with the kind of hair I covet—curly ringlets, long and sexy, cascade down her back. She's slim with a tiny waist and great boobs that she's clearly proud to show off in a low-cut dress. Her face is the kind of pretty that turns boys' heads.

"There you are," she says to Zee and steps forward, crunching my toe with a high heel and wrapping her arm around Zee, forcing me to step backward.

"Ouch." I say it low and keep my eyes down, mortified.

She pushes Zee back, away from me. A breeze blows over my skin and I shiver.

"Well, that's got to be a little awkward," a voice says. I turn my head to see a boy sitting in a patio chair behind us in the darkness.

He stands and steps closer, and as he comes into focus I recognize him. It's the boy from the pool earlier today. He's staring at me again, with those same piercing eyes, as if he's listening again to the chatter inside my head. Although what I'm thinking now is not very nice. He's holding a beer bottle and he tilts it back, then grins the playful smile of a little boy. He stumbles a little. Am I the only person at this party who's not drunk?

"Who's that?" I hear the curly-haired girl hiss to Zee. As if she doesn't know we're in a couple of the same classes at school. I don't know her name, but I recognize her. I glance back, and she's standing so close to Zee, my cheeks flame.

"Samantha Waxman," the boy beside me calls to her. "She swims with Zee, Kaitlin," he calls. "So put your claws back in."

I glance at him, surprised he knows my name.

"Sammy's my girl," Zee says with a laugh. "She's the best female swimmer on our team."

Kaitlin looks me up and down. "Oh, another swimmer," she says, and her tone implies I'm not a threat. "You people and your gills." She turns her back to me, her implication clear. Kaitlin drags him farther away. "It's cold, Zee. Warm me up." She slides her hands around his waist. Zee lifts his hands in the air as if he's trying to get away, but she keeps at him. I die a little inside.

"I'm Alex." The other boy thrusts his hand out at me. "Sorry I was spying. I came out to get some air. Some guys are smoking in the basement."

Smells like they were smoking something other than cigarettes. I stare at his hand and then laugh a little nervously and put mine inside it. His palm is big and warm and nice against my skin, but I pull away quickly.

"We've never officially met," he says. "But we go to school together."

"You were at the pool today," I blurt out.

His smile widens. "Yeah. I had to drop off Zee's iPod. I stuck around to watch you swim. I heard you were pretty good."

I lift my water bottle and unscrew the top, thankful for something to do. My body is off balance with conflicting emotions. Lust. And then rejection. Now, embarrassment.

"I used to swim," he says. "But I gave it up for baseball. My coach didn't want me doing two sports. Well, I do Parkour too. Like Zee. But that's for fun." He exhales loudly and then sucks in a big breath.

"Parkour?" I say and take a sip of water.

"Jumping off things. Like James Bond."

I nod, even though I knew what Parkour is. I was more asking why. Anyhow, I'm relieved to hear he'd been watching my swimming technique at the pool and not so much me. Unexpectedly, I giggle, a release of nervous tension.

"Parkour is funny?" he asks. "I thought chicks dug it." He inhales deeply and blows out again.

"Like how you leapt off the bleachers?"

His cute nose wrinkles up and makes me laugh again. "Exactly. Why is that funny?"

"I was kind of worried you were a perv. Hanging out at the pool. Watching strange girls swim."

He grabs at his heart. "Ouch," he says. "But I didn't hear that you were that strange."

"Good. I've kept it quiet, then." I quickly peek over my shoulder at Zee and the Amazon. My heart thunks to my toes as she leans in and kisses him. I'm suddenly feeling nauseated, but I turn back and smile at Alex. Zee can flirt with me and then make out with another girl right behind my back a few seconds later? Well. Two can play at that game.

I can do this. I can flirt with the best of them. In my head a tiny voice of reason nags at me, but the sting of rejection is louder. I place my water bottle on the patio table.

"A perv?" he says. "You really thought I was a perv?"

I lean closer to Alex. "You're too cute to be a perv," I say, trying to ignore my own embarrassment. If he hadn't been drinking, he'd probably guess I got my moves watching teen movies.

"You think I'm cute?" The wonder in his voice softens my mortification a little. "I thought you were into Zee."

I can feel the blush, and my head automatically shakes back and forth even as I'm picturing Zee behind me with the Amazon. "No." I cross my arms in front of me. "I'm not."

"Good." Alex brushes my arm with his fingers. I glance back as Zee is coming up for air with Kaitlin. Alex looks over too. "Zee's an idiot," he whispers in my ear.

My cheeks heat up again, and I lower my gaze.

"We're alphabetically linked," he mumbles and coughs.

I frown. "What?"

He tugs at his ear. "Sorry. I mean you're Waxman. I'm Waverly. And a major dork."

"Hey," Zee calls. "No moves on Sammy, Waverly. I thought

we discussed that." He tries to walk toward us, but Kaitlin tugs him back.

"Forget your stupid swim team," she says, reattaches her mouth to his, and slides her long fingers into his hair.

"Screw him," Alex says. I nod, wholeheartedly agreeing. Screw Zee and his stupid jelly beans. Screw Zee and the stupid girl.

I look up at Alex, trying to be seductive and not furious that Zee thinks he can tell Alex not to make a move on me at the same time he's making out with another girl. I'm consumed by a quiet rage that doesn't quite mask my sadness. Fighting a sudden urge to cry, I step closer to Alex and reach up to touch the collar of his T-shirt. "I've definitely noticed you around," I lie.

"Really?" He leans in, and his breath smells like booze and smoke. He stumbles again. His eyes are red. His condition takes the edge off my guilt. He's drunk. He doesn't know I'm using him to teach Zee a lesson. Maybe he won't even remember.

My frown turns up.

"You're sure you're not interested in Zee?"

"Of course not." I press my lips tight and lean closer to Alex.

He tilts his head forward, so close that our noses actually touch, and he winds my braid around his finger. I hold my breath and try to turn off the part of my brain that insists on analyzing every situation and running it through different scenarios and outcomes before taking action. Instead I press on, determined to worry about the consequences later. It's the least I can do for Zee.

Alex unweaves my braid from his finger, then moves forward, and his lips touch mine. I close my eyes and push away the thought that I'm only doing this so Zee will see me make out with his friend. I'm way too sober to be in this situation, but it doesn't mean Alex is. That has to make it all right. This impulsive thing I'm doing.

Yeah. I'm wild and spontaneous, Zee. How bad do you want me now?

Alex opens his mouth slightly. His lips are soft, and even though he's kind of smelly, it's surprisingly nice. Kissing him. I open my eyes, afraid I'll see another boy's face if I close them. Alex's hand slips around my waist, pulling me tighter. This boy knows what he's doing. His kiss is soft and sweet, with a hint of more just beneath.

I have a horrible thought that I'm turning into a slut. Maybe I've been storing up lust for so long because people thought I was gay. Because even though I barely know this boy, kissing him feels pretty darn good.

His hand travels up my side. I gasp a little. Alex pulls me in a little tighter, his lips push harder, and it becomes a little too intense. Alex, my mind reminds me. Not Zee.

The realization breaks my trance. Zee's face flickers in my brain, and my blood pumps hot shame through my veins. I pull away and place my hands on Alex's chest, pushing him and taking a step back.

"I'm sorry. This is crazy. I barely know you. I'm sorry."

Alex looks slightly alarmed, and then he sneezes.

"Shit," he says.

He begins to cough. He puts his hand up as if to say *just a moment* and then bends at the waist. He takes deep breaths, as if he's struggling to bring air in and out of his lungs.

"Uh. Are you okay?" I ask.

He doesn't answer, but it's clear this is more than dealing with my sudden rejection.

I glance around in a panic, wanting to call to Zee, but he and Kaitlin are still going at it hard, and interrupting them is too embarrassing to contemplate.

I put my hand on Alex's back and repeat, "Are you okay?"

He shakes his head and my heartbeat accelerates. I bend down to look into his face, and what I see makes me break out in a sweat.

"My puffer," he gasps.

"Zee!" I call, no longer concerned about etiquette. "There's something wrong with Alex."

"You're telling me," he murmurs. "Leave her alone." But then he looks over and spots Alex and almost comically pushes the Amazon girl away.

"What the hell?" she says, but Zee is already at Alex's side.

She glares at me and then storms back inside the house.

At this point, Alex has sunk to his knees and is making awful wheezing sounds. His face looks almost gray, and his lips are getting kind of bluish. My heart is racing, and I'm actually wringing my hands together, knowing something is wrong, but not sure what, or what to do about it.

"What the hell, Sam?" Zee yells. He grabs Alex and shakes his shoulders. "What the hell, dude? Breathe."

Alex doesn't respond.

"What's wrong?" My voice comes out shrieky and panicked.

"He's having an asthma attack," Zee says without looking at me. "Alex. Alex, you okay, buddy? Where's your damn inhaler?"

I look around the deck as if someone new will leap from the shadows and tell me what to do. I don't know anyone with asthma. I have no idea what to do. Should I pound on his back? Give him mouth to mouth?

"Go see if someone knows where his inhaler is," Zee yells at me. "Look for his sister, Chloe."

Like I even know who Chloe is. I scramble to open the patio door and pitch myself inside the kitchen. The heat and music hit me immediately. I tap the first person I see on the shoulder. "Alex is having an asthma attack," I say loud enough to be heard over the music. "Inhaler." I gesture like I'm pressing the pump on an inhaler. "Do you know where there's an inhaler?"

The boy stares blankly at me. He shrugs, continues to the fridge, opens it, and takes out a beer.

"Oh my God," I say, looking around in a panic. I loathe the thought of having to make a scene, but I glance outside and see Zee standing over Alex, who is now sitting on the ground.

"Help!" I yell. "Does anyone know where Alex's inhaler is?" Hardly anyone looks at me for longer than a curious second.

Self-consciousness no longer a luxury, I race to the attached living room and jump on the couch, almost stepping on a boy's hand. I hold up my hands like a megaphone. "Alex is having an asthma attack," I scream as loud as I can. "We need to find his inhaler." No one responds, other than a few concerned stares. "Chloe?" I yell, and people stare at me now, like I'm a novelty at the zoo. Someone yells for Chloe, and the name spreads along the crowd, and then the pretty girl in the black dress is running toward me, her face intense with concern.

"What's wrong?" she says. "Is he okay? Is he still outside?"

I point toward the patio door.

"Shit," she says, kicking off her heels and running for the deck. A couple of people follow her. Seconds later, she leans back inside. "Someone call 911," she yells. Her voice is hysterical and penetrates the party atmosphere. "Call 911 right now. Does anyone have an inhaler?"

Someone turns down the music, and people scurry in circles. Taylor rushes into the living room looking confused and upset. Justin has his arm around her. They hurry outside with some others, and from the deck I hear Chloe screech louder. "Help! Someone help Alex. Oh my God!"

There's silence, and then she yells again. Her voice is hysterical now. "EpiPen," she yells. "Does anyone have an EpiPen?"

My blood, moments ago so hot, turns to ice. EpiPen?

"Get out of the way!" Zee yells from the deck, screaming at people to step back. A crowd's gathered around Alex, blocking him. I'm frozen in place, afraid to go outside. The atmosphere inside the house transforms. No one looks sophisticated anymore. Everyone looks like kids. Scared little kids.

Outside, the noise continues and builds momentum. Girls are crying. Chloe is screaming over and over again. I'm still standing on the couch, and the boy sitting beside me shakes his head. "This is not going to turn out well," he mumbles to no one in particular. "Someone said he left his backpack at Zee's."

"What do you mean?" I ask the boy. "What's happening?"

"Oh my god," someone yells. "He's not breathing."

Chloe runs in the house then, her eyes wide and hysterical. "Did anyone give him anything that might have peanuts in it? Did he eat anything?" Her voice screeches. Tears chase each other down her cheeks. "Where the hell is the ambulance?"

I concentrate on breathing in and out. It's difficult for me, but not impossible. Like it is for Alex. I step off the couch. I want to lie down and close my eyes.

I want to pretend it's all a very, very bad dream. I want to be back in the kitchen at home with my dad. I want him to order me not to go to the party.

I don't want to be so hungry all the time. I don't want to act totally out of character and kiss a boy minutes after meeting him.

A boy who is allergic to peanuts and is apparently having an ana-phylactic reaction on the deck. I don't want to have snacked before the party even though I ate a full dinner. I don't want the snack to be a peanut butter sandwich.

I consider bolting out the back door but plop down on a nearby chair, too shocked to do much of anything else. People run in cir-cles around me. No one talks to me. No one asks me what I ate before I kissed him. My lips press tightly together.

The sound of sirens reaches the house. People cry and screech, in a panic. Two medics charge in the house and run out to the deck.

I don't have to ask. It's not good.

after

chapter three

I don't know how long it's been since the Amazon pointed an accusing finger at me as the girl who had been with Alex, but people have finally stopped firing questions at me. I've answered questions over and over again. *What did I eat before kissing Alex? When did I have the peanut butter sandwich? What happened after?*

Almost all the kids are gone. Taylor is at the kitchen table, crying softly. Justin sits beside her, looking like he's about to.

A police officer's walkie-talkie crackles. She speaks into it, then walks over to me.

"Alex died on the way to the hospital," she says softly.

Taylor moans, and Justin drops his head to his hands. I squeeze my eyes shut and shake my head. Back and forth. Back and forth. As if the motion can stop the truth from becoming real. *No.* I want to scream. This can't be real.

The police officer puts her hand on my arm. "Have you been drinking?" she asks.

I shake my head no. I wonder why it even matters.

"You're sure?"

"I swim," I say, as if that's an answer. My voice sounds foreign to me.

Her eyes soften, and I guess she's a mom, thinking about her own kid, hoping she won't drink either. Or kiss boys she doesn't know at parties. "Did you drive here?"

I nod.

"I'll drive you home in your car. My partner will follow us."

I don't argue. She pulls me up. I don't look at Taylor or Justin. I don't look at anyone. I wonder if I can stay inside my head and make it all go away.

It's raining outside and the wind is whipping leaves around. The cop asks me a couple more questions on the way home, but other than supplying my address in a squeezed voice, I can't speak. I can't talk anymore. I can only shake my head and stare at my lap. I'm holding so many emotions inside, and they're fighting hard to blast out. Swallowing is virtually impossible.

"We already contacted your dad. You won't be charged with anything," she's saying. "In a case like this there's no intent. No liability."

My joints weaken and my stomach gurgles. I should go to jail. Live behind bars. Be punished forever for what I did.

She parks in the driveway and walks me to the door, and my body starts to shake when my dad opens the door. For a second I imagine Chloe going home. Her parents waiting at the front door. No son or brother will walk inside again. Horrified, I slip past my dad while the policewoman has a hushed conversation with him in the doorway. They talked earlier, but he's just learning that Alex died. I hover behind him. Waiting.

When she finally leaves and he closes the door, my body lets go. I throw my arms around him, crumpling against him. He squeezes me harder than he ever has before and the tears I've somehow kept down gush out. I'm a snotty, blubbering mess.

Horrible sounds emanate from a deep, dark place inside me. "I'm sorry. I didn't mean…Daddy…Oh my God. I killed him."

My dad murmurs soft words that make no sense. A part of me recognizes how stiff my dad's arms are, but he's holding me close and not letting go, even as I soak his golf shirt with my groaning and weeping. I'm certain I'll never be able to stop. I rock against him, unable to process the horror of what I've done.

Time must pass, but instead of dying, like I should, I start to breathe a little more slowly. My guttural sounds turn to normal sobs. My dad tries to untangle himself, but I cling to him, terrified to be alone. He gently but firmly removes my arms from his.

"I'll be right back," he says. "Stay here."

I curl into a ball on the couch and squeeze my eyes together. I don't want to see or to hear anything. I don't want thoughts or images in my head. A notion formulates in my brain. I want my mommy. Oh God. I want my mom more than I've ever wanted her in my life.

I start another whimpering sound, but it's almost a song of sorrow that I hum to keep myself sane on some primitive level.

Dad's footsteps return and then he crouches down beside me. "Butterfly?"

I open my eyes, and he holds out his hand, flat. In the middle of his palm is an oval blue pill. In his other hand is a glass of water.

"Take it," he commands, holding the pill closer to me.

I don't have the wits to question his order. I don't ask what the pill is or protest. I can only sit up and obey. Someone needs to tell me what to do. I place the pill on my tongue, take the glass of water and swallow it down. Bitterness taints my taste buds.

Dad holds out his hand again, but this time it's empty. I recognize that I'm expected to take it. I slip my smaller hand inside and he tugs me up. He puts his other hand under my legs and swoops me up, and my arms wind around his neck. He walks slowly, carrying me, climbing the stairs with me, taking me down the hallway to my bedroom like I'm a three-year-old, not a five-foot-eight seventeen-year-old who weighs almost 130 pounds.

He grunts a little and kicks open my bedroom door. He has to step over a pile of clothes before he can plop me gently down on my bed. I immediately roll away from him and curl into a ball, but instead of tight I'm almost limp. My brain is black and emotionally spent. I'm so exhausted it feels like I'm sinking inside my head.

Dad sits on the bed, and his weight moves me a little closer to him. He strokes my hair the way he did when I was a little girl.

The pill is already working. I'm beginning to drift, and I welcome the escape with only a tiny level of awareness.

"Why, Sammy?" he whispers. "Why were you kissing a boy you didn't even know?"

I don't answer him. I'm so tired. But a lingering thought survives the weariness and travels through the dark. It goes deep and imprints on my already contrite soul.

"Why did Mom die?" I whisper.

How can I possibly get through this without a mother? Maybe

with her guidance I wouldn't have gone around kissing boys I barely knew for attention.

He doesn't say anything, and the drugs make my brain hazier. As I close my eyes and succumb to darkness, one last coherent thought flits through my head:

I wish I could join her.

My mom.

forever
after

chapter four

In theory I understand that I am grieving, but I haven't wept since Friday night. My insides give me sensory proof that I'm still functioning, but it seems likely that while I was drugged my organs were replaced with robot parts. Everything works the way it's supposed to. My heart beats. My lungs expand and contract. But it's like I'm hollow or watching a movie about someone else. None of this feels real. I can't break out of the trance.

I lie in my bed and think about poking something sharp into my skin. To see if it will hurt, to see if I'll bleed, to test whether I'm still alive. I don't, though. For one, because moving means effort. Two, because I'm afraid if start bleeding that I won't stop myself from draining all life from my body. Or worse, that I will.

I ignore my cell phone. Dad tells me Clair and Aunt Allie are texting and emailing frantically. Taylor too. He brought the phone to my room and it quickly ran out of juice. I leave it dead on my dresser and ignore the landline. Taylor calls, and Aunt Allie persists longer, but in spite of knowing how much she'll persevere, I don't want to talk even to her.

Monday morning is the first time I've missed a swim practice except for when I've been too sick to move and once when I pulled my hamstring. I ignore my dad and refuse to budge from my bed for the 5:00 a.m. swim. He stands in the hallway outside my room for a while looking confused and unsure of what to do.

"What's the matter, Dad?" I say in a flat voice. "You look like someone died."

"Oh, Sam," he says and comes in and sits on my bed, asking over and over if he should stay home with me. I shake my head and tell him to go to work. Finally he pats me on the head and says he'll leave me for a few hours but tells me to call if I need him. Clearly he's out of his league here. But so am I.

Hours later when he gets home, he comes directly to my room. I've become an extension of my bed. My hair is unbrushed, my teeth are still filmy. I've been up to use the bathroom, but other than that I've drifted in and out of sleep and, between naps, stared at the ceiling. I know a lot about my bedroom ceiling. The stains. The spider web in each corner.

"Clair called me at work," Dad says.

Nothing about that makes me react. "She offered to take you to a grief counselor. To go with you." I roll over on my side, so my back is facing him.

"But I made an appointment for you myself. Just you. I mean, I can in go with you if you want. But Clair shouldn't have to take you."

It sounds like he's asking me a question. If I do want Clair to take me. I can't deal with his uncertainty and contemplate my wall. Clair is from an old world. One I can barely remember.

"I got you in right away," he says. "Wednesday morning. The doctor made a special arrangement to get you in."

"Lucky him," I mumble to my wall. "I'm sure I'll be fascinating."

"Sam." He doesn't move from the end of my bed.

I don't answer, but I sense him staring at me. A sigh drifts in the air until he leaves. I flip onto my back again, and a few minutes later Dad walks in with a sandwich and some snap peas on a plate.

"Can you eat something?" He hands me the plate, and I take it and place it on top of the messy sheets bunched up on the bed.

"Sammy," he says. His voice cracks. "I can't stand to see you like this."

I don't answer. There's no other way to see me.

"I want to help you. Please. Talk to me."

The thing he doesn't realize is that he can't help me. And because he's so good at keeping things he doesn't want to talk about inside, somewhere along the way I developed the same ability.

"I'll be fine. Really. I just want to be alone."

"I need to do something to fix this."

"I know, Daddy." We look each other in the eyes. I haven't called him that in a long time.

"I'm sorry," he finally says, and his voice is uneven.

"Did you know that the funeral is tomorrow?" I ask, staring at the flat peas on the plate.

"I know," he says.

I pull a loose thread on my comforter. "Do you think I should go?"

"Do you want to?"

No. Yes. No. I can't imagine which scenario is worse. "I don't know." I look up at his face. The familiar crooked nose. The thinning brown hair that doesn't take away from his still handsome face. Age is being kind to him.

"I understand." He clears his throat. "But it might be good to have closure. Say goodbye. Let me know, okay? I'll go with you."

He's never used the word closure before. I wonder if he's reading psychology books.

I close my eyes to avoid thinking about that too long. When I don't say anything more, he leaves the room.

By the morning I've moved the plate to my dresser. The bread is hard and stale. The peas are untouched.

• • •

I'm wearing ugly polyester-ish black pants that Dad bought me for an awards banquet in the summer. I have on a black turtleneck with black boots. It feels like I'm playing a part in a movie, *the Mourner*. Unfortunately, I've forgotten my lines. The cues are all jumbled in my head.

Unseasonably warm temperatures drop to honor the seriousness of the day. It's cold enough that my classmates are wearing their coats zipped up. Dad and I are sitting in the idling car watching them walk by. There's no room to park in the church parking lot. We've stopped in front of a house a block away from the church. The street is lined with cars. Dead teenagers collect quite a crowd.

I'm made of ice, so it surprises me that my breath is invisible in the air. I expect white clouds to float from my lips. The heat must be on and the air must be warm, but it doesn't reach my insides.

I can't move.

"Come on, Sam." Dad reaches over and presses his gloved fingers into my arm. We touch so much lately, more than we have since I was a kid.

"We're here. We should go in." I sense his desire to push me out of the car. To make me do the right thing. He wants me to go inside and show the world he didn't completely fail raising me alone.

"I can't." I try to imagine the stares from Alex's mom and dad. I close my eyes tight and try to feel their hatred from inside the car. I deserve to let them have that, to let them pour it into me, blame me for their loss. But I'm afraid, terrified I'll never thaw out if their faces reveal what I did to them.

I'm the last person they'll want to see, I tell myself. Going inside would be for me. It's best for everyone else that I stay away. I'm unable to push myself out of the car. I want to have something useful to say to them. Something to make amends. But how do you say you're sorry for killing someone's son? What do I expect them to say back?

"It's okay. We forgive you."

Of course not.

There is nothing. There is no apology. There is no Hallmark card.

I want to tell his parents I'd gladly trade places with Alex, give my life for his. But how do you say something like that without sounding like a complete asshole?

It's too ridiculous to imagine.

"I can't, Dad. I'll make things worse. Please. Take me home."

• • •

Hours later, Dad pokes his head inside my room. "Sam? Get up. You've got to move around."

I do? I have no idea why he thinks that. When we got home I walked straight to my room and crawled under the covers. I don't know what time it is now. It ceased to matter long ago. Dad makes sounds in his throat and then walks inside my room, goes to the phone, and plugs the line back in the jack. "Your Aunt Allie wants to speak to you. It might help to talk to her."

I don't point out that he's done his best to keep us from talking in the past. He takes away the breakfast I didn't eat and returns with another plate—a grilled cheese sandwich and purple grapes. My favorite. He throws my cell phone at me and leaves the room. He's charged it. I stare at it for a minute and see a long string of texts from Clair. Taylor. Aunt Allie. I delete them all without reading them.

Almost immediately the landline rings. Dad picks it up in the living room. By the tone of his voice I guess it's Aunt Allie, but I don't listen to what he says to her.

I drift in and out of sleep, and then there's light in my room and I guess it must be morning. Dad walks back into the room and stands in front of my bed with his arms crossed.

"If you don't get up and into the shower I will pick you up and shower you myself."

He means it, and the horror of being naked in front of him forces me out of my stupor. As warm water pounds down on my body, cleansing my skin, I squeeze my eyes tight, trying to stave off my thoughts. I reach for the faucet and turn it to cold. The icy water prevents me from thinking. Shivering, I wash my hair, and when I'm done, I towel off and change into the clean clothes Dad set out for me on my bed, like I'm five years old again. I floss my teeth until my gums bleed.

As we drive to the emergency peanut butter killer meeting he's set up, Dad babbles, carrying on a nervous monologue that sounds a lot like gibberish in my ears.

I walk into the office of the counselor and figure out a few things. His name is Bob. It's written on the plastic sign on his door. Bob Kissock. Also, he wears too much cologne. It smells up the tiny room and makes me think of men wearing towels around their waists on TV commercials. He's middle aged and reminiscent of Santa Claus with his gray hair and beard. He's wearing a red sweater vest over a round belly that stretches over his black pants. He's got glasses on, but when I look closely I can see that his eyes are kind.

I sit on the leather couch, preparing to ignore him, but when he speaks his voice is gentle. "I'm so sorry, Sam," he says. "For what happened."

His voice chisels away some of my frostiness. Cold snaps in my bones. I pull my sweater tighter around me, breathing in and feeling tightness in my chest.

"You didn't do anything wrong," he says. He slides into the chair across from me. His voice is smooth and deep. Reassuring.

The tightness in my chest expands and travels up to my forehead. It pounds, and I press on my temples to try to relieve the pressure.

"I would like to help you." He says it simply but enunciates the words so that they sound authentic and sincere.

"Yes." It surprises me. I open my eyes wider, looking at Bob. "Please. Help. Me."

He leans over and pats my hand. My shoulders collapse against the back of the couch.

"I didn't mean…" I stop, unable to continue, wringing my hands around and around.

"Of course you didn't," he says, and the understanding in his voice nearly slays me. "You need help coping, Sam. And that's why you're here."

He asks me simple questions in his gentle voice. I answer in one-word sentences at first. My voice is throaty and froggy, as if I haven't used it in a very long time. Bob gently but firmly describes the stages of grief and guilt. He never takes his eyes off me. He never condescends or tries to tell me how to feel. He explains himself and why he's asking and continues with more and more personal questions. My body melts a little further. I find myself relieved to be able to feel again, though an hour ago that seemed impossible.

"Have you been bothered by reporters?" he asks after a pause.

I shake my head. "Not really. I mean, obviously it's all over the news. But none of the reports have named me. They're not coming after me. Even though it's no secret in this town."

"Good." He nods and presses his fingers and palms together like a yogi or something. "Sometimes the ethics of the news world surprise me. In this case, in a good way." And then he asks another simple question.

"Tell me about your mom." The question throws me off. I struggle not to cry and he looks me in the eye. "It's okay to cry," he says.

I press my lips tight. Swallow and inhale deeply through my nose. I wave my hands in front of my face as if fanning will keep me from giving in to everything I've been burying. His permission rips at the imaginary duct tape I've wrapped around my heart to keep the sorrow inside. A sniffle escapes, and then I can't hold it in anymore.

I use up almost a whole box of Kleenex before I can speak again.

As I sniffle, Bob talks about loss. And then asks more questions. His gentle voice and kind demeanor allow me to purge things from deep inside, and when the questions finally stop, I'm exhausted.

"What can I do?" I ask him. "What can I do to make amends? I mean, I can never do that. But I feel like I need to do…something. What can I do?"

Bob settles back against his chair. Folds his hands. "That," he says, "is a very good question." He leans toward me. "I want you to think about that. We'll talk about it again."

He stands then and tells me my dad wants to join us for our last few minutes, and then he goes to the door to invite him inside. Dad walks into the room and sits beside me, darting glances at me and then at Bob.

"What about school?" Bob asks. "Have you thought about how to continue her education in a safe manner?"

Dad glances sideways at me. "I could hire someone. For homeschooling."

"No," I say. Both men stare at me.

"I want to go back to school."

"Are you sure?" Bob asks. "Your dad tells me you've only been going there a couple months."

I nod, and he leans over and makes a note in the notebook beside his chair.

"What about the swimming?" my dad asks. "You need to go back to that too."

"No." My voice snaps, quick as a starting pistol.

They both look at me like I'm a little unhinged. They think I've got it backward. Yes to school. No to swimming. But they don't understand my need to be punished.

Bob asks me to explain in my own words why I can't swim, why I won't get back in the water. Sorrow that has been consuming me turns to anger, as if I'm being forced to say things that are vile and dark. I press my lips tight. "I can't. I won't."

"She's close to breaking records," my dad says to Bob, his voice pleading. "She's close to a national record in freestyle."

Bob nods but doesn't take his eyes off of me. "She's going through a very intense trauma, Mr. Waxman. She needs to heal."

"But there's a meet coming up. This is her senior year. She's been training most of her life for this. College scouts…" He stops.

Bob doesn't say anything, but he watches me. His expression tells me that he will support my choices.

"How will you feel if you don't make those records, Sam?" Dad asks. "You've trained so hard. You've set goals."

I turn away from him. "None of this stuff matters."

"Of course it matters," Dad says and turns to Bob. "We moved to Tadita to get her the best coaching."

I glance at both of them. Bob raises his hand, and Dad snaps his mouth shut. But his eyes flash with the anger churning inside him.

"Sam has to make that decision." Bob glances at the clock on his wall. "I'd like to see you again," he says to me and glances at my dad. He nods, but I can tell he wanted immediate results. One session to fix me. Get me back in the pool.

Bob stands. "Will you wait outside for a moment?" he asks me, and I nod. I'm emotionally shredded. Exhausted. He takes my limp hand and shakes it. He's warm, and his grip is firm. There is something in my hand when I pull mine away.

"My cell number," he tells me. "You can call me anytime if you need to talk. You're going to be all right, Sam," he says before he lets go.

I walk to the hallway as Dad writes out a check. Bob quietly tells Dad to give me space to recover. I plan on using his words to my advantage. I know how much it's hurting him, but I can't swim. Not even for him.

chapter five

Days later, I still haven't been to swim practice, even though my body is an uncomfortable mass of heaviness. It misses the feel of being in the water. Craves it. My hair smells different. My skin isn't as dry. I have pimples on my forehead. But I can't go back.

My life has become one major game of "if only." If only I had kept my damn lips to myself. And boycotted peanut butter. I can make up millions of different scenarios, all with a different outcome. Alex. Alive.

A few times, my mind wanders to Zee. I can only imagine what he thinks of me now. I try not to.

Instead I flick on the flat screen Dad installed when we moved in. A treat for both of us, TVs in our bedrooms. The TV links me to a reality I've yet to return to. The story about Alex is a big one. Not just in Tadita or even in Washington state, but all over North America. Maybe even the world.

There's a story about a school in Seattle with parents picketing and marching. "My daughter will only eat peanut butter," a woman says to the reporter. "What I am I supposed to do?"

"Try Cheez Whiz," a voice yells from behind them, and the

camera pans to the red face of a man holding a little boy. "Is your kid's fussiness really a reason for my child to die?"

"If my child had that handicap, I wouldn't inflict her problem on everyone else," the woman says to him. "Homeschool if you want a peanut-free environment. My kid has rights too."

My stomach gets queasy, and my throat swells. Handicap? Really? A few weeks ago I probably wouldn't have seen the big deal about taking a peanut butter sandwich to school, but things look different to me now. I'll never eat it again.

I turn the TV off. After a minute, the silence in the room starts to eat my brain, so I flick the TV back on and click through the channels until Alex's face fills the screen. It's a national program. The crucial thing missing from all the coverage is me. My identity. I'm both grateful and ashamed that my name hasn't made the headlines or eased into the feature stories about deadly allergies. It seems the media made a collective decision to leave me out. I have no idea whether it's because of legalities or ethics, but I wonder why I deserve that respect.

I watch as the camera cuts to some lady doctor with a fancy suit sitting stiffly in a chair facing the camera. Her name and title appear on the screen. An allergist. Her face is serious as she answers an off-screen reporter's questions about allergies. "A death of this sort is extremely rare and worrisome," the doctor says.

She goes on to explain that the likeliness of dying by a kiss is remote. "It's believed allergens can only survive in the saliva for an hour. Accidents like this, from contact with second parties, happen, but are extreme exceptions rather than the rule."

I picture Alex's face. His expression when he realized he couldn't get his breath. The way he bent over at the waist, his hand in the air, looking for help. For him, it was definitely the rule.

I flick to a new channel. Local news. They're showing a montage of pictures of Alex. My heart breaks at a shot of a cute little Alex wearing a Spider-Man costume. His mom tells the viewers he wore the costume almost every day when he was four. She laughs, but it abruptly stops.

Then the screen shows Alex, holding a giant fish and standing beside a man who has to be his dad. There's a look of joy on Alex's face and pride on his dad's. It fades to another picture of young Alex with his arm wrapped protectively over his sister's shoulder. In the background, his mom tells the camera that seven years ago, when Alex was ten, he rescued his sister from a rabid fox. He kicked the fox until it ran off. He'd been fierce protecting his sister. His mom explains that Alex and Chloe were less than eleven months apart. Born the same year.

How can his family possibly cope with his loss? How do you go on living when you lose someone like that? I lost my mom, but I was too young to really understand what was happening. I try to imagine losing my dad, and my mind goes blank. It can't go there. I won't.

The camera cuts to Alex's mom. She's in a chair across from the reporter, saying that three universities were interested in Alex for baseball scholarships. She wipes under her eyes. She's clutching a Hot Wheels car, and when the reporter asks her about it she says that Alex had collected Hot Wheels since he was a boy. She holds up a red Mustang. "This was his favorite."

I imagine it's something that would have embarrassed him. If he was still alive.

For a moment I allow my "if only" to change to what might have happened if Alex had lived. I wonder if we'd have gone out for a while. He was cute. Seemed nice. He liked me. He could have made me forget about Zee. Maybe right now he'd be on the phone with me, confessing that he still had a Hot Wheels collection in his room.

I shake my head. And I remember that I pushed him away. I look back to the TV. A girl is being interviewed by a different reporter. They're standing in front of my school with a microphone in the girl's face. She's skinny and short with fake-looking black hair and an eyebrow piercing.

"Everyone knew about Alex's allergy," she tells the reporter. "We all kind of watched out for him. He used to eat at a special table in elementary school. We were always reminded to wash our hands after eating nuts."

Yeah. Well I was in Orlie then. I'd never heard of Alex.

"Some people say she shouldn't be blamed," the pierced girl says, "but honestly, what me and my friends wonder is—if she didn't know him well enough to know about the allergy, what was she doing kissing him?"

A fair question, if I do say so myself.

The camera cuts back to his mom in the studio. A close up. She's pretty but heartbreakingly sad. Pain is written into every inch of her skin, every breath she takes. I wonder what she looked like before he died.

I do know one thing.

Alex didn't deserve to die.

The reporter asks his mom what it was like living with his peanut allergy and asthma. His mom describes years of diligence. Fighting to be the voice for her child. The underlying fear when she sent him out into the world without her. Her secret wish to find a peanut-free world and move there. She wipes her eyes again. I hear unspoken thoughts about the slip-up she couldn't prevent. The girl who ate a sandwich and then kissed her son. She doesn't mention me. She doesn't turn to the TV and declare that Samantha Waxman murdered her baby boy, but she doesn't have to. I imagine her desire to reach through the television screen, wrap her hands around my throat, and squeeze and squeeze until no air can fill my lungs.

For the rest of my life, this will be something that defines me. When people eventually find out, their opinion of me will change instantly. I switch the channel.

There's a younger mother holding a little boy's hand. They're standing in a classroom. He's cute, with lots of floppy copper hair and blue eyes that sparkle. He's grinning the face-busting, nose-wrinkling grin of a young, happy kid.

"Rusty has nut allergies and a severe allergy to peanuts," his mom says.

Beside her, he lifts his bicep and makes a muscle and does a strong man pose.

His mom smiles down on him. "We've taught him from a young age to be careful. No sharing food. No cupcakes at birthday parties.

His school has a peanut table. It's great in theory, but what happens if a child who does have peanuts or peanut butter forgets to wash their hands? And then they touch my son in a game of tag? Or holds hands with him in the hallway? They're kids. They're messy. They forget things."

The little boy turns to the other side and flexes again, grinning cheekily at the TV camera.

"I would feel absolutely horrible if a child ate a peanut butter sandwich and killed my child." The camera zooms in closer to the mom's face. "But what about you? How would you feel if it was you? Your child who killed mine? What would that do to your kid too?"

The camera cuts to the boy.

"I just want to send him to school and know he's safe. I don't want to have to worry just because there's nothing else you think you can feed your child besides a peanut butter sandwich."

Dad pops his head into my bedroom. He glances at the TV and then at the clothes and books lying all over my floor. A sock I'd been trying to throw in the laundry bin hangs off the door handle. "Turn that off, okay?" He glances around my room but doesn't comment. "I made some pancakes. You need to eat. And you could clean up this mess."

"No." I don't look up or untangle my limbs from the sheets on my bed. He walks inside, takes the remote from my hand, and presses the power button.

I stare at the black TV screen as if it's fascinating. My stomach growls, but I ignore it. "You going to swim tonight?" he asks.

His voice is hopeful, but underlying anger ripples the edges. He's trying not to be pushy. He's trying to give me time. I can only imagine the strength it takes for him to stay calm about my refusal to swim.

"It'll help to get your blood flowing again. Make you feel better."

"No." I wait, hoping he'll get mad. Yell at me. Instead, he takes a deep breath. We both know how much speed and endurance I'm losing.

I stare at him, but he's the one looking into space now.

"Why don't we ever talk about Mom?" I ask.

"Your mom?" He looks me in the eyes and seems surprised, as if he's forgotten a woman was involved in my creation. His back straightens, and he rolls out his neck. "She died a long time ago, butterfly."

I move my gaze back to the blank television screen. "Obviously, I know that. But we never talk about her. I don't even know what she was like. Did you love her?"

"Of course I loved her." He's pressing his lips tight, and his forehead explodes into wrinkles. His voice does not convince me that this is a fact. His lips disappear, and then he exhales and they reappear. "What do you want to know?"

"Lots of things." I wait, but he says nothing. He isn't going to make it easy. "Am I like her?"

"No." He says it so quickly and with so much force it startles both of us. He turns away and studies the bulletin board on my wall. The first thing he hung up when we moved in. Layers and layers of different colored ribbons are stuck onto it with equally colorful pins. Above the board are pegs with medals dangling from them, and the wall is almost full with framed swim certificates. Club records I've broken. State records.

Dad gets everything framed. He keeps everything I've accomplished up on display, but he hides memories of the woman he created me with.

"Your mom was a glorious swimmer." He turns and looks into my eyes. "And you look like her. But you're different. She…" He glances away. "Had difficulties."

He's never told me that before. He steps forward and runs a finger over the top ledge of the TV, and then rubs it against his thumb to wipe away the dirt. "You're different from your mom," he repeats. Then he sighs and walks to the doorway. "We'll talk about it another time. Come on. Come and get some supper."

His footsteps clomp down the stairs, but I stay where I am.

"You told Bob you wanted to go back to school and it's time," he calls up the stairs. "You'll go back to swimming soon. But first, back to school. Tomorrow."

"I'll never swim again," I whisper to myself.

I shudder thinking about going back to school, but a small part of me almost wants the finger-pointing. Even though none of the newspapers or TV shows named me, everyone in Tadita knows it was me. Social media isn't as polite as traditional media. It's time to face the haters head on. The kids on Facebook who've dubbed me the Peanut Butter Killer.

We'll see what I'm really made of when I am forced to face their wrath.

chapter six

Walking has become a skill to relearn. Nothing about it comes naturally anymore. The cloud of despair has spread from the top of my head and surrounds me completely. My heart beats at triple pace. My hands quiver and I make a fist to still them. My eyes stay hidden behind long hair dangling in front of my face. I'm thankful Dad pushed me to keep my hair long even though short would be easier for swimming.

The horrible anticipation of running into Zee keeps my shaky steps moving through the hallway. Everyone veers around me as if I'm a live bomb about to go off, yet at the same time I might as well be naked, the way everyone stares. Their looks are either horrified or relieved, as if they're glad it's me and not them in this mess.

I cross my arms in front of me, clutching my backpack, trying to hide behind it. When I glance up and catch the eye of a short boy, he drops his gaze fast. Feeling isolated in the crowd is worse than the isolation in my room, but this is what I signed up for. My head hurts from the intensity.

"Hey, Sam," a voice calls, and I glance up. A boy stares down at me, which means he's pretty tall. Amazingly, his smile is bright and seems authentic. I recognize him, but my brain is mushy and sluggish and his name won't come to me. I blink like a blank computer screen as my nose fills with the scent of an expensive, overpowering cologne.

"Casper," he says.

An image pops into my head.

"And now you're totally thinking about Casper the Ghost."

A smile turns up my lips. Quickly I put my hand over my mouth to cover it.

He reaches over and touches my arm and without meaning to, I pull away.

"How you doing?" he says softly. "It's okay to smile, you know." He's clearly a guy who's familiar with the gym—and a number of styling products. Nothing about his tousled hair looks accidental.

Other students whiz past us, their dirty looks and disapproval so potent I don't even have to look to feel them.

"Under the circumstances, not really," I mumble. I move away, eager to get to my classroom. The first class of the day is a safe one. But it's bringing me closer to the inevitable.

Fingers dig into my shoulder. "Ouch." I turn.

Casper. He's staring straight into my eyes. His expression is kind. "You didn't know, Samantha," he says softly, and the sympathy in his voice almost finishes me.

I blink quickly and successfully keep the tears behind the shutters, out of sight. "Thanks," I whisper. His niceness makes me feel worse because I so stupidly judged his carefully planned appearance. "Um. I gotta go." I shrug away from him and run-walk through the hall and hurry into my classroom. Safe for at least another hour. Everyone watches me as I take a seat near the front. By keeping my eyes lowered and staying deep inside my head, I pretend not to notice the hostility.

The bell rings, and Mrs. Elliot walks toward the front of the aisle where I'm sitting. I know she's coming toward me, but I duck my head and dig inside my backpack to pull out my textbook.

"Everyone please get out your book and turn to page 65," she calls as her shoes clack toward me.

Backpacks unzip and bodies shuffle around to get their books. She bends and touches the top of my head so I'm forced to look up. She smiles, and the turn of her lip and tilt of her head express so much compassion I kind of want to crawl into her arms and cry.

"We missed you the last couple weeks," she says, her voice barely above a whisper. "You okay?"

I nod once and then drop my gaze, studying her feet. She's wearing awesome brown leather boots with a long boho skirt. She's youngish for a teacher, and I wonder if she has any little kids at home. I imagine her with an apron on, oven mitts up to her elbows, pulling a steaming pan of chocolate chip cookies from an oversized oven, and I almost smile. Then, with a start, I wonder if her child has an anaphylactic allergy to peanuts, and my whole body flushes.

"Let me know if you need some help catching up. Although with your grades, it shouldn't be a problem." She spins and click-clacks to the front of the class to begin her lesson.

After class, I take my time gathering up my things, waiting until everyone is gone before standing. It's hard to breathe, knowing that they're all out there. In the hallway.

Mrs. Elliot glances at me from the desk, where she's grading papers. No doubt an exam I missed while hiding out at home.

"You okay?" she asks.

I pause before I stand. "Yeah. Thanks."

She brings the red pencil to her chin, studying me. "Alex was a good boy, and the kids around here miss him. We all do. But no one is blaming you, Sam. You know that, right?"

My lips quiver. She's wrong. They do blame me. How can they not? There's blood on my hands that can never be scrubbed away. There is no forgiveness for this. None. There is nothing that can bring back a life. A real person is gone. A real person who will never speak again.

"The school had a memorial in the gym, did you know that?" she asks.

I nod. It was on Facebook. I've stalked his page. Thousands of condolences complete with updates on events. The memorial notice was posted.

"I was hoping you would come. But I guess it was…hard…"

I clutch my backpack closer and start inching toward the door.

"I can do the make-up test Friday," I say.

Her expression changes, and she glances down at her work. When she looks up she nods. "Fine. Come see me at noon on Friday," she says. A flash of something crosses her face. "Take care, Samantha." Her voice is soft. She bends her head and returns to her work, dismissing me.

My heart dips, and even though it's me who brushed her off, I can't shake a twinge of disappointment. I want to go admit that my insides feel hollowed out. Tell her I worry I'm turning into a statue or an ice block chiseled into shape with a chainsaw.

An almost paralyzing desire to talk to my mom stops me in my tracks. Her face turns into Mrs. Elliot's. Mrs. Elliot is way too young to be my surrogate mother figure. She doesn't even know me. I wonder if I'll keep looking for someone to mother me in every woman who's nice to me.

I force myself to start walking and step into a tidal wave of people. Some glare at me, and the hostility is palatable. Someone elbows me in the side. Hard. Another voice calls, "What's for lunch, Samantha? Peanut butter sandwiches?"

"Reese's Pieces?" Someone else calls.

I blink faster, and the bodies become blurry roadblocks. I'm suddenly missing every single person from my old school. At least there people knew me as more than the swimmer who killed Alex.

"Sam!" a voice calls, ringing with familiarity.

I spot the hair first. Taylor lifts her hand, and relief flows into my blood and gives me extra oxygen. She runs at me, throwing her arms around me, squeezing me hard. I nestle my head against her shoulder, wanting her to absorb some of my pain but not wanting to hurt her. Yet I find I'm too weak to turn her away. I'm not as masochistic as I thought.

She is the first to let go. "You've ignored all my calls and texts," she says. "And there were a lot of them."

"I know." I duck my head as people walk by and gawk when they realize who Taylor is talking to. "I'm sorry. I just…" My mouth clamps shut, unable to continue.

"I know." Taylor places an arm over my shoulder and pulls me close. I inhale the clean smell of shampoo, a hint of chlorine. "You should have told me you were coming today. I would have come with you?"

"Really?"

"Really. God, Sam. You don't need to face it all alone."

I don't? I inhale deeply and close my eyes. "Thanks," I whisper. She's thrown me a lifeline, and surprisingly, I grasp onto it, digging my fingernails in tightly. I didn't realize how frightening it would be to be alone with this. I didn't realize how much I want someone with me. Taking on the blame might be more than I thought I could handle.

"Take a frickin' picture," she snarls, and I glance over to see a group of freshman girls blatantly staring at us. I almost smile at the way they break up and scatter, running off in the other direction.

Taylor takes my hand and leads me. We walk slowly, and the crowd parts to let us through. Taylor seems oblivious. "We miss you so much at the pool."

I attempt a smile, but my lips quaver and instead I duck my head down to keep from bawling. "Thanks," I whisper.

She snarls at a couple more gawkers. "Get over it, bitches," she calls and then turns to me. "Clair is nagging me to help get you back in the pool."

"Not yet," I say. *Not ever*, I think. I drop her hand, but we keep walking together.

"Well, hurry. I need you to keep my slow ass moving."

She's lying. Taylor set a club record at a swim meet on the

weekend, beating her best time in the 100 breast by over two seconds. She also beat my best time by half a second. Dad read me the results posted online.

"I heard you did great at the meet. Congratulations." I swallow back my competitive juices and try to be genuinely happy for her. I want to be. I'm supposed to be. But happy is a stretch.

When Dad read off the winning times my legs itched. I did my best to ignore them. With neglect, my drive would eventually fade away the same way I would start disappearing off record books. Alex would never hit another home run. He'd never leap over a railing and pump his fist in the air while doing Parkour. Why should I be allowed to defend or break swim records?

"Thanks," Taylor says. "It was kind of awesome." She smiles. "Of course, as soon as you come back, you'll beat my time. Me. I am destined for second best."

"That's not true," I frown at her. "You're not second best."

She shrugs a shoulder and then flicks back her thick hair and runs her fingers through it. "It's not a big deal. It's where my mom would prefer me to be."

The expression on her face changes. Her lips press together. Her eyes narrow. Interesting. I think of our swim meets. Neither of her parents is usually there. I've seen her dad around the pool, but I can't remember seeing her mom. They never volunteer for the team. They're what Dad calls "cutters" instead of "doers." They cut checks instead of doing the work.

"You're just as good as me." I'm surprised to realize it's true. I never questioned that I was better, and that's probably what kept me in front of her in the pool. I've always believed I would win. And apparently she's always believed she would come in second. It's inexcusable that she felt this way and I was just too involved in my own life to notice. My shallowness surprises me.

"Whatever." She shrugs again and then pulls her phone from her jacket and glances down at it. "Only a couple minutes left." She stops abruptly, and I almost crash into her. "I have to go this way. Biology with Mr. Bruster."

Reality hits with a thunk. I want to go back to thinking about her life. Go to class with her. I want to shrink her and carry her around in my pocket. I don't want her to leave me. She leans in closer.

"Sam," she says, lowering her voice. "I saw you and your dad parked outside at Alex's funeral," she whispers. "I waited for you, but you didn't come in."

I blink furiously as memories from the funeral day pop up.

"Sam?" Taylor's voice pulls me back to the school hallway. "Are you okay?"

My hands shake, and I make fists to stop the trembling. "I couldn't," I whisper. "I didn't want to upset his family." I'm afraid the bigger truth is that I couldn't made amends and I chickened out. And it shames me to the core. I never felt the quitter in me as much as I did that day. I didn't like it at all.

Taylor reaches for my hand and squeezes it and then lets it go.

I open my mouth to say something, but my thought vanishes when something behind Taylor catches my eye. The air around me thins. I can't talk or even breathe. I wonder if there's a funky smell coming off me. I wonder if fear has an odor.

My vision goes blurry. My moment of reckoning has arrived. I can only stare. He's walking toward me, someone at his side. There's no way for me to escape. He's seen me. It can't get any worse.

chapter seven

It gets worse.

Zee's so tall he's impossible to miss over the crowd of students roaming the hallways. It seems that the world slows down. His face changes when he spots me, and then every person around us stiffens, as if they sense a faceoff. Heads turn toward me and then back to Zee. The crowd parts slightly and my stomach pricks with another sharp shock of pain. Walking beside Zee is Alex's sister, Chloe.

The blood in my veins freezes. I grab for Taylor and lean against her for strength.

"It's okay," she whispers into my ear. "You can do this, Sam." I'm so happy she's with me I'd give her my kidneys. Both of them.

Zee glances sideways at Chloe. He leans down and whispers something in her ear, and she lowers her eyes and nods.

I hold my breath. Waiting for her to look up. Yell something at me. Thrust black horrible words into the air and make me suffer. I wait for her vicious accusation. My heart thumps, and I feel like a boxer waiting for the first punch to be thrown. When our eyes finally meet, she blinks. The blink is slow and exaggerated. And then her gaze purposely moves past me as if she did not even see me standing there. Staring at her. She dismisses me.

Zee grabs Chloe's hand and pulls her along. They pick up their pace. Zee drags her through the hall as if they're pushing through water.

"Zee!" Taylor calls, but he ignores her.

In a few hurried steps, they're gone. Nothing is said. No words are exchanged. They don't even look at me again.

I am nothing.

As if a hole has been jabbed in me, my body deflates. Taylor's cheeks redden, and she stares after them and grabs my arm, her fingernails digging into my flesh hard enough to leave half-moon imprints.

"They need time is all. Alex was like a brother to Zee. And Chloe, well, of course she's messed up. But they know it wasn't your fault, Sam. Deep down. They'll come around." She removes her fingers from my arm, and I press my lips tighter and nod as if I believe her.

Taylor clears her throat and glances down at her phone. "The bell is going to ring any second. You have advanced English, right?"

I nod. The class I've been dreading. Apparently for good reason.

"Shit. With Zee." She glances down the hallway. "Screw it, I'm going the other way, but I'll walk you to class." She puts her arm around me and pulls me down the hallway, fending off onlookers with fierce stares. It feels like someone else is wearing my body, and my head is foggy and confused. I've never felt so grateful to someone for their support and so incapable of expressing my appreciation at the same time.

She walks me to the door of my class and gives my back a gentle push. "It's okay," she says quietly. "You've got to face it sometime, and it's going to be okay."

But it's pretty apparent how his jury voted, and we both saw it.

I'm as guilty as can be. With Taylor whispering support, I attempt a smile, mouth her a *thanks*, and take a deep breath as she jogs off.

I step inside the room. Kids are slumped in chairs, some texting, or sitting on top of desks. Almost everyone is chatting, but no one says a thing to me. They duck their heads if I accidentally catch their eye. A quick glance to the corner, and I see the teacher isn't at his seat yet.

I slide into the first empty desk without looking around, thankful this teacher isn't obsessed with assigned seating. There's noise as someone takes the chair behind me.

The bell rings, and groans float up in the air.

"Hey, Sam," a voice says.

Casper. I try to fake a smile but fail, so I just lift my hand and turn around, wondering why he's being nice to me. The English teacher rushes into the classroom, his face still buried in his BlackBerry.

"Turn off your phones," Mr. Duffield calls.

"Turn off yours," someone calls back.

"Psst, Sam."

My eyebrows push together, and I pretend not to hear over Mr. Duffield chewing out the smartass.

"Sam," Casper calls again.

I ignore him, hoping he'll take the hint.

"I do not like green eggs and ham," Casper whispers, but this time it's noisier. "I do not like them, Sam I am.

"I do not like green eggs and ham, I do not like them, Sam I am." He says it louder, so I finally turn to him and he grins. "If you will let me be, I will try them. you will see."

"Seriously? Dr. Seuss?" I say.

He laughs a squeaky, high-pitched laugh loud enough to attract attention. I scrunch up my shoulders and bury my chin into my chest as eyes turn toward us.

Mr. Duffield glances our way. Great. I don't want any more attention, but fortunately he's decided it might be more valuable to spend class time teaching. I say a silent prayer of thanks to the teacher gods.

"Be my partner," Casper says.

"For what?" I whisper.

"We have to do a joint study on *1984*. I was thinking that we could do a paper on double thinking as it applies to our world versus the world in the novel."

"Casper?" the teacher calls. "Is there something you need to share with the class?"

"Not so much, Mr. Duffield. Catching Samantha up on what she missed," he tells him. Every eye in the room turns to me, and my face boils to hot tub temperature. "We've decided to work together on the team assignment."

We have?

The teacher eyes us both and then nods. "Fine," he says and reaches toward his desk. He types something on his laptop keypad and then looks up. "All right, who else is pairing up?"

Other kids raise their hands, and Mr. Duffield one-finger types names into his laptop.

With my hands folded, I stare down at my desk, but my skin tingles with the feeling that someone is staring at me. I look up and glance over a couple of rows. Zee's eyes are narrowed and shooting virtual bullets into my brain. He lifts his chin slowly and, with a purposeful look straight at me, raises his hand.

"I'll partner with Kaitlin, Mr. Duffield," Zee calls out and looks away.

Kaitlin practically purrs with approval, and a few boys around them whoop like overgrown monkeys.

Zee grins, but the edges of anger don't leave his face. Behind him, Kaitlin flashes me an evil sideways smile.

"Typical Zee. More interested in scoring than grades," Casper says quietly, and then he laughs.

My heart flops. Of course Zee is interested in Kaitlin. I blow out a big breath. As if it matters. Zee already made his choice pretty clear. And I killed any chance I ever had with him. The thought chokes me and I squeeze my eyes tight. No pun intended, indeed.

Casper taps me on the shoulder. When I turn around, he passes me a piece of paper. "My phone number," he says. His voice isn't deep, and it has more cracks it in than an old sidewalk, but it's a pitch that carries. I know every person in the room can hear us.

"I'd like to get started right away. I want an A-plus on this." He glances purposefully around the room. "And who knows what else we might get…"

My spidey sense tingles. Is he actually flirting with me?

"Can I get your number?" he says, as if to promote the idea.

The creepy sensation on my skin returns, and I glance over. Zee looks like he just got disqualified in a swim race. I lift my chin.

"Sure." I jot my number down in my notebook, rip the page out, and hand it over to him.

"Better not get too close," someone behind him mumbles. "She'll take you down the way black widows eat their prey."

"Hey, dickhead," Casper says. "Did you listen to what they said at the assembly? You're supposed to be compassionate."

As much as I'm mortified to have it confirmed that I was discussed at school, it doesn't surprise me. Unlike on the news reports, my name is on everyone's lips here. My heart warms to Casper. I'm almost inclined to hug him.

"She didn't know, and obviously she feels bad, so back off," he says.

I turn and focus on my desk top again.

"Sam can get as close to me as she wants," Casper continues, and I wish he would have stopped a sentence ago. His voice carries across the room.

Kaitlin coughs once into her hand. It sounds very much like she coughed out the word "killer." There's a few low laughs but also a couple of dirty looks thrown her way.

A girl beside me smiles at me with sadness in her eyes. It's supportive and makes me want to cry. Fortunately, Mr. Duffield finally moves away from his desk and starts a lecture about George Orwell.

• • •

After school, I make an emergency phone call to Bob, feeling overwhelmed and not sure I can face another day with everyone staring at me and making such nasty comments. He talks me down and goes over the good things I accomplished. I don't really believe him when he tells me I'm brave and resilient, but I like when he tells me he's proud of me. I hang up feeling somewhat stronger.

That night Dad and I sit down to eat a roast he made in the

crockpot. "Your aunt is coming for a visit. Hopefully a short one," he says between bites. It's tough and chewy, but at least he's actually made an effort to cook something that didn't come frozen in a box. Since the accident I haven't been in the mood to cook. Or eat. My clothes are baggy. When I do eat, all I can manage is canned soup or scrambled eggs with plain toast. I threw out the peanut butter jar.

I stop gnawing on the meat and put down my fork. "Really?"

"I can't stop her from coming. God knows I've tried."

I grab a snap pea and bite off the end of it, and then I pick up my glass of milk. I'm overwhelmed by the emptiness in my middle that food won't fill. I wish she were already here. "It'll be nice," I say, pretending nonchalance, and sip my milk, watching the expression on Dad's face over the top of the glass.

His eyes shoot fireworks, and he makes a face. "Nice if you like to have all the oxygen in the room sucked out before you can take a breath," he mumbles. He sounds like a belligerent little boy, and in spite of myself, I smile.

"She's dragging along that little mutt she carries with her all the time too."

He pretends to hate dogs, but Aunt Allie told me he's been deathly afraid of them since he was a little boy. The thought of him being frightened by a tiny black Chihuahua makes me cough into my hand to hide a smile. It feels odd and out of place on my face. My cheeks crackle with the effort.

"She doesn't go anywhere without Fredrick," I remind him. "He's traveled all over the country with her."

"Who names a dog Fredrick? Especially one the size of a rat." He shapes his hands into claws and lifts them into the air. "Her and that little dog too," he says, imitating the witch on *The Wizard of Oz*. We probably watched that movie a hundred times when I was a kid.

Aunt Allie brings out sides of Dad that usually lay dormant. He drops his hands and scrunches up his face. "I'm hoping she won't stay too long, but who the hell knows?"

"You don't mean that."

He sticks his fork into the pile of lumpy potatoes on his plate. "Don't I? If that dog pees on our floor, I'll scalp him." He puts his fork down, lifts his wine glass, and takes a long sip.

"Fredrick uses a litter box, Dad," I remind him.

"And that's not weird? He's a dog, not a cat."

"I like Fredrick."

"Yeah. Well, you also like your aunt."

"So do you, Dad. You just hide it better."

He snorts. "You didn't grow up with her running your life the way I did."

The twelve-year difference suggests he was kind of an "oops" baby, and it sounds like she ran his life because his parents were busy living theirs. Like most unpleasant things in his life, he deals but chooses not to talk about it. "Anyhow, she's been calling and calling, and I couldn't put her off any longer. She's arriving tomorrow. Of course, now I have to take time off work to get her from the airport. "

"I could go pick her up," I offer immediately.

"You've missed enough school already." He pours himself another glass of wine. "How was today?" he asks to change the subject.

I shrug and use my finger to pick up a piece of roast and shove it in my mouth. "You think she'll give me a reading?"

"God, I hope not." He takes another long sip of wine and pushes his plate away. "You think I can stop her? It's embarrassing the way she believes in that stuff."

"I don't think it's embarrassing. It's cool." I don't tell him I'm hoping she'll read my cards and maybe a death card or something will show up to claim me. Or at least the disaster card, dooming me to a horrible fate.

"I don't know why you're interested in that stuff. Don't even think you'll ever be allowed to follow in her footsteps."

"I'm not the psychic type, Dad. It's not exactly in my cards." I make air quotes at "cards," but instead of laughing he makes a face like he smells something rotten.

"Anyhow, Aunt Allie has three degrees and is fluent in three languages. I'd say that makes her kind of a genius." Smarter than him, even, but I know better than to say that out loud. "She does it because she loves it." I pick up my plate, walk over to the garbage, and empty my leftovers into it.

"She's wasted her brains doing that wacko stuff." Dad sips at his wine again, and I frown, worried he's going to pound back the whole bottle the way he's going.

"She hated working in an office," I remind him, opening the dishwasher to push my dish inside. "She's happier doing what she loves."

Dad gives me a funny look. I usually keep my opinions about Aunt Allie to myself, and he's taken my silence as an implication that I'm on his side. But with my guts hanging out for everyone to see, the truths about most things are closer to the surface than usual.

"Well, apparently corporate America hated her back." He sighs. "Besides, being responsible isn't the same as being happy."

"Being responsible doesn't mean you have to be an accountant," I say softly.

Where Aunt Allie is about spirituality, growth, and healing, he's all about balancing ledgers and controlling spreadsheets. His world is black and white, hers is filled with blended colors. But she makes lots of money. I know that. It's not what motivates her, though. She travels with an international psychic fair and helps people deal with their lives.

I think she forces him to look beyond his tightly controlled world at the messy things that can't be added or subtracted in the correct column. And he doesn't like it. Aunt Allie drives him crazy, but even though he never admits it, I know he loves her. Me, I love Aunt Allie more than anyone else in the world. Besides him. And I kind of have to love him.

Auntie Allie whirls in and out of our lives like a living cyclone. Dad is her moon. I am her sun. That's what she tells me. She travels around, but she always orbits back to us. They drive each other crazy fighting, and she's not around as much as she'd like to be, but she always has my back. Like in first grade, when I'd been upset about a Mother's Day tea. I couldn't stop crying and stuttering about being the only girl without a mother to take. Dad had planned to take me, but one of the girls in my class lifted her bitchy little chin to declare that dads shouldn't be allowed because it was girls only. As my tears flowed, he'd held me, and when the hiccups started, he got up and went to the phone and made a call. The next day, Aunt Allie showed up. She'd flown halfway across the country to have tea.

"Well, I'm glad she's coming." I look forward to being diverted by her crazy tales of other places and other people's lives. Or past lives.

The landline rings. "Get that, would you, Sam?" Frowning, I walk over and stare at it. A private number. I pick it up.

"Hello?"

"Samantha?" I recognize the voice right away.

"Casper?"

Dad looks over, his eyebrows rising. I catch his eye and he looks away, but I can tell by his straight back and unblinking gaze that his full attention is on me and the caller on the other end of the phone. Boys call me, like, never.

"You recognize my voice? I'm flattered. So. How's things?"

With my dad watching, making small talk with Casper is just about the last thing I want to be doing. "Fine. Um. It's not really a good time for me to talk." Nothing like me getting right to the point, then.

Dad clears his throat and picks up his wine. I turn my back to him.

"Okay. Straight to it. I'll have to tell you how beautiful your eyes are another time."

My cheeks burn, and I'm glad my face is hidden from Dad.

"So? My place or yours?" he says.

"What?"

"We need to start working on our English project. Remember. An A-plus-plus."

"Yeah. Um. Yours." I don't want to invite anyone into my house. It's too embarrassing to think of anyone seeing what I used to be.

"Good choice, Sam. You're off to great places! You're off and away!"

I wish he could see me rolling my eyes. "Dr. Seuss again?"

He laughs. "See, that's what I love about you. You totally got that. So how about Friday night?"

"Friday night?"

"You got a date?" he asks. There's a bit of a nasty edge to his voice.

"Friday's fine."

"Great. Give me your cell number, and I'll text you my address." The friendliness is back. Casper the friendly ghost.

He says good-bye, and the phone clicks in my ear before I say the same. I hold the dead air to my ear, thinking about how much it bothers Dad when people hang up without waiting for him to say good-bye first.

"Good-bye," I say to no one and put the phone back on the cradle.

"That was a boy?" Dad says.

I turn to look at him. "An English project."

"Hmm. That's not what we called it in my day."

"Not funny, Dad. We're doing a report on *1984* and it's going to be a big part of my grade. Casper is smart, and he wants to work with me because I'm smart too."

His lips turn up, and he sits up straight and tries to look contrite by scrunching up his eyebrows. "Sorry," he says "Smart is right. Especially in English. My worst subject. I was a math guy."

"I never would have guessed that." Except I've heard it, like, a hundred times before. I walk to the table, take his dishes to the garbage, clear them, and load them into the dishwasher. I come back to put the condiments away, and he's still staring at me. "What?" I ask.

He tilts his head, and his eyes crinkle in the corners. Concerned. "Are the kids at school being…you know, okay?"

I frown, lift my shoulder, grab the salt and pepper shakers from the table, and stick them in the cupboard.

"Did they…" He pauses and I spin around, frowning at him as I grab the milk carton from the table.

"What?" I demand when he stops.

"Your swim team didn't start rumors, like they did in Orlie?"

"Dad!" My mouth drops open. I hurry to the fridge, shove the milk inside, and then stare at him, shocked. My face is hotter than the sunburn I got in California at an outdoor swim meet last year. He knew about the rumors?

He looks around the room, as if he'd rather be somewhere else than having a convo with me about my sexual orientation. "I knew it wasn't true. I mean. It isn't. Right?"

"I'm sure if the dead could speak, Alex would back me up on this one."

"Oh, butterfly." He stands and takes a step toward me but I step back and press my back against the refrigerator.

"No, that rumor is gone. Now I'm just a murderer. A straight one."

He takes a step toward me and then stops. "Are the kids bullying you?"

"No. They fucking love me, Dad. Why wouldn't they?"

I wait for him to yell at me for saying the F-word in front of him. He says nothing. A part of me realizes I want him to yell. To talk about what's happening, even in anger. But he stares at me as if I'm someone he doesn't even know.

In some ways, he's right.

"Do you need to go back and see the counselor?" he calls.

I head for my bedroom. "Bob and I have an appointment in a week," I call back. "I'm good."

I need to talk, but as usual, there's so much Dad and I don't say. So much we need to say. Like the F-word. Over and over and over. Until my throat begs for mercy.

chapter eight

A couple of days later, I walk in the door from school and Aunt Allie jumps up from the kitchen table and whirls toward me, a blend of turquoise and browns, as her skirt and billowy sweater blow all around her. She's holding Fredrick in one arm. He has a tiny little head with pointy black ears, and he's wearing a miniature bandana with autumn leaves all over it.

Fredrick stares at me with a slightly entitled expression shining in his eyes and barks a high-pitched squeal, but his tail wags as Aunt Allie pulls me toward her with her free arm. He maneuvers around us and licks my face to renew our friendship.

Aunt Allie crushes me into her shoulder. Her flowery scent is both familiar and comforting. She never changes much. Skirts, scarves, blouses, vests. When she lets me go, she lifts my chin and stares into my eyes with her intensely green-blue ones, so much like Dad's and my own. Hers are enhanced with eyeliner and see much more than I ever want them to. Whether it's because of her spirituality and dabblings in all things psychic or just because she knows me so well, I'm never sure.

"I'm so sorry about what you've been going through, butterfly." Her voice is low and gravelly. "I would have come sooner, but I was in a convention in Houston. Keynote speaker." She lets my chin go and hugs me close again.

Behind us, Dad is sitting at the kitchen table, visible from the foyer. He clears his throat and mumbles something, but we both ignore him.

"It's okay," I say into her shoulder.

"We knew you'd come eventually," Dad mumbles a little louder.

She gently pushes me back so she can look over to the kitchen and glare at him, but she keeps one arm around me, Fredrick tucked up in the other. I slide off my shoes and slip out from her.

"No, it's not okay. Sam needed me. I don't care what you say, Jonathan. She did. Does." She narrows her eyes and shoots him a look so evil that if I were on the other end of it I would sleep with one eye open for the rest of my life. He merely rolls his.

"The truth is, I would have flown here the minute I heard about the accident, but your dad said to give you space. I came as soon as your father would let me."

"Way to"—Dad makes air quotation marks—"hold your tongue."

Aunt Allie makes a *pshhaw* sound. "I don't want to darken the energy in this house with more lies. She needs to know I love her and would drop everything for her."

"She's my daughter," Dad says.

"And she's my niece. Also a girl who desperately needs the love of a woman right now. A relative, not a nanny. And unfortunately, I'm the closest thing she's got."

I know she auditioned hard for the role of surrogate mom, but Dad went with a nanny from the time I was little. She still brings it up every once in a while, even though the nanny days are behind me. It's not the first or the last time they'll bicker about me.

Dad studies the table and brushes away imaginary crumbs. "I didn't ask you to lie to her. You just don't have to blurt out every thought on your mind."

"I'm glad you're here," I say before she can answer.

I reach out to pet Fredrick. He snorts happily and licks my hand, wagging his tail. His head is out of proportion with his body. Pencil-thin legs support his bloated tummy. He paws at my arm, demanding that I take him from Aunt Allie and give him the attention he deserves.

"*Hola, mi amiga*," Aunt Allie says in a Spanish voice, pretending she is the voice of Fredrick. "You are so beautiful."

She holds him out, and he uses my arm to crawl over and prop himself up to my face and then sticks his tiny tongue inside my nose. It makes me laugh, and it's a relief to have the dark clouds parted, even for a brief moment.

"Fredrick loves you," she says. "He doesn't take to many people."

"He always growls at me," Dad says.

"Like I was about to say, he has very good taste," Aunt Allie says.

"Ha ha," Dad says, regressing in front of my eyes.

Aunt Allie takes Fredrick from me, places him on the floor, and then grabs my hand and leads me to the kitchen table. There's a plate of giant cookies in the middle, and she gestures toward it.

"Please. Eat them. They're for you." She glares at Dad as he's taking a big bite of one.

"You baked them yourself?" Dad smiles a bratty smile. I don't think he notices how much more laid back he is when his big sister is around. She's not all bad for him.

"Of course I did. At the Starbucks bakery. At the airport." Aunt Allie waves her hand in the air. "Just eat them. They cost a bloody fortune."

"You inherited your cooking gene from Mom," he says.

"As did you," she answers, plucking a cookie from the pile and nibbling at it.

"Didn't Mom tell you boys aren't supposed to cook?" Dad says.

"I may have heard that once or twice." A tiny smile turns up the corner of her mouth, and they stare at each other for a moment across the table. They don't speak, but a whole conversation seems to happen.

"You going to eat, Sam?"

I wonder if the cookies are peanut free. "I just ate at school," I lie. "Dad's not that bad a cook," I add to defend him.

"Well. He's improved then," she says and flashes him a grin.

"You're one to talk," Dad says. I half expect him to stick his tongue at her like a five-year-old.

Aunt Allie takes another bite of her cookie. "Have you talked to them? Mom or Dad?" she asks, her voice softer than usual.

He nods. "Mom. A few days ago." He glances at me and then back at Aunt Allie. "They're doing okay. Well, getting old. Dad is on heart medication. Mom's osteo is worse. They're cranky and self-centered, as always." He smiles. "They asked about you. Whether you'd be coming to see Sam."

"They didn't offer to come, of course?"

Dad shakes his head.

"Of course not," Aunt Allie says. "That would require actual human compassion."

Both of them stare off into space. "At least we don't have to worry about me being spoiled by grandparents," I say.

Aunt Allie shakes her head and turns to me and smiles. "That we don't."

Fredrick runs over and paws at her legs. Aunt Allie bends to scoop him up in her lap. She breaks off a tiny piece of cookie and gives it to him.

Dad makes a coughing sound in his throat. Aunt Allie glances at Dad. "At least you and Sam cook. I hated cooking when I was a kid." She holds out another piece of cookie for Fredrick, but he turns up his nose at it.

"I know. I remember."

She eats the piece she offered to Fredrick, and I gag a little inside. Then she turns back to me. "Your dad looks tired, Samantha. I don't suppose I can hope it's from getting too much action."

My mouth opens, but I'm lost for words. Dad shoots me an "I told you so" look, but then he actually laughs. "Allie, please. You'll scar Sam for life. And seriously, do you need to have your dog in your lap at the table? And share your food? You're making us sick."

"Of course I do," Aunt Allie says, flicking her hand in the air. "And it would take a lot more than that to shock teenagers these days. Probably shock Sam if you had a real conversation with a live woman. You're the most stubborn man I know. Single for over sixteen years." She makes a sign of the cross, lifts Fredrick, tucks him under her arm, and then stands and walks to our gigantic fridge. "I might borrow Sam's laptop and set up a profile for you on one of those dating services."

He glances at me. We both know he was seeing a woman from work back in Orlie, even if we didn't talk about it much. Rose. She wore yoga pants and ugly sweaters. She was nice, mostly quiet, kind of a female version of him. I couldn't imagine them doing anything except having dinner together and bonding over spreadsheets and chose to believe their relationship was purely platonic, even though some mornings when I got up she was still there. Too much to drink, I told myself.

He hasn't talked about her since we moved, and neither have I. The fact that he never mentioned her to Aunt Allie doesn't surprise me in the least. He's good at keeping secrets.

"You're one to talk," he says to Aunt Allie, but his voice is bouncy, as if he's enjoying the break in the seriousness that's been clogging the air in our house. "When's the last time you went on a date?"

I hide a smile behind my hand. "Yeah. We've never met any of your man friends."

Aunt Allie scowls at both of us. "I was meant to be alone on this planet. I have Fredrick, and he isn't threatened by my intelligence. Nor does he hog the remote or tell me my butt is getting big. Besides, according to my angels, my soul mate passed before I was born."

"Bullshit," Dad coughs into his hand again, but she ignores him.

"But you. An attractive, relatively young man in a town of

divorced woman. Unlike me, you need someone." She tugs on the door of the stainless steel fridge. It's heavy.

"I don't *need* someone, and how do you even know there are divorced women in this town?"

She pops her head and arm inside the fridge and emerges with a bottle of white wine in her hand. "This is America, isn't it? Divorced women are an epidemic." She holds up the wine bottle for my dad's approval. "Shall we?"

He glances down at his watch. "It's not five o' clock yet."

She gives him a look that would give me nightmares if it were directed at me. He stands and grabs the wine bottle from her hand and digs in the kitchen drawer for the corkscrew.

He grabs a wineglass, fills it halfway, and hands it to Aunt Allie. She sticks her nose inside the glass and sniffs appreciatively. "Mmmm. Sauvignon blanc. You going to have some, Sam?"

"No, she's not," Dad answers. "She's underage."

"European children drink wine with their families all the time."

"Last time I checked, we were living in the United States of America."

"You always were an observant child," she says to him and shrugs as she turns to me. "And what about you, butterfly? I heard you've had your eye on some handsome young swimmer?"

The levity in the room vanishes. Reality crashes hard. My whole body converts back to ice. For a moment, I'm incapable of movement.

"Allie," Dad says and glances sideways at me. "She's still getting over this…thing."

"Of course she is," my aunt says. She sips her wine and watches me over the rim of her glass. "I'm sorry, Sam, but you're not going to give up on boys forever, are you? Just because your father and I live like a priest and a nun doesn't mean you have to."

My knee bounces up and down under the table. I bend my head down and put my elbows on the table. "Dad had a girlfriend in Orlie. She stayed the night a couple times," I mutter.

"Sam!" Dad says. "That's private." I look up, and he's glaring at Aunt Allie. She's grinning at him.

"You just got here. We don't need to discuss this right now," he tells her, but I know he's not talking about his girlfriend.

"Yes. We do." She takes a few steps to me, reaches down for my shoulder, and squeezes it. "I'm just trying to show you that life goes on," she says softly. "What happened to that boy was awful. But not talking about it isn't going to make it go away."

I lift my hands and press my palms into my eyes. "Nothing will make it go away. It's on every TV channel and all over the newspapers. It's even on the radio when I drive to school."

"Samantha, you kissed a boy. That is far from a crime at your age. There was a horrible, horrible accident." I hear her place Fredrick on the floor, and his nails tap the tile. "It wasn't your fault. Your life will go on. You will go on to kiss other boys."

My earlobes feel like they're about to spontaneously burst into flames. I wonder if it's possible for them to melt my brain.

She sips her wine again. "I have a client up in Canada who heard about it. But I'm so grateful your name isn't being splashed all over the place."

"Why? Because it would be an embarrassment? If people found out I was your niece?"

"Sam!" Dad says, and it's clear he's not on my side on this one.

I lower my chin. "Sorry," I say to the table, but we both know I don't really mean it.

"Of course not, Samantha," Aunt Allie says. "You're innocent. All you did was something that almost every teenage girl has done or will do. I just want to make sure you're protected from crazies. 'Cause there are always some of those out there. We don't need your name inviting them in."

I push my hands into my eyes to block her out.

"Have you started swimming again?" she asks.

I pull my hands away from my eyes and glare at Dad, wondering if he's put her up to this, but he looks about as comfortable as I feel about this conversation.

"No." My lips press tightly together.

"Why not?"

I shake my head.

"Why not?" she repeats.

"Allie," Dad says. "You're pushing her too hard."

She ignores him and keeps her focus on me, narrowing her eyes.

"I can't," I whisper to her, afraid she can see what's in my head. The feeling is familiar, and my stomach tumbles into coils.

"You can." Aunt Allie sits. "You choose not to." Fredrick paws at her legs and whimpers, and she lifts him back into her lap. She sips her wine, watching me. "You don't think you deserve to go on with your life?"

"Leave her alone," Dad says. "Her doctor said to give her time."

"Her doctor doesn't know her. Swimming is as important to this child as breathing and eating. Why do you think you can't swim, Sam?"

I lift a shoulder and concentrate on breathing, feeling the control I've built up start to slip. She's trying to force me to admit something I can't even put into words. I can't admit I miss the pool. Swimming. I have all this free time and all this anxiety. And nothing to do with it.

"Survivor guilt, Sam. You're suffering terribly from it. And I knew your father would not be much help." She turns to him and frowns. "No offense, Jonathan, I know you love her and want what's best for her, but she needs to deal with this. Talk about it. Not pretend it never happened. Not pretend it's all going to go away. If Sam is going to get her life back, she has to face some things."

"She's seeing a therapist," Dad says. "Bob."

"And that is a wonderful start." She looks back at me. "But Bob doesn't live with her. He doesn't speak to her every day."

"I can call him if I need to," I mumble. "He gave me his cell number for emergencies."

"And that's great too. You have to deal with everything as it comes. Head on. And I'm sure he's a great help. But guess what? I'm here to help too. Twenty-four seven. Any way I can. I'm not going to trivialize what happened or your right to be upset, but you need to learn how to go on with your life as well."

"Allie. Really. Do we have to talk about this now?" Dad says. "We're not professionals."

"Yes, Jonathan. We do have to talk about it now. No. We're not professionals. But we love her. This is one of the reasons I came. Sam needs to talk about it. Now."

I don't say anything. I stare at the table. My mind is fogged up.

"Her aura is very disturbed. I think we could do a few Reiki sessions. I want to consult with her angels."

"Her aura is fine," Dad says and stands up, smacking his hands on the table. "Don't start with the woo-woo stuff already, Allie. You just got here."

"Um. Hello? I'm sitting right here," I remind them.

Suddenly I'm not so sure her visit was a good idea either. The air in the room seems darker. For a moment I picture myself under water. Getting pushed down without being able to fight back or move my arms. I'm struggling not to drown.

"Your aura is very dark too, Jonathan. There's a lot of repressed emotion in this room."

"There's a lot of bullshit in this room." He stomps out of the kitchen toward the back stairs that lead to the basement. I watch him disappear into his man cave with the big-screen TV and La-Z-Boy chair. I kind of want to follow, run behind him, away from things I don't want to deal with either. But I'm pinned to the spot. Saturated with emotions I've been stuffing down and unable to move under the weight of them.

Aunt Allie breathes out loudly. "I'm sorry, Sam. Your dad and I are not always good at communicating." She sips at her wine. "Well. He is good at storming out on me. I'll give him that. But he'll come around. I know him better than I know myself sometimes."

She lifts Fredrick up to look at me. "*Nosotros tenemos que ayudar a*," she says in her Fredrick voice. "We have to help." She places him back on the floor, reaches over the table, and places her large hand over mine. Her skin is thin and spotty. Older than it used to look.

"If there's one thing I know, it's that repressing feelings only makes them come out in other ways. And I don't mean healthy ways."

She pats my hand and then lifts it and places my palm in hers. She studies the lines and clicks her tongue. I want to ask her what she sees, but I'm afraid of what it might be. What my destiny has become. She traces her finger over my palm and presses her lips tighter. Her hand twitches slightly.

"We need to do a proper reading," she says.

"How about now?" I offer, focusing on her hands, with mine tucked inside.

"First we need to cleanse your essence. Things need to be done on this plane before we look to the next." She squeezes my hand and then lets it go. "Before we speak with your angels, before they will be willing to reveal anything, you'll need to confront your feelings. You need to look deep in your heart. There are things you need to do."

I pull my hand away and twist my braid around my finger. "I don't know what you mean. I just want a reading."

"I'm going to have to cleanse this house too," she announces as if I hadn't even spoken. "Clean out the bad vibes. It's time to start healing. To begin, we'll purify the air in this home."

Aunt Allie purses her lips together and smiles at me. "You have to deal. Starting with the boy. You have to tell him how you feel."

"Aunt Allie, I don't know if you noticed, but he's dead." My attempt at a joke falls flat. I stare at the kitchen table.

She reaches over and pats my hand again. "Talk to him. No. Write him a letter. You don't have to show it to me. You don't have to show it to anyone. But it must be done. It's part of your healing." She pauses, tilting her head to the side and staring off as if listening to someone or something.

"I don't want to write him a letter. It's not like he'll be able to read it."

"No. But you will. It will help." She lowers her head. "And so it is," she says. To someone. Or something.

I glance around the room. But there's only me, her. And Fredrick at her feet.

"This is necessary. Can you do it?"

I shrug. I don't want to lie to her, but I can't do what she asks.

"Do you want to get better?" she asks.

I can't honestly answer that question with a yes.

"Please?" she asks. "Can you do it for me? Your kooky old aunt?"

"Let me think about it," I tell her. Maybe I don't need a reading after all.

"Good." She sips her wine and makes a face. "We also need you to talk about your mother."

My mouth drops open, but nothing comes out.

"She's been gone a long time," she says, her voice lowered but loving. "But you two still haven't dealt with it as a family."

She takes another sip of wine. "Your mom watches over you, Sam. She always will. But she's not an angel. There's a difference. Angels guide. Your mom can't do that anymore." She stands and walks to the sink and pours out the rest of her wine. "The energy in this house is affecting the taste of the wine."

"If there are angels, then why did Alex have to die?" I ask.

She sighs. "Angels don't control destiny."

She leans against the counter and puts down the empty glass. "Sometimes a tragedy opens more old wounds. You have a door opened to you now, Samantha. The healing's been put off for long enough. You have a chance to heal more than one wound."

I close my eyes and inhale deeply. "I would like to know more about my mom."

"And you will. I promise you that. She's been a silent ghost for years. I can show you parts of her. And so can your father. It's time you got to know her. And what you lost."

I frown, wanting to believe she's just a fake. A flake. But in my heart, I believe in Aunt Allie. I always have.

"Start with the letter," she says. "And then we'll go further."

I can pretend I don't, but I want a reading. So much. Aunt Allie's contact with angels always gives me tremendous relief that there is something bigger out there. That there is someone or something on my side. I believe in her angels. And I need them. For me and for Alex. I want to know that he is okay too.

The problem is I can't imagine what I could write to Alex on this level. What would I possibly say? It's too scary to face what I did to him.

Aunt Allie presses her lips together and sighs, about to say something, when we're interrupted.

Boom!

We both jump at an unexpected loud noise outside. It almost sounded like a gunshot.

chapter nine

W hat the hell was that?" Dad yells, as his footsteps tromp up the stairs. We all reach the front door at the same time. Fredrick growls low in his throat but doesn't bark, as if he's wary too.

Dad puts up his hand, motioning for us to get behind him. Aunt Allie tries to step in front, but he gently moves her back. "This is my home," he reminds her.

He presses his eye to the peephole in the door. "I don't see anything."

He unlocks the deadbolt and turns back to us. "Stay there." He pushes the door open and steps out on the porch, pulling the door, but it stays open just an inch.

"Son of a bitch," he mumbles.

I flinch at his words. "What? What is it?"

"What, Jonathan?" Aunt Allie asks. "What's going on?"

"Stay there, stay inside," he says instead of answering.

A moment later, the door reopens. He's holding something behind his back. He won't look at me.

"What is it?" I repeat.

His lips press tight, and he glances at Aunt Allie and then at me. I almost see actual wheels turning inside his head as he tries to think of something to say. "Stupid kids," he mutters. "Just stupid kids."

Invisible spiders race up and down my arms, leaving shivery bumps behind them. I wrap my arms around myself. "Tell me what you saw."

Slowly, shaking his head and mumbling, Dad pulls his hand out from behind his back. His hand grips a small jar of peanut butter. Red lid. Extra crunchy, extra peanuts.

Icicles crystalize my veins.

"Oh." The sound comes out in a puff as my mouth forms the shape of the word.

"Take that shit outside and throw it in the garbage," Aunt Allie says, in a fierce voice so unlike her that my eyes open wider.

I don't know that I've ever heard her swear before. Dad stands in place, holding the jar.

"Go on, Jonathan, get rid of it. It's covered in bad karma. Get it out of the house."

For once, Dad doesn't argue with her. He snaps to action and hurries back out the front door, holding the peanut butter in front of him as if it is deadly poison. Which, as a matter of fact, it is. To some people.

My stomach presses in, and I bend over as if I've been punched.

"No," Aunt Allie snaps. "No." She puts an arm around me and pulls me tight beside her. "We will *not* let this harm you."

My shoulders shake with the effort of holding in sobs trapped in my core. Breathing like a woman in labor, I force it all down, fighting the pain. As I try to calm myself, Aunt Allie directs me to the kitchen, pushing me toward a kitchen chair.

"We start with peppermint tea." She gets the kettle from the stove, takes it to the sink, fills it with water, and places it on a burner. "Too much negativity. It's hard to breathe."

Dad walks back into the kitchen, his hands empty and his face full. Our equally weary gazes meet.

"You okay?" he asks.

I lift a shoulder with effort, too weak to do more.

"That was a really sick thing for someone to do," he says. "Do you want me to call Bob?"

I nod. Fredrick trots over to me and jumps up, pawing at my legs, so I lift him to my lap. He circles around, digging his little nails into my legs.

"This is a sign of Mercury in retrograde," Aunt Allie says. "Tricksters abound. Unresolved issues come to light. Things are in flux."

Fredrick jumps up, licking at my face, chasing at my closed mouth with his tiny tongue. I move away, but he tries to make out with me. As if that might help.

"*No se preocupen. Yo te protegeré*," Aunt Allie says in her Fredrick voice. "Do not worry, my butterfly. I will protect you."

I scratch his tiny head, wishing it were true. That he could protect me.

Dad watches, not moving, not saying anything until the whistle on the kettle starts singing. "When does this retrograde thing end?" he asks Aunt Allie.

"Not soon enough." Aunt Allie pours water into the teapot. "Sit, Jonathan. I'll pour you a cup of tea and explain the basics."

Later, after I have a lengthy conversation with Bob on the phone, they quiz me to make sure I'm not going to off myself. Finally, they leave me alone, and I go to my room and log on to the computer. My Facebook page is filled with comments, but one stands out.

Samantha Waxman sat on a railroad track, her heart was all a flutter. A boy came along so she kissed him. TOOT TOOT Peanut Butter.

chapter ten

The next day, I wake early and open my bedroom door and tiptoe down the hallway. Aunt Allie and Dad are talking in hushed voices in the kitchen. I stop and tune my ears in to what they're saying.

"She says she's fine, but that's all she ever says. She's not fine. This is not a fine situation. She keeps everything inside, just like you. I'm worried about her. She needs to get some of it out."

"I'm worried about her too, Allie. Sam is my baby. I'd do anything if I could change what happened. Anything."

My eyes water at the concern in his voice. His baby?

"Of course you would. But you can't. You can't protect her from this forever."

"Bob said she's handling things okay."

"Bob didn't know her before this happened."

I clear my throat and take loud steps in the hallway, and they stop talking.

"Morning! Breakfast is almost ready," Aunt Allie calls

"Lord save us all," Dad says. He's in a dark shirt and dark pants. The accountant uniform.

Aunt Allie smacks him with the spatula in her hand. With an apron over her clothes, she looks practically maternal.

"I can handle adding water to pancake mix."

"But can you flip them before they burn?"

She smacks him again, and he holds his hands up in self-defense. The truth is she's far from a natural chef, but when she visits she likes to take over for us in the kitchen, and we both let her. Familiar roles. Anyhow it's not like we'd complain about anyone cooking for us.

"Did my mom like to cook?" I ask as I take a spot at the kitchen table across from Dad. The table's loaded with flavored syrups and jams Aunt Allie picked up on shopping trips in town.

They look at each other and then back at me.

"She was okay," Dad says, lifting a shoulder, grabbing an empty glass on the table, and filling it with orange juice.

Aunt Allie snorts as she flips a pancake over in the pan. "She was a terrible cook."

Dad looks shocked for a second and then pushes the full glass at me and laughs. "You're right, she was. She would have said the same thing." Dad chuckles. "She had a good sense of humor."

"She had to, being married to you," Aunt Allie says as she flips a pancake.

They laugh, and Aunt Allie gets into a story about my mom making dinner for her and almost burning down the kitchen. She'd turned on the wrong burner and started the grease for gravy on fire. The microwave melted, the curtains burned, and two fire trucks arrived at the house before Dad even got home from work.

I smile as Dad adds to the story, and before long he has tears rolling down his cheeks, he's laughing so hard. It's music I haven't heard in a long time. Aunt Allie puts a plate in front of me. I choose plain syrup and dig in.

"I'm glad you're here," I tell her. She rumples my hair and smiles. Dad sips at his coffee and glances up. "I am too, Allie."

• • •

That night after school I have a session with Bob. I'm feeling a little more peaceful by the time I get home. I'm at the kitchen table doing math homework when the doorbell rings. The droning sound of the vacuum cleaner doesn't stop from downstairs. For the past few days, Aunt Allie has been cleaning everything in our house, scrubbing down walls with lemon juice, vacuuming, leaving every single window wide open despite the crisp fall air. She's working on a full-house cleanse to rid us of negative energy. Dad's been holding his tongue about it, mainly because I think he appreciates the free cleaning. We haven't lived in the house long enough for it to be really dirty, but he and I aren't exactly clean freaks, so her efforts can't hurt.

The other thing Aunt Allie seems intent on doing is buying up most of the fresh flowers left in town. She's got them sticking out of vases in every room, and she even put them in juice jugs and old milk cartons when the vases were all used up. She tells me the flowers negate bad energy.

Dad bugs her about the money she's wasting on things that die in a week, but she explains that they have a purpose that lingers long after they're gone. Besides, she adds, material things never last. Anyhow she's got more than enough money from her settlement when she was let go from her corporate job, and she does well on the psychic circuit.

The scent in the house is fresh and soothing. The bell rings again, and it's polite and less threatening than a *thunk*, but I flinch anyway. When the bell rings a third time, I glance around for someone to save me from answering it. Even Fredrick is downstairs, deafened by the vacuum and not curious enough to come up and check out the visitor for me.

Sighing, I walk to the door and slowly open it.

Coach Clair is on the porch.

"Samantha," she says and steps forward and hugs me. I lose my ability to speak for a second, I'm so surprised to see her. "I've missed you," she says.

Even though we've only been training together for a couple of months, I realize how much I've missed her too. My relationship with my coach in Orlie was so different, more formal. I can't even imagine her ever coming to my home. She hasn't been in touch since this whole mess blew up. I know from emails from Gillian that my Orlie swim club knows I am the girl from the news, so my old coach must know too. Clair lets me go and hands me an envelope with my name on the front. "Can I come in?"

"Sorry, of course. Come in." I hold the door for her, and she steps into the house. "Come inside and sit." I hold out my hand and point, gesturing for her to go forward to the living room.

"Open it," she commands, nodding at the card in my hand. I follow her to the living room.

It's a miss-you card, signed by my team. The vacuum cleaner drones on downstairs. I scan the signatures but don't see Zee's.

My heart sinks, but I sit on the loveseat across from her and smile. "Thanks."

"We need you back, Sam," she says.

All I can do is press my lips tight, hold in my fear, and shake my head. She's here to take me back. I need to stay strong.

"Yes, we do. I do. And you need us, Sam. Swimming is who you are. I know what that's like. You'll wilt without it."

I pretend to listen to her as she presents positive affirmations. I notice the vacuum shut off downstairs. "Remember what you said when I agreed to coach you, bring you on with the Titans? You said that nothing would stop you from trying to be the best."

I nod as if I'm agreeing but can't stop my next words.

"Well, I didn't foresee this whole murder thing."

She inhales quickly. "Sam. It wasn't murder. You know that."

I shrug. "I know," I tell her, because that's what she wants to hear. "But you've seen the news, right? The story about Alex is everywhere. Everyone in the swim world will know it was me. The Titans don't need that kind of attention."

"All of us will stand behind you. Every single member of our team."

She's wearing a dark blue Titans polo shirt, capri pants, and a pair of expensive sneakers. I wonder if she ever wears dresses. What her boyfriend looks like. He never comes to the pool or to meets, but rumor has it he exists in real life.

She's in good shape, but she's starting to get thick around her waist. I wonder what she looked like when she swam. Will I start getting lumpy in the middle? Right now I'm skinnier than I've ever been as a result of losing my appetite, but it's coming back.

Clair's mouth keeps moving, but I don't hear her words. Cold creeps right inside the marrow of my bones and blocks out sound.

"Sam?"

I smile and tilt my head.

"I'll do whatever it takes to help you. I want to see you back in the pool. You need to be there."

I nod, but my heart isn't in it. I watch her face as she struggles to find the right words for me, trying to motivate me, get me back in the pool.

"It's not even about winning, or a scholarship. Or how hard you've worked to get where you are," she says. "It's about taking your life back."

She stands up and tells me a quick story about champions who get going when the going gets tough. And then she leans down and hugs me again.

"I'm so sorry about what happened to you."

The choice of words surprises me. What happened to me is nothing compared to what happened to Alex.

I stand up and walk her to the front door.

"Getting back in the pool will help you to heal."

She keeps talking, but I tune her out. What she doesn't know is that I don't want to feel better. I don't want to go on with my life as if nothing happened. Something did happen. Something big.

"Okay?" She smiles, and it changes her face, making her look younger and prettier.

"Sure," I say, and her grin widens and reaches her eyes. I wonder what the hell I just said to cheer her up.

"Things are really okay?" she asks. "At school? Taylor said the kids are being tough."

I want to ask her what Zee's said. "It's okay. You know," I say instead.

She hugs me again and heads out. I stare at the closed door.

"You want to go for a walk?" Aunt Allie says. I'm not surprised she's behind me. I nod while she puts on Fredrick's coat and Harley Davidson collar and then slip on shoes and a jacket. We stroll out to the sidewalk as the streetlights turn on. It's getting dark so early now. Too early. Finally Aunt Allie glances at me. "That was your coach?"

I nod.

"So how are you feeling about swimming these days?"

I lift my shoulder and push my braid behind my ear. "Is Dad making you talk to me?"

She shakes her head. "No. You're my family too, you know. The best part of it."

I imagine she gets lonely on the road sometimes, even though she appears to have everything she wants. "I wish he would have let you be around me more when I was growing up," I tell her. It's the first time I've admitted it to her. I don't feel like I'm betraying Dad anymore. It's the truth.

"Your dad is stubborn," she says. "Sort of like his daughter. But he had his reasons, I think."

"It's not that I'm stubborn," I say.

"It's just that you don't feel you deserve to go on with life?" Aunt Allie stops and waits while Fredrick lifts his leg on a neighbor's lawn. She doesn't seem concerned about ruining anyone's grass.

"Maybe you're getting something out of not swimming? Some control? Not doing what your dad wants for the first time in your life."

"No." I don't agree with her. A man passes us on the sidewalk with a big black dog on a leash. Kind of a giant Fredrick. I notice the man smiling at Aunt Allie, but she doesn't even look at him, and Fredrick ignores his dog. Aunt Allie is staring up at a dark streetlight above us. It's broken; probably a kid threw a rock at it. For no reason other than to see it break. People do senseless things all the time.

"I dream about swimming all the time," I tell her. "Sometimes I'm standing on the platform and I dive in, but there's no water. I keep falling and falling. And then I wake up."

"Oh, butterfly. It's okay for you to go back. Not swimming isn't going to change what happened. Don't let the guilt break you." She stops again while Fredrick turns his back on us and squats. "The letter to Alex will help." She waits and then bends and scoops with her baggie.

"Let's go home. I'll make you a hot chocolate and throw away this dog poo."

"Hopefully not in that order."

Aunt Allie laughs, and the sound of it echoes in the street. "Want another bit of advice."

"Not really."

"Stop listening to the news. Start living your life again. There are things you can do to start taking it back. Do them."

But I don't even know what I want from my life anymore. Or how I can deal with what I did.

chapter eleven

On Friday night, I pull the car up to the address Casper gave me, a little surprised by the freakin' mansion-ness of his home. It's about the size of three houses and is built across a ridge, so the view of the mountains behind it is amazing. It's even more gorgeous this time of year, with the reds and oranges on the trees. I turn off the ignition and sit in silence for a moment, studying the huge house, trying to imagine living in it.

Finally, I grab my backpack and close the car door behind me. The age and condition of our car suddenly seems kind of embarrassing. As I walk, my boots crunch over leaves from the many trees on the lot. Raking must be a full-time job. Trees line both sides of a back yard that includes a full-size tennis court that seems small in the surroundings.

I don't want to be intimidated or impressed by the sheer size and cost of the house. Money shouldn't make people seem better than those who don't have as much, but it's hard to remember that while staring up at such a majestic building. I feel like I'm wearing a ratty bathing suit in a room full of girls in expensive prom dresses.

Inhaling deeply, I focus on the slightly sweet scent of decaying leaves drifting to the ground to rot in the gusts of wind. The little girl inside me wants to stretch my arms out and twirl around. It's my favorite time of year, even though it means that the dampness and cold of winter is around the corner.

I think how Alex will never have the luxury of a gray, soulless, cloudy day, and I close my eyes and breathe in and out through my nose slow and deep, the way Bob's been teaching me.

"You okay?" a voice calls.

I open my eyes and see Casper looking tiny in the doorway of the house, especially from the long brick driveway where I'm standing. I realize he must have been looking out the window, watching for me. Seen me hesitating.

"Come on," he yells. I scramble up the driveway, walking fast, but it takes a long time to reach him.

He smiles and flicks his hair as I approach, and I push at my braid as the wind whips it into my mouth.

"Wow," I manage, wanting to pretend I'm cool and used to this. "Wow," I repeat, not able to pull it off.

"Yeah. What can you do?" He lifts his shoulder as his gaze goes from one side of his house to the other. "My parents invested in technology back in the nineties and got out just in time. You should see my mom's house, where I live the other half of my time." He grins and makes a silly face, and it's slightly charming. Some of my unease fades. "They have a competition going." He holds the door for me. I step inside and am reminded of fancy museums. The entranceway has huge ceilings, tile floors, and lots of echoic space. There are no framed family pictures or even piles of books or bills on end tables. It's spotless and organized and makes me want to whisper, like a show home for pretend people who never make messes.

I slip my shoes off and adjust my backpack strap on my shoulder, wishing I'd worn something a little fancier than yoga pants and a hoodie. Casper has on jeans and a polo shirt. I guess this is his casual look.

"You mind working upstairs?" he asks. "In my room?"

"Um. No." I look around, expecting his parents to come out to meet me.

"My dad and stepmom aren't home," he supplies. "They're at a party."

"Oh."

"Poor little rich boy," he says. "Left all alone."

I'm not sure where to look or what to say.

"Don't look so sad, Sam, I'm just kidding." He laughs. "And Theresa is here."

I don't ask who Theresa is, assuming she's a maid or cook or something.

"You're quite safe, don't look so uneasy."

"It's just that your house is so…"

"Big?" he supplies.

"Yeah. That. And…"

"Expensive?" he says.

I nod again, trying to shake off my feelings of inadequacy.

"It's just a house." He waves his hand at the vast hallway that leads to a spiral staircase. "Theresa promised to bring up some food and drinks in a while. She wants to check you out."

"Who's Theresa?" Curiosity gets the better of me as he leads me down a huge hallway, past a dining room with dark wooden chairs lining each side and a fancy table with vases of fresh flowers on them.

"Family," he says as we reach a huge spiral stairway.

"Wow," I say again, and we tromp up the stairs and weave down another long hall, past a couple of closed doors, and then he leads me into his bedroom. I step inside and glance around. It's the size of our entire top floor at home, and it's nothing like I'd expect a boy's room to look. No posters of rock bands or girls in bikinis, no clothes on the floor. There's nothing personal about this room either. It could belong to anyone. For some reason, it makes me a little sad for Casper.

The floor is dark wood, and there's a king-size bed on the opposite end from the door. It's covered by a comforter with gray and black geometric shapes that looks fluffy and pricey. To the far right is an archway leading to a bathroom that makes Dad's look like a dollhouse. The curtains on his window match the comforter. I'll bet it's the work of a professional designer. I think of my own room, with posters of Rebecca Soni and the Olympic Swim Team on the wall and my bulletin board of swimming awards. Clothes piled everywhere. Mayhem.

Casper points to the left, where there's a sitting area with two black leather couches and, pressed against the wall, an office desk. It's perfectly neat, with a laptop on it.

"Cool spread," I say trying to sound like the coldness and sheer size are wonderful.

"You get used to it." His voice is nonchalant.

"So," he says and points to a couch. "*1984*. You need to plug in?"

"Yes." I slip my laptop out of my backpack, and he points to an outlet. I plug in and sit. While the machine I've had since middle school is firing up, I glance around. Casper pulls his Mac from the desk, moves to the couch, and puts his feet up on the coffee table.

"We're going to ace this thing," he says.

I don't respond, but I want to ask him if working with me and getting a good grade is more important to him than Alex's memory.

A light tapping behind us startles me.

A striking woman steps into the room, holding a tray. Or is she a girl? It's impossible to tell her age, and I stare at her, because it's weird to have such a beautiful person breathe the same air as me.

"Hi, Theresa," Casper doesn't look up as he types something on his keyboard. "This is Samantha Waxman. Samantha. This is Theresa."

"Hello, Samantha." Her mouth widens, but her eyes don't smile. She glides forward and places a tray on the coffee table between us. She's brought us four cans of soda and one plate of oversized muffins, and another plate with an assortment of fruit.

"Sam," I manage, but her beauty steals my ability to say more.

"Casper said you were very smart. He didn't mention you were pretty too."

My cheeks warm. Me pretty? She could be on the cover of *Vogue*.

"I would have said she was pretty, but you'd accuse me of being shallow. Again. I like Sam for her brains. Her looks are merely a bonus." His voice is affectionate and teasing. "And stop giving away all my secrets."

"Not all of them, Casper," she says, talking as if he's a little boy, but one she's fond of. "The muffins are nut free," she says, and I realize she knows exactly who I am.

"Don't make a mess, you know how Mavis gets." She smiles at me. "Not you. Casper. He's a slob." She smiles again, but it's not warm. "I'm going out," she says, and slips out the door, leaving a floral scent in the air.

"I am not a slob," he calls, but she's gone. Based on his room, I'd have to agree. He looks at me. "I'm actually pretty clean. I mean, for a guy, you know. Not a neat freak or anything"

I hold in a smile. It's kind of funny that he's defending himself both about not being a slob and about being a slob. As if he can't decide which one is worse.

"Theresa is beautiful," I say and eye the muffins. Even if she's not tactful. My appetite is returning. I'm not sure it's a good thing, but I'm starving.

Casper lifts a shoulder and gestures to the tray. "Take one."

"You said she's a relative?"

"Long story. Kind of a sister." Casper grabs a muffin, takes a bite, and brushes his crumbs to the floor. He glances down and bends to pick them up, then looks at me, straightens his back, and sits up, leaving them on the floor. I notice him look down again, but he doesn't touch them. It's none of my business what his messed-up relationship with crumbs is.

I pluck a muffin from the tray, rip off a chunk, and wolf it down. Casper watches me and grins. "You eat. Another thing I love about you."

I chew, suddenly self-conscious, and the muffin lumps up in my throat. "You love that I eat?" I ask.

"Well. You know. Most girls are all, 'oh I can't eat that, I'm on a diet.'" His high-pitched voice goes even higher imitating a girl. "When they weigh, like, ten pounds. You don't pretend not to like food."

I shrug, not wanting to think about the reason I've always been able to throw back a lot of food. Swimming burns a lot of calories.

"I like a lot of things about you," he says.

Whoa, this boy has guts. His forwardness unnerves me. I can tell I'm not the love of his life or anything, but he's good at flirting. I put the muffin on the tray, take a can of soda, and pop the lid, rationalizing what is happening. Casper is cute. He's being nice to me, but I'm definitely not crazy over him either. Not like with Zee. I swallow, wondering about attraction and how it works. Why Zee? What decides who people fall for? Is it only based on looks? Personality? Or is there some connection in previous lives, like Aunt Allie believes?

"So are you back to swimming yet?" Casper asks.

I put the soda down. "No."

"Why not?"

"What about you?" I ask instead of answering. "What's your sport?"

"I play football, but I dislocated my shoulder." He rubs it, moving his fingers in a circular motion. "I need to get back, especially for college applications. Ivy League calls. Oh. I also do some free running. With Zee and Alex."

I stiffen as if he's thrown cold water in my face.

"Sorry," he says softly. He gets up and sits beside me on the couch. "Sometimes I still forget about Alex."

I keep my gaze down, refusing to look at him. "I don't know how you can be nice to me." I focus on the coffee table and blink and blink and blink.

"It was an accident." His leg presses up against mine. It's muscular, but mine is too and almost bigger than his. "He's not the kind of guy who would want you to suffer because of it." His voice is almost a whisper. "I mean, he wasn't."

"Under the circumstances, he might." I sniff, and my nose accidentally drips. It should be mortifying but, how can I really care?

"No. He wouldn't," he says. He gets up and snags a box of Kleenex that I can't help notice matches his décor. I try to wipe up the mess on my face as best as I can. My eyes aren't leaking, but my nose makes up for it.

He sits down on the couch, but not so close he's touching me this time.

"It was really bad luck," Casper says softly.

"Luck? I only kissed him to—" I stop, realizing I'm about to say something I'll regret later. "I'm a mess," I point out, but it's not like he didn't notice that already.

"Why did you kiss him?" he asks quietly.

I shake my head. I won't admit the truth.

"Alex thought you had a thing for Zee," he adds.

I crumple into myself a bit. Shake my head. "Zee hates me."

Casper slides closer and puts his arm around me and pulls me close. "Zee is kind of an ass. He's pissed at everyone right now. Don't let him get to you."

Yeah, and I'm at the top of his hate list. Casper slides his hand under my chin and turns my head toward him. His fingers are strong, but I move my chin away. I can only imagine how blotchy my skin looks. Red eyes. Red nose. A beauty queen.

"What happened to Alex was awful. But it was awful for you too."

I stare down at the box of Kleenex.

"You know, it easily could have been any one of us. I mean, obviously the guys wouldn't be kissing Alex, but I know we've had nuts and stuff around him before. We could have, you know, touched him or something. Same thing could have happened."

"But it didn't." I stare at my lap.

Casper reaches over and takes my hand. "Seriously. Even Chloe doesn't blame you. Not really."

"You talked to Chloe about me?" I cringe, imagining what she might have said.

"She doesn't hate you. She actually kind of feels bad for you."

I let out a breath of air. "If I were her, I would hate me."

He leans back, sinking into the thick leather cushions. "It's complicated, I give you that." An expression I don't recognize crosses his face. Pity? "Did you know the coroner ordered an autopsy?"

The image makes me sick to my stomach. "Why?"

He shrugs again. "I guess because of the way he died. Chloe said it's common in a sudden death."

I let it sink in, but the image is so horrible I shiver and wrap my arms around myself.

Casper taps the couch with his fingers. "You want some free advice?" He doesn't wait for an answer. "Talk to Chloe. It might be good for both of you."

He leans over to the table, picks up a Coke, and chugs it.

"I don't want to make it worse."

He puts the can down and wipes his mouth with the back of his hand. "It won't."

I sniffle, no longer even embarrassed at being such a hot mess.

"If you ignore her because you feel guilty, the weirdness will keep building and building. Her anger, I mean it has to go somewhere, right? If you don't talk, it might be you."

He points his finger at me and then drops it down to my arm.

"How'd you get so smart?"

"Valedictorian, remember?" He smiles, scoots closer, puts his hands on my neck, and starts massaging.

"Relax," he whispers. "Turn around so I can give you a proper massage."

My insides mix with unease and pleasure, but I tilt my head to one side and slowly move so my back is to him. His fingers knead my shoulders, digging deep. It's both painful and exquisite.

"Man. You're tighter than a pair of football pants," he whispers. He's leaning forward, and his breath tickles the outer shell of my ear. I close my eyes as he moves his head closer to my skin. I wonder if I should stop it, stop him.

I don't.

When his lips press against my neck, a shiver runs down my spine. His fingers keep moving, and then his mouth presses against my shoulder. My body fills with longing while my heart aches, but my brain turns pleasantly fuzzy and warm. He can make Alex disappear from my head. He can make me forget Zee.

Everything dissolves except the feel of Casper's hands and lips on my skin.

I ignore a voice in my head trying to tell me it's not right. That I should stop him. That I'm not even close to being in love with this guy, I'm not even truly sure how much I like him. Or that I'm not the kind of girl who goes around kissing boys she hardly knows. And I'm not doing a good job of proving that to anyone. The trouble is, maybe, just maybe, I need him right now. He's making my pain go away and erasing thoughts from my head. And how can that be bad?

I ignore my guilt as his fingers stop massaging, and he turns me slowly around. He presses his lips against mine. For a moment, I'm reminded of Alex, but Casper pulls me closer and keeps kissing, and the image recedes further and further. All I can think of is right now. This moment. It's such a relief that he isn't reacting badly to my kiss. I inhale his powerful cologne and run my fingers through his light hair. I want to stay entwined like this forever. I want to hide in his bedroom, sleep in his closet, and be pulled out only to kiss him. I'm losing myself in his arms.

My body starts aching for things, asking for things my heart isn't sure of, but before we cross any more lines, Casper abruptly pulls back.

"Whoa," he says. "You are a great kisser." Between him and Alex, he must think I go around making out with random dudes all the time. Heat floods my cheeks, and I press my face into his shoulder so he can't see me. "We better stop now, while we still can."

My cheeks get even hotter. He obviously doesn't know I'm

a virgin. A total virgin. All he knows is that I seemed ready to do almost anything he asked. He's more of a gentleman than I thought, showing restraint when clearly I didn't deserve it. The old me would have been grateful. This me is just empty inside.

Casper is not the boy of my dreams. We have little in common except some genetic quirk that makes us both smart. His voice doesn't send thrills through me. Catching a surprise glimpse of him doesn't fill me with excitement. And just like Alex, he's not Zee.

And just like Alex, I'm using him to try to forget. To try to show Zee that I am worthy. That boys want to kiss me. I shiver, thinking about what happened to Alex because of me. I suppose I'm trying to prove something. That kissing me isn't the most horrible thing in the world. I wonder if the experience with Alex realigned my value system? I want it to mean something more. I want *me* to mean something more. I want to be held and I want to allow a cute boy to stop me from thinking.

Aunt Allie said I'd go on to kiss other boys and she was right, but it's happening faster than either of us probably imagined. Casper strokes my hair as I drift back to the real world, hiding the conflicting emotions threatening to burble out of me. I want to kiss him again, lose myself and forget my thoughts.

"I'm sorry, Sam." He lifts his arm and glances at his watch. He's one of the few boys I know who wears one. "I have to be somewhere in about fifteen minutes." He grins sheepishly. "And it takes me at least twenty to get there, so technically I'm already late."

He leans his head forward and kisses me again. "As much as I don't want to, I have to get going."

I'm being dismissed.

"God. I'm sorry." I untangle my needy arms from his.

He stands but reaches down and grabs my hand and squeezes it. "Don't be sorry. It's totally worth being late for you. You're amazing."

I frown. "I am?"

"Sam I am." He grins. "You are." Then he bends and picks up my laptop, unplugs the cord, and slides it into my backpack for me.

"I'll walk you to the door? Okay?"

He takes my bag and leads me out of his room, and we silently reverse our steps through his house. I can't think of a thing to say, but Casper whistles under his breath, the kind of whistle that someone does when they're not even aware of it. When we finally reach the front doors I quickly slip my shoes on.

"Uh. I'll see you at school, I guess." I take my backpack from him, wishing he'd ask me what I'm doing tomorrow. If I want to hole up in his room again and make the outside world disappear.

"I'll walk you to your car," Casper says in a calm voice, as if nothing out of the ordinary happened.

"You don't have to, you're late." My face burns. Reality is rushing back. He thinks I'm the type of girl who does things like this all the time. First Alex. Now him.

He reaches around me, holds the door handle, and waits. "I want to."

He opens the door and then slips his hand inside mine. It fills my heart enough that it doesn't feel completely empty as he walks with me down the long driveway. I want to believe it's a sign that this means more. There's more to this than me making out with the wrong person again. When we reach my car, he opens my door for me after I click the lock open.

When I'm in the driver's seat, he bends down, closes the door, and waves through the glass. "See you Monday. I'll call you."

I attempt a smile, but I don't answer as I pull on my seatbelt. Carefully, I back out of the driveway while he stands watching. I pray I don't run over a gnome or something and then wave, put the car in drive, and drive away.

I wonder where he's going. Why he didn't ask to see me again this weekend. But of course, who do I think I am? The perfect girlfriend? I swallow and swallow and swallow, but a lump is back in my throat. A hollow ache settles back in my chest.

Casper helped me forget. How sorry I am about everything. I want to be in Casper's arms again. Forgetting.

And what does that make me?

chapter twelve

I see Bob early Saturday morning, but I don't tell him about Casper. I think I'm afraid he'll talk me out of what I'm doing. Later, when I'm home, Dad freaks out when I refuse to go to swim practice. As far as I'm concerned, he has no right to act surprised. It's not like we'd agreed today was the day it would magically happen. At no point did I tell him any such thing.

While we're arguing, Aunt Allie puts on her coat and boots and dresses Fredrick in his sweater vest. "You two need to talk," she says.

"*Adios*," she says, holding Fredrick up to me. And then she carries him to the door and hooks him up to his Harley Davidson leash.

Dad storms out as soon as they're gone, and for the first time since Aunt Allie arrived, the house is quiet. It's good for about three seconds, and then images and thoughts boom too loudly in my head. I think about the letter Aunt Allie wants me to write. But I can't do that. I decide a run is the only way to liberate some of the edginess from my body.

After a quick change, I find my running sneakers at the back of the closet, put on my sunglasses and ball cap, and clip on my iPhone. I head slowly down the street, jogging toward the school yard. My lungs tighten almost right away, and I fight the rapid breaths and burning sensation. It's embarrassing how quickly I've lapsed out of shape, but instead of slowing down, I sprint harder. My lungs scorch trying to pump in more oxygen, and I pant, but the pain is good and I don't slow my pace. The streets are empty. No one is outside enjoying the beautiful fall weather. I run down a pathway across the street that leads to the school yard and keep running until I reach the field.

As I head across the grass to the playground, I see someone running toward the flight of stairs beside the school. From the back, I can tell it's a boy with long hair sticking out of the bottom of his cap. His track pants hang low, and the butt looks familiar. I keep running and watch as he vaults over the railing with a huge drop. He disappears. I run to the wall. The boy rolls on his shoulder and then leaps up and turns my way. As suspected, it's Zee.

We stare at each other, and as much as I want to turn and run the other way, I can't now without looking like a complete jerk. He lifts his hand. "Hey," he calls when I almost reach him.

I slow to a walk and pull out my ear buds. "Hey," I say. "You trying to break your neck?" I hold my side, as the stitch I'd been ignoring slices into me. I blow out slowly and bend toward the cramp, trying to stretch it away.

"Hardly." He actually grins at me. "It's called Parkour."

"That's what you call jumping off steps and almost breaking your neck?" I lift my arm and stretch it over my head, opposite the stitch.

He jumps up and down in place, bouncing high as if he's on a trampoline. "Maybe to an untrained eye. Parkour is about using the body efficiently to quickly get from one place to another. We use the obstacles in the way to help the journey."

"So you had to get"—I point to the top of the stairs and then to the drop—"to there quickly?"

He grins for a second, but it's gone so quickly I'm not sure it even happened.

"Um, why?" I ask.

"I'm tracing. The official definition of Parkour." He stops bouncing and punches at the air, as if he's boxing. "For those uneducated in our ways."

"I see." I push back my braid, which got stuck in my sunglasses as I ran. "So that's Parkour." I don't want to bring up the fact that Casper was talking about it. And Alex. My cheeks flush.

"Look it up on YouTube," Zee says as he shadow boxes, ducking from an imaginary opponent. "I mean, if you're interested. You can see the basic moves there. Like monkey walks and cat leaps and kong vaults."

I smile and nod, pretending to know what he's talking about.

"The first time I tried Parkour, I ended up face first on the pavement with a bloody lip," Zee says. "My ego hurt more than my face, though I pretty much resembled a cat's scratching post. I wiped the blood away and got up and tried again."

"Doesn't sound so fun to me."

"But it is. Even David Belle falls, and he's the greatest free runner in the world. He makes basic Parkour moves look easy, but trust me, they're not."

I start bouncing on my heels with him as a gust of wind rips right though me. "I'm surprised Clair lets you do it. You know. In case you get injured."

He shrugs. "I don't do everything Clair says."

"I know that for a fact." I quickly bend over and touch my toes, not wanting him to see the look on my face since I was talking about his drinking. And we both know what happened the only time I saw him do that. I don't want to think about or talk about that night.

"What about you?" he says as I straighten up. "You're not exactly following Clair's training schedule, now are you?"

I grab my ankle and stretch my leg back behind my back, keeping my expression neutral. He doesn't need to know how much I miss the pool.

He stops faux boxing. "At least you're cross-training," he says. "Keeping in shape for when you come back?"

I change legs. "No. I'm going for a run. That's it."

"Hmm," he says. "Sounds like cross-training to me. Can't keep a fish out of the water for too long, Sammy."

I turn from him, ready to jog away, back to punishing my body.

"Clair hates it," Zee says quickly, and his deep voice catches at the end. I slowly turn back. He starts jumping, but lower to the ground.

"She thinks it's stupid to do Parkour during swim season."

"And? Is the jury still out on that one?" I ask. Another gust of wind blows my ponytail straight up.

He pulls his cap lower. "A jury is made up of twelve people not smart enough to get out of jury duty."

I hold in a smile. For a moment, the old chemistry bubbles between us, below the surface.

"Why would I let anyone decide whether what I do is stupid or not? I kind of run my own life," he adds, and the light Zee-ness is gone.

"She's your coach," I say.

"She's your coach too."

I roll my neck to loosen it and ignore his comment. "You could get hurt. She's looking out for your best interests." Leaves billow up around my feet.

He stares at me, squinting his eyes, and the scrutiny makes me squirm. "It doesn't seem as important as it used to."

I glance at him and then down at the grass under my shoes, brown and stagnant. "What about your parents? They're not worried you're going to get hurt doing Parkour?"

"My parents have never seen me doing Parkour. They don't get it. They like swim meets because it makes them feel good about themselves when I win."

I look up at him. "You can't win at Parkour. It can't get you into Berkeley."

He runs his hands through his hair. "I think that's your dream, Sam. Not mine. Not anymore."

"What's changed?" I ask.

"Everything."

I know what he means. I realize how much I've really missed Zee. We used to have great talks about what we wanted.

"Swimming came easy for me. Body type or genes. But with Parkour, I have to work at it."

"You have to work at swimming too." I can't help defending my old sport.

"True. But I don't get roughed up swimming. Actually, I think my dad liked the bruises and cuts. He played hockey. He's used to injuries. Manly, you know." He grins, but he's staring off into the distance and it fades from his lips almost as quickly as it appeared.

"How'd you learn Parkour?" I ask, even though I'm starting to freeze and need to get moving.

"They have drop-in classes at the gymnastics place downtown. But mostly we learned from watching YouTube." He starts jumping up and down again, springing from his toes, reaching for air. "We practiced on scaffolding at first and then vaults and horizontal bars at the gym, but mostly outside. Free running. Me and Alex."

At the mention of his name, we look away from each other.

"Casper came to the gym sometimes too, but his dad didn't really like him doing it. No glory in it, I think. Casper used to swim too, but since he wasn't the best, his dad made him quit. Anyhow. He's not that good at Parkour. He doesn't follow the rules." He sounds kind of pleased.

My cheeks burn. I want to ask why they're angry with each other, but that would be as stupid as sticking my hand inside a hornet nest. I don't want him to know about Casper and me. Whatever it is we are.

"Alex wasn't much good either. He had ball practice all the time."

It's there again. His name. An anchor that drops between us.

"I'm sorry." My words come out in a rush. "I'm so freakin' sorry about Alex."

"I know." He flips his head back and stares at the school wall instead of me. "He came to the pool to see you that day, you know. He had to drop off my iPod. But mostly he wanted to see you swim."

I bend my head. "I'd do anything to take it all back…"

"Well. You can't." His voice cuts deep. It drips with harsh reality. Nothing can change what happened that night.

I take a deep breath. "I didn't know about his allergy."

I wince, realizing I'm practically begging for forgiveness from the best friend of the boy I killed. My body stays tense, waiting. Zee says nothing. I try to imagine how much he must miss Alex. His best friend. They had years together. I barely knew him.

"I never should have kissed him," I say softly.

My feet feel as heavy as my heart, but it's time for me to leave. I take a step away from Zee, about to sprint away.

"I shouldn't have been with Kaitlin that night," he says.

I freeze in place.

His voice is almost a whisper. "I was wasted. But it was a shitty thing to do to you."

My ears burn. My instinct is to pretend not to know what he's talking about. To deny that he and I had a thing. I'm flooded with the memory of how I'd been so sure that he was going to kiss me.

It's too late for us now. But for a moment I remember being on the deck. Before Kaitlin showed up. Before I knew Alex was watching.

"Kaitlin and I had this weird history of hooking up. That sounds bad, I know, but she was pretty aggressive, and…it was before." He curses under his breath. "I'm sorry."

Zee spins then and runs from me at full tilt, heading toward a play structure nearby. He jumps on top of a planked wooden bridge. He leaps to a higher level and then, while my heart pauses in fear, he does a flip to the ground, landing on both feet.

"See you around, Sam," he calls, and he jumps up on a play boulder and disappears over it in a blur of motion.

Just like that, he's gone. Things can change so quickly. One second you're in the present, the next you're remembering the past. My insides ache, staring at the empty spot where he stood.

Pushing my ear buds back in place, I jog off in the opposite direction. Fast beats pulse in my ear, and I press the volume button to full, so loud my hair vibrates. I break into a straight-out run and concentrate on nothing except the beat of the music and the pounding of my feet.

I run and run, trying to get rid of the angst icing up my belly. My body finally quits on me, so I circle back and start heading for home. I bring down my pace. I have no choice but to take the route that passes the school, but I stay on the perimeter of the school grounds until I hit the field I need to cross.

Zee is still on the playground, but he looks tiny and far away. I squint and frown, watching as he runs to the parallel bars at full steam. His foot must slip on his takeoff because he ends up slamming his head straight into a metal bar. The sound of it echoes across the schoolyard, and my head stings in sympathy.

Zee stays down for a minute, rubbing his head, and then gets up and goes back and runs at it again. This time he swings his body up but misses the second bar completely. His hands are down and don't break his fall between the two bars. He flips off the side onto his back. I watch as he lies still, not moving. Inhaling deeply, I start running toward him. My legs ache, but I move them as fast as I can.

Before I reach him, he pushes up. I watch as he runs at the school wall, stopping at two posts that run parallel to the roof. He stares up and then puts one foot on a post and the other foot on the other post and shimmies up to the roof like Spider-Man on a rescue mission.

Wind blows through me and I shiver, but it's not from the breeze. I'm just close enough to see Zee as he flings his body onto the roof and stands. He glances down at the drop, then looks up to where another wall juts higher with another roof about four feet above the one he's on. He backs up, staring at the taller wall.

I realize what he wants to do and shout his name, but the wind catches my voice and carries it away. Zee doesn't even look my way as I get closer. He backs up and then charges, like a bull running at a target. My belly is on fire from a rush of adrenaline.

"Zee! Don't!" I holler.

My toes touch pavement on the school ground as he leaps off the edge, jumping and reaching for the taller wall. His fingers grip the ledge, but his feet flail against the stones. He's thrown off balance and slips. I gasp as he loses his footing. He stops moving, pushing his feet against the wall, and then tries again. In slow motion he manages to crawl up the side of the wall and scrambles to the higher roof. He collapses on his back when he's on top of the roof.

"You asshole!" I yell.

He looks over the edge at me standing below him. "Thanks for noticing," he calls.

My hands clench into fists, and I make a sound in my throat instead of yelling profanities.

"What are you doing back here?" he asks.

"I need to go this way to get home. You scared the crap out of me." I'm shaking from his near miss. "You could have been hurt," I yell. *He could have been killed*, I think. *Doesn't he get it? We're not invincible.*

"I didn't know you cared." A gust of wind blows as he jumps to the lower roof and shimmies down the poles on the side of the building.

"Would you stop that already," I yell at him.

When his feet touch the ground, he holds one hand in front of his stomach, puts the other behind his back, and bows.

Instead of going at him with both of my fists, I spin on my heels and use the last of my energy to sprint away. I glance over my shoulder to make sure he hasn't jumped back up on the roof, but he's moving across the field in the opposite direction.

After keying in the code to get inside the house, I stop, swallowing hard, trying not to cry. I'm so sick of crying. Aunt Allie is sitting in the family room with Fredrick curled up on her lap. She takes one look at me and puts the dog on the floor. He gives her a look of disbelief but tilts his head and runs at me. As he's jumping on my legs, Aunt Allie rushes in and embraces me in the hallway.

"What happened?" Her warmth and concern make me shiver harder. She murmurs comforting words while Fredrick rubs against my legs, like the cat he's hiding inside his body.

Aunt Allie pushes me down the hallway. Fredrick trots along behind us as if he's been invited. "We need to warm you up outside and in," she says and pulls me inside my bedroom. She sits me on the bed, and Fredrick jumps like a Mexican bean until I pick him up and nestle him in my lap.

"Oh, *amiga*," she says in Fredrick's voice. "We need to fix you up."

"Wait here," she says in her own voice, and she goes into the bathroom, starts the bathtub, and then goes to the guest room. She comes back in seconds, holding a fluffy purple robe, and hangs it on my back. "This was your mom's."

She scoops up Fredrick and pushes me to the bathroom. "Okay. Go get in the tub. Warm yourself up and put this on when you're finished. I'll grab you some clean underpants from your drawer."

I actually giggle when she says "underpants," like I'm a seven-year-old girl. She's treating me like a child, and in response I'm acting like one, but it's exactly what I need. I'm not about to fight it. I want to be babied and looked after, even it's for a little while.

She puts her hand under my chin, kisses my cheek, and then walks out, leaving me alone. I pull off my sweaty clothes and slowly lower myself into the hot bath, breathing in the steam and letting the hot water caress me.

When I come out, there are a bra and panties on the counter. I dry myself, slip them on, and then pull on the huge robe, tie up the belt, and roll up the sleeves. I pet the fuzzy sleeves, thinking of my mom. It makes me feel vulnerable and protected at the same time.

"Come to the kitchen," Aunt Allie calls.

As I slide into a chair at the table, she hands me a steaming cup of mint tea. Cupping it in my hands, I let the heat seep through my body and inhale the fumes, willing them to relax me and draw the tension from my head. Aunt Allie leans against the stove and crosses her arms, her face wrinkled up with concern.

"What happened?"

I take another sip of the tea. "I ran into Zee. At the school."

"Zee is the boy you have a crush on?" She pours hot water into another mug.

My cheeks get warmer. "Zee is the boy I used to swim with."

She presses her lips tight and cups the mug in both hands. "Whatever you say."

I want to fight her on that, but know it's not worth it.

"Zee was practicing Parkour at the school. He almost frigging killed himself, right in front of me. It scared me." I take a sip of the tea and glance at her over the top of the mug. "Parkour is when kids jump over things—"

She walks to the table, still cradling her mug. "I know what Parkour is."

I lift my shoulder and sigh. Of course she does.

"And?" She puts her mug down, pulls out a chair, and sits close beside me so our knees touch. Steam rises off my tea and I inhale the scent. It reminds me of her. Aunt Allie. Who is always digging deep inside people's souls. Helping them see what they need.

"It scared me," I whisper. "Zee was taking stupid chances."

"Oh, butterfly. Mortality is a hard lesson at your age. Life is very fragile." She pats my knee. "It sounds as if your Zee is dealing with his feelings by taking risks. You're doing it by avoiding them."

I want to tell her he's not "my" Zee, but I swallow instead. "How did you know about Zee?" I ask in a soft voice.

"You talked about him when I was in Houston."

"I did?"

"You did. You told me he was your partner. The angels told me he was a good match for you."

I think back to our phone conversation. "I told you he was my swim partner."

"Your voice told me more." She waves her hand in the air. "Oh. A boy named Casper phoned while you were out. I was nice to him. Is that okay? Should I be nice to him? Is he a nice boy? Or do I want to run him off?"

I shrug. "I'm not sure." I get up and pour myself a glass of water. "Want some?" I ask her, but she shakes her head.

I'm not about to tell her that Casper is trying to get into my pants. For a second, I wonder whether the angels will reveal it to her. Do they tell my aunt things like that?

"Poor baby," Aunt Allie says, tsking me. "Boys are hard. So what about Casper?"

I wrap my braid around and around my finger. "We're working on an English project together."

"That's all?" She lifts her brow, and a deep blush starts in my toes and travels up. I walk back to the table and sit.

"I don't think he's all he appears to be," she says.

I tilt my head. "How would you know what he appears to be?"

She smiles at me and points up.

I roll my eyes, even though I believe her. "Casper is just being nice." I pause and stick my braid in my mouth, chewing the end of it, not wanting to admit what we're up to. How I'm getting involved in something that might be over my head. I decide to shift the conversation.

"He said I should talk to his sister. I mean, Alex's sister."

Aunt Allie doesn't react to obvious diversion. She nods in agreement. "*That* I do approve of. You need to talk to her. Can I make a suggestion?"

I wait. "What?" I ask when she doesn't respond.

"Write it out to her in a letter. You'll be able to say everything you want. I'm a strong believer in the written word."

She doesn't ask if I've written to Alex yet. We both know I haven't. Won't. Can't.

I think about her suggestion. Take a sip of tea. It's cooled down, and I swallow a large mouthful and the flavor of mint lingers on my tongue. "What if she doesn't want to hear what I have to say? I know you're trying to protect me, Aunt Allie. But what about Chloe? Maybe she doesn't want to hear how I feel. Maybe she doesn't want to hear my excuses."

"My heart is filled with sympathy for her, Sam. But you come first for me. I'm your person. But I think the sister needs to hear from you too. They're not excuses. There is heartfelt sorrow in you too. Like hers."

She stands, goes to the pantry, and opens the door. "She has a void. And yes, she may be angry with you. Maybe even guilty about feeling that anger, because she knows you didn't mean for it to happen. But how can she begin to not hate you if you don't speak to her about it?"

My head falls to my chest. She grabs a bag of pretzels from a shelf and brings it to the table. "I don't blame you. Alex doesn't blame you, and even his sister probably doesn't, but you need to face up to the people he loved. Help them let go of their anger by talking to them."

I reach for a pretzel and nibble at it. "But what if she doesn't want to? I'm no good at confrontation. We actively avoid it in this house."

"Well, that's why I'm here."

I nod.

"What do you think?" she asks.

I close my eyes, concentrating. Trying to put on Chloe's shoes. "If I were Chloe and I knew I roamed the same school with her every day, well, it would be weird. Hard." I open my eyes and look at Aunt Allie. "I guess we're both kind of connected by this horrible thing."

"And…" she prompts me.

"And if I don't talk to her, she will start to hate me because I am not allowing her to deal with it. I can't change what happened. But I can at least apologize for the part I played in it."

She nods, purses her lips out, and taps the bottom one with her finger. "Good, butterfly. Good."

"But how do you tell someone that you're sorry for something like that?" I ask.

"I honestly don't know. But you're a smart girl. Dig deep inside. Write it out. And then afterward, talk to her. You need to talk to her." She takes another pretzel and bites into it. "But explore it on your own first. Write the letter."

"Do you always make people write letters?"

"As a matter of a fact, I think it's a great way to deal with things. I suggest it as a tool when it's appropriate. Sometimes it's all we can do."

Like with Alex. We sit quietly for a while longer, munching pretzels and gulping down tea. When I'm done, Aunt Allie takes my cup from me and looks inside at the leaves on the bottom.

"Yes," she says.

"What?" I ask, but she takes the cup to the sink, dumps the loose leaves out, rinses it, and says nothing.

I get up from the table and walk to the sink. Without a word I wrap my arms around her and squeeze tight. "Thank you," I tell her.

She wipes a tear from her eye as I leave her and head to my room. I check my cell phone and text Taylor to turn down an offer to hang out with her and Justin. They don't need me hanging around, but I do appreciate the offer.

On Sunday Aunt Allie suggests an afternoon matinee, but Dad begs off, saying he's too tired. We go to a romantic comedy, but it's bad and we sneak into the next theatre and watch an action flick.

Afterward I climb into the driver's seat as Aunt Allie opens the passenger door. When I put the key in the ignition, I notice something on the window of the car. I open the door, slide my arm to the front window, grab it, and pull it inside.

My heart stops when I look down at the lumpy package. It's a bag of Jelly Bellys.

"What's that? An advertising gimmick?" Aunt Allie asks.

"It must be," I whisper. Coincidence and nothing more. Nothing more. I toss them over to her lap as if they're poison ivy leaves.

"Not my favorite," she says. "I'm more of a chocolate person. But you love these, don't you?" She picks up the package and rubs it between her fingers. "Hmmmm. Interesting."

"What?" I yell.

"Nothing." She glances sideways at me with a tiny smile. "They're obviously meant for you. That's all."

"Why?" I try not to shriek and ask her what she knows from rubbing the package.

She studies my profile for a moment. "Well you're the one who likes them. Right?" She smiles when I turn to her. "Plus," she says. "There's a message written on the package." She holds it in the air and then puts the bag down on the console between us.

"What does it say?"

"*Sorry.*"

I swallow and swallow.

"The swimmer?" she asks.

I don't answer.

"Is there a health food store nearby?" she asks softly. "I need to pick up some things."

She punches information into the GPS and finds a store nearby. In the store, she wanders with a shopping basket over her elbow, mumbling and throwing things into it.

When we get home, she starts mixing herbs and spices in jars and pans and Dad mumbles something about witchcraft. She doesn't mention the Jelly Bellys. But I can't stop thinking about them.

chapter thirteen

It's getting easier to block out the angry stares and ignore the nicknames haters whisper when they walk by in the school hallways. Maybe my heart is hardening, but a part of me wonders if it really does have to do with the small sachet of herbs Aunt Allie made me promise to carry in my backpack at all times. Or the message scrawled on the Jelly Bellys. It does seem like there's a smile and wave of support here and there. I hate to admit it, but it's nice to know some people don't think my entire entity sucks.

I'm early and at my locker putting away books, when I look up and see Zee stalking toward me, like a predator about to take down an enemy. I have a terrible feeling the enemy is me and wonder what's changed from when he almost killed himself doing Parkour. At least then he'd been cordial, if also stupid. Now the intensity of his gaze freezes me in place like a paralyzed bunny. I can only blink as he pounces closer, about to rip me apart limb by limb. He looks scary and I secretly mourn the loss of how he was before.

Zee stops directly in front of me. His hands are clenched. "Seriously?" he says. "You're hooking up with Casper?"

The breath I was holding whooshes out. "Whaa?" I manage.

"Casper Cooper uses girls, Sam. He chews them up and spits them out when he's finished."

I have an image of Casper biting off my head and nervously laugh. Zee frowns and pushes back his floppy hair.

"We're working together on the English assignment." I blow my braid out of my eyes. "He's smart," I add. As if that matters.

"You were working on an English assignment on Friday night?"

My mind immediately conjures up memories of Casper kissing me. I push the images away, wondering how Zee even knows about Friday night. He certainly didn't when we ran into each other Saturday afternoon. Someone told him after that.

"I never said I was an exciting person. Doing homework on the weekend is not out of the ordinary for me." I slam my locker a little too hard, and it bangs. Nearby, a girl giggles and whispers something to her friend. They're leaning against a locker opposite mine, surrounded by guys.

"Well. It is for Casper. No matter how smart he is." Zee stares at me, and the flashing emotion in his eyes muddles his anger.

"You plan on coming back?" He scowls at me and cracks out his knuckle.

His negative energy seeps into me. "Why do you care?"

"Clair asked me to talk to you," he spits out. "This morning at five o'clock. At practice. The one you didn't bother to show up for. Again."

I spin around and start walking away from him, but he's on my heels. "She's worried about you. You're missing out on the chance of a lifetime if you stay out much longer. The finals are only weeks away, and you're going to be out of shape. Even if you are running. It's not the same. You need to swim."

I walk faster. "No. I don't."

He grabs my arm and pulls me to a stop. "You need to come back."

I try to shake his arm off me, but he holds tight.

"I can't."

"Why? Is there lead in your ass? You suddenly allergic to chlorine? What's stopping you?" He squeezes my arm a little harder and it pinches, but I don't flinch.

A freshman walks by, trying not to look like she's witnessing prime gossip and taking mental notes to deliver to her friends.

He lets go of my arm and I automatically rub where he was pressing.

"It's not just about you, Sam. The Titans need you to help us win our division. This is the first year we can actually do it." His deep voice growls. "Clair deserves it. She's the best coach in the state, and she should get this. But she needs you back." My face turns red, but I don't answer him.

I glance around the hallway, looking for someone to save me, but there's no friendly face. No one in this school is going to run to rescue me. Taylor's my main ally, and I've hardly talked to her. Who knows, maybe she's pissed with me for not coming back too. I'm letting the team down. I want to help Clair. But it's not like I have a choice. Not really.

Zee's lips turn into a snarl. "You afraid? I thought you were tougher than that. I didn't know you were a quitter."

"It's not that," my voice snaps with anger.

"Then what is it?" Zee's upper lip turns up in a sneer.

I glance straight into his dark, storming eyes. "Do you really need me to spell it out for you?" I ask.

"Yes," he says, and his lips quiver. "I do."

"Fine." I take a deep breath. "Alex won't ever get a baseball scholarship, will he?"

Zee's angry expression changes to disbelief.

"So why should I get my chance? Why should I swim and keep on with my life when he can't do the same?"

Zee's swagger deflates. My heart hurts for putting that look on his face.

"What," he says, his voice barely a whisper, "is that supposed to mean?"

"Exactly what I said. Why should I go after my dreams, when Alex can't go after his?"

Zee opens his mouth. Shuts it. "Alex wasn't like that," he says, his voice low. Almost hollow. "He would never have wanted anyone to punish you." He drags a knuckle back and forth over his eyebrow. "Not even yourself."

He turns abruptly to leave, stops, and then turns back. "And so you know, Casper's not as nice as he pretends to be." He stomps away and disappears around a corner.

I stare at the empty space, wondering how we got here.

"Hmm," a voice says. "Zee doesn't like you much, does he?" Kaitlin steps up beside me in high boots and a short skirt that show off model-worthy legs. She's got a smile on her face, and she blinks slowly and opens her eyes wider. "Too bad. I know you have a crush on him."

She holds up her hand and inspects her nails. She's got a perfect-looking manicure with pink nail polish to finish it off. "Too bad you killed his best friend. Not exactly the best way to get on a boy's good side."

A surge of anger gets the best of me. Who says things like that to people? "Shut up, Kaitlin," I growl.

She laughs as she walks away. "I heard you were much sweeter when everyone thought you were a lesbian." Her leather boots clack along on the tile floor and I wonder how she heard, but the swim community is small. And she knows lots of swimmers. My hands shake from the confrontation, and my stomach flops like a dying fish.

"Everything okay?" asks a voice.

I turn the opposite way and see Casper. Great.

"You look upset," he says. "Kaitlin being her usual self?"

"It's nothing," I tell him. "She heard the old rumor about me."

"That you're a lesbian? Well, we've proved that wrong, right?" He bumps my shoulder with his, but I step away from him.

Casper puts a hand on my arm. "Hey? You okay?"

"Fine."

"Ouch," he says. "Never trust a woman who says 'fine.'"

I pretend to smile. "She just said some really ignorant things about me and Zee."

"She's jealous. She knows you're friends from swimming."

"Were friends," I correct him.

He nods, and it breaks my heart that he agrees with me. "You know how they talk about girls with daddy complexes in psychology?" Before I can answer, he continues.

"Kaitlin is a classic example. She's damaged. She chases boys who clearly aren't interested in her. Stalks, really. Her dad is an asshole. Belittles her. She cries about it when she's had too much to drink. It's kind of sad. She's focused on Zee right now. But trust me. I've been in his shoes. She gets kind of crazy."

He waits for me to start walking, and it's obvious he's planning on going to class with me, so I start moving. I want to feel sorry for Kaitlin, but it's hard.

"Speaking of Zee. I saw him at the school yard on Saturday. He was doing some dangerous stuff," I tell him.

Casper shrugs. "Zee always does dangerous stuff."

"But this was pretty risky. It looked like he was taking real chances. Like he could have hurt himself. You know. Badly."

"That's just Zee, Sam. He's nuts."

I wonder. I never saw nuts in the pool. I saw dedicated. Focused. I can't imagine him being much different in Parkour.

"Maybe you should talk to him." We turn a corner, and a new wave of students heads for us. We both dodge out of the way.

"We aren't talking much lately," he tells me.

I glance at him, surprised. "I thought you were friends?"

Casper lifts a shoulder and waves at someone down the hall turning into our class. "We were friends because of Alex. With him gone, it's complicated.

"He's been spending a lot of time with Chloe these days," Casper continues, as if the two subjects are somehow connected. "You think Zee would hurt Chloe. You know. With his reputation with girls?" he asks.

I frown. "I don't know much about his reputation." These two guys each seem convinced that the other is a bad ass.

"Come on. Zee didn't make moves on you?"

I have an urge to punch him in the arm. I want him to be quiet. To shut the hell up. I develop an interest in my braid, winding it around my finger, stroking the smoothness, making sure the elastic is secure and intact. "It's natural that Zee is hanging out with Chloe," I remind him. "You shouldn't worry. It's possible for boys and girls to be friends, you know."

"It is not."

I frown. "Of course it is."

"Well. He better not hurt her is all." We pass a group of girls huddled around the water fountain, and they narrow their eyes at me but call out hello to Casper. He waves, then he places his hand on my back as we reach the classroom and pushes me through the doorway first. No one looks surprised when the two of us stroll in together. No one calls me a name. They keep talking or texting, ignoring me. Some of them wave or say hey to Casper, but it's like I'm not even there.

"Our essay is awesome," Casper says loudly as we head to our seats. His voice is friendly. There's nothing in his inflection to give away that we were swapping spit doing our "awesome" assignment.

"Everyone knows you're friggin' brilliant," calls a girl in the front of our row. She stares at me. I have no idea who she is.

"Whatever it takes to get the best grade." He grins a lopsided grin at her. "You know it, Callie."

She raises her middle finger at him and turns back to her notebook. I slide into my desk. Casper slides in behind me.

"Callie Zibler," he says under his breath. "She's pissed off because in the past I used to work with her. But I'll get a better grade with you."

Cold.

I glance up at Callie, but she's paying no attention to me. As if I need to give anyone another reason to hate me.

Zee's seat is empty. Kaitlin turns her back to me, then leans forward to the girl in front of her, and they both turn and glare at me. I try to imagine her crying over her dad, but it's not easy to imagine her with real emotions.

The bell rings, and phones get shoved away so they won't be confiscated. Mr. Duffield, who has been quietly lurking at his desk in the corner, stands to start the class. Zee's seat stays empty.

• • •

Later, I'm walking down the hall with my eyes cast down when a noticeable hush falls and people step out of my way. I glance up and spot Chloe. We see each other at the same time and lower our eyes simultaneously. I wish I could disappear instead of being a constant reminder to her of what she lost. How can I justify rubbing my existence in her face? I know I should reconsider homeschooling.

A friend uses her body to shield Chloe from me, and they veer off and walk away in a big circle. My heart races like I've just finished a sprint. I wonder how Chloe manages to go on with day-to-day stuff with the threat of seeing me around every corner. I hope her friends are helping her.

She's an only child now. Like me.

Taylor swings up behind me and latches her arm around my elbow. I do my best to smile at her.

"Hey, friend," she says.

I think about how she was the fastest breaststroker on the team until I showed up. Instead of being pissed off, she told me she improved her times after I joined the team. I lean close to her and soak up some of her body heat and feel ashamed for the times being around her made me turn an unattractive shade of green. And not from the chlorine in the pool. She's a true friend. Better than any I've had before.

"I don't know what I'd do without you," I whisper to her.

"You don't have to find out," she says.

"You're my real-life angel." She gives me a funny side-eye, but pats my arm.

chapter fourteen

When I get home from school, Aunt Allie and Fredrick are out and Dad is still at work. Instead of being enjoyable, the solitude only exaggerates my isolation and boredom without swimming. I glance at the clock on the wall, but I know the Titans will already be pulling through their first sets. It's a double day. Early-morning and after-school swim.

My bones ache from underuse. My muscles crave the water. I debate with myself and decide it's okay to go for a run to release some of my tension. As I head to my room to change, my cell phone cheers to let me know I've gotten a text. I pull my phone from my backpack and glance down.

Casper: Parents are out. Can u come over?

I stare down at the screen. It cheers again while I'm watching.

Casper: We can work on our assignment.

I stare for another long moment. It's not due for a week. When? I text back, instead of *No*, like I should.

Casper: Now.

I wait before I type an answer. Is this what I want? Casper?

I don't even know what I want, but my brain automatically supplies an answer: to forget.

Okay. I'll be right over.

• • •

Casper gently runs his finger along my cheek. We're sitting side by side on his huge bed with books and laptops around us. I'm cross-legged, a pencil in my mouth, thinking about the modern implications of a totalitarian society. I glance up when he touches me.

"I love watching you work." The flirty tone is back in his voice. I lean away a little, not sure of what to say or do.

Until that moment, we were all business. I'd been sure I'd imagined our last time together and that the kissing must have been an anomaly. We've worked hard for almost two hours.

"I'm kind of sad we're almost done," he says, and his grin is lazy and sure. "I like your brain."

He should talk. The boy has mad brains; I'll say that for him. He's right about the A-plus we're going to get. We've argued and philosophized and come up with amazing arguments for our paper. All we have to do is transfer everything to our computers and proof our respective pages.

There's a knock at the door, and Casper jumps to his feet, his eyes wide and almost frightened. "What?" he calls.

"You need anything? I'm heading out." It's Theresa's voice from the hallway. I wonder if she has snacks. I hate to admit it, but I'm starving. The bottomless pit has apparently reopened for business.

"You scared the shit out of me. I didn't know you were home," he tells her. "We're working on our assignment." He sits on the edge of his bed, his back straight.

She pops her head in the door. No snacks. "I'm going out," she says. She doesn't say hi to me.

"I thought you *were* out," he says. "Where you going now?"

"Out, Casper," she says and closes the door. Her footsteps move loudly away from the door, down the hallway and then the stairs.

Casper stares at the door for a moment, his eyes narrowed, his lips pressed together. Then he turns back to me and his expression completely changes.

He scoots his butt closer, puts his hand on my shoulder, and presses his mouth to my ear. "I've been wanting to kiss you since you got here."

All righty then. He could have fooled me, but I guess it wasn't such an anomaly after all. I have no idea how to read boys.

He kisses my ear lobe, and shivers tread over my skin. Heat flows and temporarily melts my icy insides, but my brain stays frozen and words won't form. I have no idea what to say, so I shut my eyes as his tongue flickers out and gently nips at my ear. I tilt my head closer to him, and the pencil falls from my mouth and plops onto my lap. With a sudden boldness, I turn and press against him and find his lips with my own.

This, this takes away some of the emptiness. My head fills with nothing but sensation, and it helps me forget everything else.

He pulls his head away from me and I try to reclaim him, but he moves away. He carefully takes the books and computers off the bed and carts them to the coffee table. I wait, too shy to say or do anything but watch. He finally crawls back on the bed beside me. "Lie back," he says. As if I have no will of my own, I lower my back onto his bed. He leans over me and takes my braid in his hand. "I love this," he says and pushes it behind my ear. "So sexy. So hot."

He presses his lips on my neck. His hand wanders, and I inhale and hold my breath, almost squeaking when he runs his fingers over my shirt, over my bra. Warning bells fire from my brain, alarms sound off, and I wonder why he can't hear them. I squeeze my eyes shut and ignore them. I accepted his invitation. Now it's time to go through with it.

His other hand reaches under my shirt, and my fogged brain kind of registers that he's pushing forward quickly, but I force myself to relax. This is what I want. To forget.

I breathe a little faster, trying to downplay the panic, when he reaches around my back and expertly unhooks my bra. I want to hold it in place, but his hand reaches up and scoots under the material, and he touches me for the first time on the skin. Right on my boob. I fight off an urge to giggle. The sexiness is kind of evaporating as I analyze his moves, calculate his next step. As I suspected, his other hand reaches for the button on my jeans and his lips reclaim mine. I cringe. No. I want to do this. I want to be his girlfriend. I'm out of the gay closet. This is what seventeen-year-old girls do. They're not lame virgins who have been too busy breast-stroking in the water to get any breast-stroking out of the water.

Gross. Even when I try to be flippant about sex in my head, it's an epic fail. I pull my head back from his and stop kissing him. He moves his lips back to my neck, but the feeling is no longer pleasurable. It feels like he's suffocating me. I picture Alex's face as he tried to get his breath.

I use both hands to push him away, and he struggles for a second, groans, and then collapses against the pillows behind him.

"What?" There's an edge to his voice.

I stiffen, but in a minute he gently lays his hand on my arm. "You okay?"

"I'm sorry," I whisper. I quickly reach behind my back with both hands and do up my bra.

He blows out air loudly. "I thought you wanted to."

Heat rushes to my cheeks, and I push myself off the bed and stand. "I'm sorry," I repeat. "I thought I did too." I open my mouth and close it, not able to think of what I want to say.

He swings his feet over the side of the bed and pats the spot beside him. I don't sit.

"It's okay. I'm not going to touch you anymore. I just want to talk to you."

I glance at him, and he half shrugs. "Trust me."

I plop down on the bed and put my head in my hands. "God. I'm such a dork."

"No, you're not." He puts his arm across my back and holds it there. It's not sexual, it's kind of tender.

My shoulders start shaking, and I'm mortified to realize that I'm crying and shivering.

"Hey, Sam. Don't." He sounds kind of uncomfortable, but he doesn't take his arm away. He moves closer so our legs are pressed together. I'm so cold. So, so cold.

"It's okay," he says.

Finally, my heaving stops and the tears slow down. I wipe under my eyes. "I don't even know why I'm crying."

Casper takes his arm away from me, and instantly I freeze from the loss of body warmth when he stands. I wrap my arms around myself.

"It was so much easier when I was a lesbian," I say with a sigh.

His eyebrows press together and he frowns.

"Remember? All the boys at my old school thought I was gay."

The look on his face makes me laugh. He must think I'm completely crazy now. Crying uncontrollably one moment, laughing hysterically the next. But he shakes his head and grins and sits again, patting my knee. "You're something else, you know that. And since you're not a lesbian, do you want to go the Fall Festival with me?"

My laughter slowly leaves my lips. "The what?"

He tells me about the town fair that goes on every year in November. Scarecrow-building contests, baking contests, rodeo, the list goes on and on. There are even rides and games. A real county fair.

"Seriously?" I say, wondering why I haven't heard of it before. Probably I wasn't paying attention.

He frowns. "You don't want to go with me, just say so."

"No. I just never knew about it. I swear."

"Well. It's a big deal. Every year." His voice is a tad sharp.

"We didn't have a fair in Orlie. We had to go to Seattle."

"You want to go, or what?"

"I guess. I mean. Sure." I smile at him, kind of surprised that he's asking me out. In public. Does he want to announce to the world that we're a couple?

I wonder if we are. I've spent the last half hour or so kissing him, and I have no idea whether we're a couple or not. Or if I even want us to be. Is he more than a distraction or relief that someone is paying attention to me?

There's no fluttering in my stomach when I think of him when we're not together. I don't get all giggly and itchy around him, not like with Zee. I chew the inside of my cheek, wondering what he'll say. I don't want to think about Zee. Or before.

"Don't sound so enthusiastic," Casper says, but he smiles.

"It's not that. I didn't know."

"Cool…" He pauses and taps his fingers on my leg, as if he's playing a song. "We used to all go together with our dates." He takes a breath. "Alex, me, and Zee." The words refreeze my thawing skin. "Zee's taking Chloe this year. You want to go with Taylor and Justin?" He taps my leg. *Tap tap tap.*

I try to keep breathing normally.

"Zee's taking Chloe?" I manage.

He lifts his shoulder. "He's hanging out with her a lot. He's into her, I think."

I nod. Maybe they are becoming more than friends?

"So," he says and stands up and stretches his arms high in the air. I have the feeling I'm being dismissed.

"Can you type out your final draft of your part of our essay by

Friday? We can trade and proof each other's and hand them in to Mr. Duffield on Monday. That doable for you?"

"Sure." I stand up and head to the coffee table, where I grab my books and start putting everything in my backpack. He walks to where I'm standing, bends down, and lightly kisses my cheek. "I know how hard everything must be. You're handling it great."

I don't answer, but I sling my backpack over my shoulder and fake a smile.

Casper walks me all the way outside to my car and holds the door while I climb inside. "I'll pick you up. For the festival. I'll text you the details. Wear something warm. It gets cold."

The house is still empty when I get home. Or empty again. There's a note on the fridge held by a magnet. I skim Aunt Allie's writing. She and Dad have gone to his doctor. Fredrick's along for the ride. I'm not to worry. There's leftover pizza in the fridge.

I feel dirty, like the kissing and touching tainted me. There's no dreamy afterglow. It's almost like I'm cheating on someone. But who? Alex? Am I mocking his memory by making out with another guy? His friend.

I shiver.

I want to tell Alex I'm sorry I kissed him before I had a chance to get to know him. Maybe I would have liked him. We might have dated or something. I try not to think about Zee.

I want to tell Alex I'm sorry he had a crush on me. That I feel bad about what happened to him, and don't want to forget him, not really, but the thought of putting my words on paper horrifies me. I'm not ready to write him a letter.

I open the fridge, but food doesn't appeal to me. I pick up my cell phone, but there's no use texting Taylor. She'll be swimming. No one in Orlie texts me anymore. There was a rush of messages to try to find out more about the accident. But they've died off. Gillian seems to have written me off. I shut off my cell phone. There's only one thing I can think of to do. I dart to my room and change into yoga pants, a T-shirt, and a pullover running jacket, grab my iPhone, and head out on the road.

I start off with a light jog, my body responding with a rush to the exercise. Quickly, though, it feels like I'm swallowing acid in my throat. My lungs hurt, but I run faster and faster. I miss the sensation of water on my skin. Running doesn't use my whole body. My shoulders are stiff but limp, and my body struggles to get a breathing groove, so different from breathing in the water. My legs ache, but it's not like kicking. Trying to forget what my brain cannot, I turn the music louder, so loud I can't hear anything else, not even my own breathing.

I push myself, running fast and farther than before. It's dark when I get home, and my lungs feel clogged and uncomfortable. The house is still empty, which is weird but kind of good, since I'd probably be in trouble for being out running alone in the dark. I shower and while hot water runs down my back, my thoughts somehow drift to my mom.

I pull on the purple robe Aunt Allie gave me, and when I reach around to tie the belt my hand brushes over a small lump in the pocket. I reach inside. My fingers wrap around something metal. It's thin and light. I pull it out. It's an old-fashioned silver necklace with a locket.

With my heart beating fast, I slide my nail in and open it up. There's a tiny picture inside. I bring it up closer to my eyes. It's my mom. Holding a baby. She's staring down at the baby, and the look on her face is exquisite. Mom love. I've never seen the picture before, but of course the baby is me. My heart pounds and pounds, and I can't decide if I'm afraid or excited.

I close the locket and squeeze it in my fist. Somehow I'm compelled to stand and creep down the hallway to Dad's room. I push on the door and stare at his neatly made bed. There's folded laundry on his dresser. Aunt Allie's taken over the laundry since she's been here. He hates doing it and pays me an allowance to handle the chore, since I've never been able to get a job with my swimming hours. It's the only time I go into his room. To put his laundry away.

Listening for Dad's car, I creep inside, closer to his other dresser. The tall one. There are pictures in frames on the top. Mini me on a diving platform. A bigger me on a podium, three gold medals around my neck. Me last year, emerging from the water in a butterfly stroke with my shoulders looking as big as my head. My insides ache. For how much it must hurt him to have me refusing to swim. No pictures of him. None of Mom.

Swallowing jitters, I pull open the top drawer. His black work socks are shoved inside, unsorted. I refuse to match them up and roll them together. Instead, I throw them on his bed in a big pile on laundry day. It's very un-Dad-like that they go in the drawer the same way.

I run my hand under the socks, searching the bottom of the drawer for something, but there's nothing secret stashed away. I repeat this in his other drawers, not aware of what I'm looking for but sensing there's something to find.

Ignoring my bad feeling, I look around his room and then take a step inside his walk-in closet. Dress shirts line the inside racks, displayed on cheap white coat hangers with the protective plastic from the drycleaners. I don't do work shirts. I hate to iron.

Above the hangers is a long shelf that runs the length of his closet. Sweaters are folded neatly in piles and then, at the end, there's a long white storage box. I stare at it for a moment and then tuck the necklace in my pocket, walk over, stand on my tiptoes, and pull it down.

SANDRA is written on top in thick black marker.

My heart pounds. I've never seen this before. I have no idea what's in it. I carry the box to the bed.

Slowly, I lift the lid. A pale pink baby sleeper lies on top of a pile of cards and pictures. There's a sweater under it that looks home-made. Knitted or crocheted, I can't tell the difference. It's so tiny. I pick it up and hold it to my nose. It smells sweet. I reach for the stack of pictures and pick one up. My heart skips a hurried beat. It's my mom, and she looks so young. Maybe not much older than me. She's wearing flared jeans that go all the way to the top of her waist with a tight, short T-shirt. Her hair is huge. I peer closer. She's smiling at whoever is taking the picture.

I flip to the next one. Her in a retro Speedo bathing suit. I flip and flip. There are so many more. Younger versions, and gradually shots of her with Dad. Arm in arm. In one they're wearing matching hiking clothes on a mountain. They're smiling. Happy.

In another she's sitting on his lap, and they're smiling into each other's eyes. Under the pictures is a frame, and I pull it out. It's her. Sitting in a rocking chair. She's wearing a yellow hoodie with bright red sweat pants. She's holding a baby to her chest, half swathed in a blanket. Leaning up against her feet is a black Labrador retriever. She's smiling, but there's sadness in her eyes. Tired. She looks tired.

I put the frame down and look back in the box. A set of candles in a plastic see-through box. Baptismal candles. My name and birthday are printed on them. There's a white sleeper with a silk cross on the front. I recognize it from my baptism pictures from the album Dad keeps out for me with pictures from my childhood. Before everything went digital and got stored on his computer.

In the picture, Mom's holding me facing the camera, the only baby girl not wearing a frilly white baby dress.

The box is empty now except for an old VHS tape. I take it out. On the spine, in Dad's handwriting it says "Sandra." And a date close to when I was born.

I put everything back in the box, everything except the framed picture and the video. I plunk the lid on and place it back in the closet where it was.

I sit down on the bed for a moment, thinking, and then I take the frame and place it on top of Dad's dresser. I tuck the tape under my arm and go down to the basement, wondering where Dad would stash the old VCR, knowing it wouldn't be thrown out. Not yet.

There are a few unopened containers in the storage room. Each one is labeled. Dad's organizational skills are reliable. Inside a box marked "Electronics" I find the VCR. The cords are still attached.

Triumphant, I carry it to the TV, hook it up, plug it in, and nod in satisfaction when the TV switches over. I put the tape in, waiting impatiently while it whirs and beeps, taking forever to load. I listen with one ear for sounds from upstairs to indicate that Aunt Allie and Dad are home, but it's quiet. I wonder if they went out for dinner. An image flickers on the TV and then a voice speaks from off camera. The image wobbles and then a woman, blurry and out of focus, appears on the screen.

"Sandra, Samantha, look over here," Dad's voice calls.

I hold my breath and the picture comes into focus.

My mom sits on the edge of a pool. Her feet hang in the water. She's wearing a black one-piece suit and has long, pale legs. Her hair is pulled back into a ponytail, and she turns and smiles at the camera, but her eyes don't smile along with her mouth. The baby in her arms is chubby, with rolls for arms and legs.

Compared to the roly-poly baby, my mom looks too thin. The baby—me—I look too big to have come from her body. But she holds me under my arms and dips my toe into the pool. The baby—me—I squeal, and then a giggle erupts from my lips. Off camera, the deep voice of my dad chuckles. "Just like her mom, a natural in the water."

The baby shrieks again, but the giggle turns into an angry wail. I watch my mom stand, pulling the baby up with her as she gets to her feet. The baby shrieks. Loud and angry cries.

The look on my mom's face makes my heart sink. She looks angry, terrified, defeated in the span of a second. "Take her," she says. "Please, Jonathan. Put down the camera and take her. She hates me." She's holding me out, with her arms straight, her eyes opened wide, her lips pressed together.

"Sandra," my dad's voice says off camera. It's changed. He's talking in a low voice, I recognize the sound. He's angry, but he's trying to remain calm. "She's probably cold. She doesn't hate you. Just hold her close. Warm her up."

The baby howls louder.

"Take her. Please." On screen there's a close-up of baby me, with squinched-up eyes and an angry, toothless mouth wide open and hollering.

"For God's sake, Sandra." The camera jiggles around and then turns off. There's blackness and then a hissing and horrible pop from the TV. I jump and press mute on the remote, then I find the fast-forward button on the VCR and press it. Another image wobbles on the screen, distorted until I let go of the button.

The baby again. Older. Wearing a goofy flowered dress. Baby me is sitting up on my own.

"Sam?" Dad calls.

Noises come from upstairs. The front door's opened, and Aunt Allie and Dad's feet thump on the floor above. Fredrick's little paws scrape along the hardwood.

I turn the VCR off. "Down here. I'll be right up."

Fredrick hears my voice, scrambles down the stairs, and jumps at my legs. I pick him up and he attacks my nose and mouth with his little tongue until I spurt and move him away. I carry him up the stairs with me while he grunts and snorts and noisily greets me. He's wearing a new bandana covered in orange pumpkins.

Aunt Allie is at the top of the stairs with a sour look on her face. Her eyebrows are pressed together, her lips tight. Dad smiles, but it wavers and quickly fades. Immediately guilt plops into my head. Do they know? About me and Casper? About me snooping in his room?

"Where'd you get that robe?" he asks when I walk into the kitchen.

"Aunt Allie gave it to me." I glance at her.

"It was your mom's," he says and presses his lips together and shakes his head.

"I know." I stare at Aunt Allie. She glares at my dad.

"I thought she should have it. She has so few things from her mom."

"It's fine." He waves his hand in the air. "Fine. Sorry we're late," he says to me with another sigh. He squeezes my shoulder as he walks by me to his wine cupboard. "We went for dinner and texted and called your cell to see if you wanted to come, but you didn't answer."

Aunt Allie swoops in and pulls me close and tries to squeeze the stuffing out of me. When she lets go, I reach into my pocket and pull out the necklace.

"What's that?" she asks, narrowing her eyes to peer closer. Dad has a wineglass in each hand, but he stops moving and his face goes almost white.

"Where'd you get that?"

I glare at Aunt Allie. "You put it here."

She shakes her head. "No, I didn't." She holds out her hand. "Let me see it."

I close my fist.

"What is it?" she repeats and shakes her hand at me.

I open my hand and dump the necklace in hers. She sucks in her breath and her eyes open wider. She lifts the open locket up close to her eyes.

"It's Sandra's. Jonathan. Did you see this?"

He's put the wine glasses down and is walking toward us. "Where'd you get that?" he repeats.

"It was in the pocket."

He glares at Aunt Allie. "Did you find it and put it there?"

She shakes her head. "No. I washed the robe before I gave it to Sam. I know the pockets were empty. I've never seen that necklace before."

Dad's face is almost white. Aunt Allie hands him the necklace. His face crumples.

"She lost this," he whispers. "She was so upset with herself. It disappeared right before she died." He looks at me. "I gave it to her for her birthday. And when she was wearing it, it slipped off. We never found it."

Shivers run up my spine.

"Allie. You must have put it in the pocket," he says again.

"I didn't, Jonathan."

"Then how?"

The three of us look at each other and then down at the necklace.

"Sometimes things happen," Aunt Allie says.

"Don't start with that stuff," Dad says, but his voice is low and gravelly. He wipes his finger under his eye. "Really, Allie. You never put it there. Sam? You're sure you found it in the pocket?"

I nod. "Take it, Dad. Take the necklace."

Dad looks at me. "Oh, butterfly," he says, and he steps forward and takes me in his arms. And then he opens the clasp on it and secures it around my neck.

He pushes me gently back, studies the necklace, and glances at Aunt Allie. "Your mom must have meant for you to find it. She wants you to have it."

"But how?" I ask.

"Not everything can be explained," Aunt Allie says. "Sometimes we just have to go with it."

Dad doesn't try to come up with a logical explanation.

Maybe there is one. But maybe none of us wants to find it.

chapter fifteen

I make it through classes with an invisible bubble around me that
keeps me safe from onlookers. I suspect it has something to do
with the locket.

Taylor texts me, but we miss each other in the halls. I wonder
if it's possible to get through the whole day without speaking to
anyone other than teachers. But I have English after lunch, and I'll
see Casper, so probably not. I'm surprised I haven't gotten any texts
from him, which I'd both expected and dreaded.

At lunch I take my brown bag outside to eat alone. I try not to
remember earlier days of sitting in the cafeteria with the swimmers,
close to Zee while he made jokes about my three sandwiches and
Taylor threw crusts at him.

The air outside is chilly, so there aren't many kids around. I stand
in the entranceway and lean against a railing, not wanting to sit on
the damp grass. I watch the usual groups hang around the outskirts
of the school like they do at school grounds all over America. Dad
always says teenagers think they're original, but other than having
a lot more technology, they're not so different from their parents.
I can't imagine that he's right. It has to be harder now than when
he was a kid.

I chomp on my sandwich, down to one from three. I've cut back on the huge portions, afraid of eating too much. Without swimming, I'm afraid of ballooning up. For the millionth time, my fingers go to the necklace, and I rub the locket and stare at cars passing the school, making up stories in my head about the people inside.

"I hope that's not peanut butter." My mouth stops chewing, and chunks of bread and ham stick to the roof of my mouth.

A girl is staring at me. She walks close, her long legs perfect for the black skinny jeans she's wearing. Her arms are crossed over a thin black sweater with no jacket to keep out the chills. She's either freezing or has lava running through her veins. She snaps her gum, and even though she's pretty, with her short whitish blond hair and big hoop earrings, she reminds me of someone from a TV commercial about troubled youth. She's the girl from English class. The one Casper dropped as a partner for me.

She uncrosses her arms and squints as if she wants to give me a beat-down. I force myself to swallow the food in my mouth and stare back at her, trying to look tough and not terrified.

"It's not peanut butter," I tell her. "I don't eat it anymore." My cheeks turn red, realizing how stupid that must sound.

"Yeah? Too bad you didn't put that into practice a few months ago."

I want to say something snarky back, but don't have the energy or will. I drop my eyes and look at her scuffed-up ankle boots.

"You know who I am?" Her voice challenges me to something I'm not sure of.

I push off the railing, drop my hands to my side so I'm standing taller, and look straight into her eyes. We're about the same height, but I've got more muscle and bulk. I can't believe I'm sizing her up and noticing all this. I've never had to fight to protect myself in my life.

I swallow and think Xanax-y thoughts.

I am not afraid. I am not afraid.

The anxiety in my belly tells a different story.

"Callie Zibler," she says. "I'm Callie."

"You used to partner with Casper in English." I twist my braid around my fingers.

"Used to." She shifts her weight, juts a scrawny hip out, and lifts her thumb to her mouth to gnaw on the nail. Her bottom lip quivers just a little, enough for me to notice. "He thinks you're smarter, and that's all he cares about. He's desperate to be valedictorian. As if he needs scholarship money. He wants bragging rights."

She sighs and doesn't look like she wants to beat me up anymore. "He's an ass."

It's such a relief that I put my hand over my mouth to stop a giggle. I crumple the rest of the sandwich I'm holding in my other hand and wait for her to say more.

She pulls her thumb from her mouth. "Alex and I used to go out. We split up a few months ago, before he died. But we stayed friends."

I glance down. A ladybug crawls on the pavement by my shoe. It only has two spots and is more orange than red. She's out late in the season, and cold weather is coming. Stupid ladybug facts live in my head. Useless information stored for no apparent reason. They hibernate in groups in the cold. I wonder where the bug's friends are.

"I'm sorry. I wish I could have known him better." I stare at the ladybug, thinking about Alex's friends. He had a lot of them. "That probably sounds horrible coming from me."

"No. He was a really good guy. You would have like him," she says. "And actually, I kind of screwed him over," Callie says.

I look up, surprised. "Alex was good about it," Callie continues. "Chloe's my friend. From softball. She's really good. Like Alex was. I think he and I kind of went out by default. Both of us ball players, you know?"

I hide my surprise. She's a jock? She doesn't look the part. But what do I know? Until recently I was a fake lesbian. Now I kill boys with my spit and make out with my study partners.

"I like Alex, but we were better as friends." She pauses. "Liked." She shivers, and her knees wobble together. "He was cute. Cool. We just weren't each other's type. He was so good about it. He was a great guy. Like I said, you would have liked him."

A boy in the school yard whoops as his friend tackles him. We both watch them goof around for a minute.

"I'm sorry." I manage again and let out a huge sigh.

She reaches out and touches my arm. "I know," she says. "It must be awful. I mean. I miss Alex so much. It's hard to believe he's gone. But for you." She shakes her head. "It could have been me too. You know. I mean, I ate nuts and stuff when we dated. I wasn't always a hundred percent safe."

I swallow again and again, but my throat feels like it's growing and stretching out of my skin. The boys are play fighting; their friends are gathered around watching.

Callie stares at me as if she's waiting for me to say something, and I wonder what I could possibly say. "I wasn't at the party," she says. "The night it happened."

"Lucky you."

She half smiles, but it fades quickly. "Yeah. I heard it was pretty awful."

I nod and look toward the street. An old truck rumbles past. It's white, but the body is covered with orange rust. A girl is squished up close to the driver, and she has her head tilted back and her mouth open, laughing. The boy driving is smiling. I wonder what he just said to make her laugh. I want to run after the truck. Hop in the back. Ask them to share and take me away from this conversation.

"He talked about you. Said you're a swimmer. I heard you're awesome."

I glance at her, almost surprised. I shrug. I was a swimmer. I'm not sure what I am anymore. But it's nothing she needs to hear.

"Anyhow." She narrows her eyes. "Alex was a good guy, but sometimes he did stupid stuff."

I frown. It's not nice to talk about a guy who's no longer around to defend himself. It doesn't matter so much anymore if he did stupid things.

She shivers and rubs her hands up and down her arms, avoiding my eyes. "I'm only saying so because some people are being pretty ignorant, acting like everything is your fault."

I look across the school yard. The kids horsing around look tough, kind of like druggies. The boys' pants hang halfway down their butts. The girls' makeup looks like war paint, and they're heavily pierced. I imagine them mocking me and my clean lifestyle the way the druggies in Orlie used to. I judged them too, and what they did to their bodies. We're all judging each other and trying hard to find someone to fit in with.

"That's kind of to be expected," I tell her. "Under the circumstances."

"It's not right," she says.

A gust of wind blows a cluster of leaves toward us, and I pull my hoodie closer. She wraps her arms tighter around herself; her thin sweater is for fashion, not warmth.

"Frick. It's cold. Listen, the reason I followed you into this freezing weather is to tell you something."

"What?" I finally ask when she doesn't say more. "Can you enlighten me?" I try to sound patient.

"They're investigating his death. Like, a coroner is."

"Yeah," I say. "I know."

"You do?" Her brows furrow together, and she seems genuinely surprised.

"Casper told me."

"He did?"

"We're—" I pause, but a sliver of shame creeps onto my face. "Working on that English project together."

She tilts her head as if she smells embarrassment and glances past me toward the group of kids who are now heading our way. She narrows her eyes, and the toughness I saw before is back. "I didn't think you'd know. Alex's friends are all pretty messed up by all this."

"I know," I tell her.

"Everybody deals differently, right? I'm glad Casper told you.

We're all kind of watching Chloe's back. But you don't deserve to be reviled."

I almost chuckle at her word choice. Why wouldn't they revile me? But I have Chloe's back too. She just doesn't even know. I would do almost anything to protect her.

She peers closer at me. "She doesn't hate you."

"I would," I say automatically. "Hate me."

"No," she shakes her head, and her earrings bob around. They're so big it looks painful. "I don't think you would. Especially if you knew everything."

I frown.

The kids are getting closer. One of the boys waves to her. She waves back and jumps up and down on the spot. "God. It's cold out here. I gotta go back inside."

"If I knew everything?" I repeat.

She jumps. Up, down, up, down, up, down. A human pogo stick. "Talk to Chloe," she says, her eyes on the boy, and then she hurries to the front doors of the school and disappears inside.

I weave my braid around my finger. What the hell was that supposed to be about? What don't I know?

My pocket starts to vibrate. I pull out my cell phone and frown at the caller ID.

"It's Dad. You got anything important next period?"

"Not really."

"Then come right home."

chapter sixteen

I hurry to the school parking lot and drive straight home. My nerves jump, trying to figure out what would make Dad ask me to ditch class.

When I run in the house he's sitting in the living room. He's holding the framed picture of Mom that I put on his dresser.

I pause at the threshold to the living room, where the tile from the kitchen and hallway meets the hardwood. The house smells like vanilla and fresh cookies, and it gives my head a mixed message. There's no noise or sign of Aunt Allie or Fredrick.

I stare at the frame in his hand, and my cheeks burn. My fingers immediately go to the locket on my neck. I asked for this, but now have an urge to turn around and run back out the door. Confrontation. Here it is now, in front of me.

"You were snooping around in my room," he says. His voice sounds odd. Devoid of emotion. "You could have asked me about your mom."

Heat flushes from my feet and rockets through me. "No," I remind him. "I couldn't. You never talk about her. You never let me ask about her." I lift my head higher, reminding myself I wanted this. His anger. This confrontation. "We never talk about her."

He doesn't say anything, and I can tell he's carefully considering his words. His eyes go to my hand. The locket around my neck that I'm clutching. "Did that really just show up?" he asks.

"I swear." I take my hand off it and lift my head as he stares at the necklace.

"I watched the video. The one from when I was a baby," I tell him.

He brings both hands up and rubs at his head, scratching his scalp furiously. "I know. You left the VCR out." He points at the spot on the couch opposite him. "Sit."

I do as he asks. The fireplace light is on, and the blinds on the window are open. It's bright and cheery in the room, but he isn't.

"The first time I met your mom was at a swim meet. We were both fifteen. We both lived in Seattle, but at opposite ends. She swam for a different club than me. Like you, her butterfly was famous. Poetic." His head is down, as if he's talking to the hardwood.

He glances up. A soft smiles turns up the corners of his mouth. "Inside the water she was fierce, unstoppable. But outside the water...she was kind of fragile." He places the picture frame he's holding on the sofa table beside him. He turns it so it faces me.

I listen to the words he's unwrapping like gifts and hear the emotions in his voice. Love. Hurt. Sadness. I try to relate them to the person who was my mother. Not the woman frozen in time in a picture.

"She was pretty. Blond hair, with eyes so much like yours. Her eyes made people stop and stare. Like Elizabeth Taylor's. Almost purple. And of course, the perfect swimmer's build." He chuckles and stares off into space, and my cheeks redden as he remembers her in a way that is sweet but kind of embarrassing.

"But what was she like?" I whisper, afraid to stop the flow of memories, but afraid he won't go on if I don't prompt him. I stare at the vase of flowers that Aunt Allie placed on the fireplace mantel. The leaves are browning, but the flowers are struggling to hang in.

"Quiet. Your aunt told me to watch out for quiet ones, but I didn't listen to her. I couldn't. I fell in love with your mom almost the first time I saw her."

There's a noise from the basement, a rustling and then a burp-growl, and I realize Aunt Allie and Fredrick are home but hiding out downstairs. Giving us privacy.

"Your mother was beautiful."

I twist my braid and put the end of it in my mouth, bite down on it. "I saw that. But what was she like? Why was she unhappy?"

He leans back, sticks his feet out, puts his hand behind his head, and sighs, and the force of it goes right through him. "She lived in her own skin. In her own head. Aunt Allie called her an old soul."

I frown. "Like reincarnated?"

He laughs, but it's dry. "Allie might say so, but no, I meant she was deep. A thinker. She analyzed everything but kept most things inside. She was quiet and soft except when she got into the pool. And then she was fiercely competitive. She didn't like to admit how driven she was. But she loved to win." His mouth turns up into a smile again.

I wish I could see inside his head, see the person he is remembering. "She was introspective, but she did have a good sense of humor. I don't know." He blinks, and his eyelashes glisten. "I loved her so much, but I always wondered if I wasn't enough."

My heart opens to him. "Oh, Daddy. Of course you were

enough." I wish I were little again and could sit on his lap and comfort both of us. I wait for him to go on. When he says nothing more, I have to ask. "Why did you think that?"

He stares at me. Through me. Blinking. I can see he's trying to figure out what to tell me. How much.

"It's okay, Dad. I can handle this. I can."

He presses his lips tight and sighs, takes his hands away from behind his head and sits up straight. "I suppose you can. She was ill. A little while after we got married, she got pretty sick." He shakes his head. "They put her on meds to try to help, but it made her lose speed in the water. By then she was only swimming for herself, but she hated it. So she quit swimming."

My stomach drops as I feel how wrong it was for her to do that. And it's very familiar.

"What was wrong with her?"

"Her doctor said she was bipolar, only back then they called it manic depression. Her highs weren't crazy or out of control, but her lows flattened her. It affected her energy level and self-esteem. The medication was brutal. They didn't have the kind they have now. It was strong, with side effects, and she hated taking them. But after a while, she did feel better. And then she wanted to get pregnant. So." He smiles at me but sighs. "She went off them. Her doctor wanted her to stay on, but she didn't want to risk your health. There were so many unknowns, taking the meds while pregnant. And she seemed so much better."

I close my eyes. "Why are you only telling me this now?" I ask in a soft voice.

He stands and looks as if he's about to leave the room, but then, just as abruptly, he sits back down. "Your mom didn't tell people about her disease. She didn't want anyone to know. I guess I got used to covering up for her."

"But I'm her daughter."

"Yes. And for a long time you were too young to understand. The way you worry about things. I never wanted you to blame yourself. I thought it would be worse for you to know."

"Why would I blame myself?"

"Because. You're you." He stops and rubs his eyes. "She loved being pregnant, she wanted a baby so much. She was so excited. But it brought back the depression with a vengeance. She struggled. She had a horrible time with postpartum blues. We had her in and out of doctors' offices. They were playing with her medication, trying to get the doses right, but she wasn't getting better."

He reaches over, picks up the picture frame again, turns it toward himself, and studies it. "I was working, trying to keep things together. We didn't have a lot of money. Your mom's mom, Grandma Catherine, was sick then. It was right before she passed. She couldn't help out."

"What about Grandpa Ned and Grandma Karen?"

He makes a grunting sound. Puts the picture down flat on the table. "They weren't ready to help. Not really. For one, they didn't believe your mom was sick." His voice hardens. "They thought she should just get more sunlight. Take extra vitamins. Aunt Allie came to stay with us, but I think it made your mom more anxious, if anything. She felt like Allie was judging her. She wasn't, but the illness…Well, she wasn't herself."

"Why didn't you tell me, Dad?" I say softly.

He holds his hands out flat. I stand from the sofa and walk over and sit down close to him. "Maybe I was waiting until you were ready to talk about it. Maybe I was waiting until I was."

He pats my knee, and I nod. Both of us were so wrapped up in my world. Swimming. I'd let my questions about my own mom wait.

As if he senses my guilty thoughts, he puts his arm around my shoulder.

"It was never your fault. It was never about her not loving you. She loved you so much. So much. More than she ever loved anyone." He smiles. "Even me."

"So…when she died?" I can't help the thoughts trying to sneak in.

He squeezes me tighter. "No. It was an accident. They investigated. The road conditions were terrible. The other driver was at fault. Your mom couldn't have done anything different."

I breathe out. Relieved. I twist my braid around and around my finger.

Dad takes his arm away from me and reaches for the frame again. He picks it up with one hand. "She was a good woman, your mom. She would have gotten better. I know that. She would have loved being with you as you grew up. She would be so proud of your swimming." He holds it out to me.

"Take this. She would have been so proud of the way you turned out, butterfly."

I shake my head. "No. I have the necklace. You keep it. On your dresser. With the other pictures."

His lips turn up, and he nods.

"Is it hereditary?"

He puts the frame down on the couch and turns to me. "Honestly? It can be. When you were little, I worried. But you're stronger, Sam. You're not like your mom that way. You're healthy as a horse."

I close my eyes and think. No. I don't think I'm sick like her. I'm wounded, but not down.

"You calling me a horse?" I open my eyes.

He chuckles. "I loved your mom so much. And she loved us. Especially you."

He pulls me in then and holds me tight. His warmth spreads to me.

"Are you afraid it's happening to me?"

He puts his chin on top of my head. "You're keeping it together pretty well, considering. The worst thing you're doing is punishing yourself by not swimming."

I close my eyes.

"You've always had an active imagination. Swimming has helped. Believe it or not, it's not always about being the best. Or getting into the best university."

I pull my head out from under his chin and glare at him.

He laughs. "Okay. Guilty. I've been interested in those things too." He pats my head then, as if I'm Fredrick. "Maybe too much."

We sit in silence for a while, and then I realize I have to get up. Burn up some energy. Do something. I pull away from him. Stand. "You pulled me away from my gym class. I'm going to go for a run. You want to come with me?"

His face reddens. "I haven't run in a long time." He looks like he's about to lapse into another long speech.

"It's okay, I'm more of a lone runner anyhow."

He nods. "Okay. Be careful. Take your phone with you."

I go to my room to change, stopping in the living room on the way out and pointing at my arm band holding my iPhone. A one-stop entertainment center and Dad-approved safety feature.

• • •

I run toward the pool. The south wall of the recreation center is a glass window. The blinds are open. I can see my team on deck, and I slow down. Watching them. It looks like they're lining up to do sprint races. Light glimmers off the water, reflecting and shooting up pretty colors from the sunbeams. The colors dance on top.

Clair is on deck. As if she senses me watching, she slowly turns her head. I lift my hand. She stares at me and then lifts her hand in return. I jog faster until she's out of sight. I think of Alex. His baseball and where he was headed in the future. I think of my mom. Crippled by her mind. Unable to get back to the pool. Am I doing the same thing?

I run farther. Faster. Until I'm home.

In my room, I google bipolar disorder and go over the symptoms. A website lists a page about a group working to lessen the stigma of mental health issues. I notice a link that advertises a five-mile run to raise funds and awareness for mental health. I click on the link, sign the online form, and click Send.

And then I type in "peanut allergy." I read and explore, and then I hit a website that gives me an idea. A way to do something. A way to finally do something more than mope in my room.

chapter seventeen

I barely notice Halloween arrive. I've ignored the houses on our street turning into haunted mansions with fake spider webs dripping from trees. I've ignored zombies hanging off porches. Carved pumpkins. I've glossed over huge candy displays in the grocery store.

It's always been my favorite holiday, ranked even ahead of Christmas, but when Dad offers to pick up pumpkins to carve, I turn him down. For the first time ever.

At school, Taylor tells me she's having a small get-together even though it's a weeknight. For the swim team and a few other friends. Her mom will be chaperoning to help the kids work through bad memories from her last party and show them life goes on. Taylor pleads with me to come, but we both know I won't.

It's the first time I've missed a Halloween party since I stopped trick-or-treating. But I can't imagine being at Taylor's with Alex's friends. I'm the last person who should be there.

What I really want to do is sit in my room and read, but Aunt Allie is consumed by Halloween excitement and makes me sit on a stool in the kitchen while she cooks. "Keep me company while I make dinner. Well. Breakfast for dinner. Perfect for Halloween."

Fredrick sits in the middle of the kitchen and stares intently up at her. She ignores him and moves to the counter to chop up onions. She picks up a handful of the chopped onions and throws them in a frying pan. A sizzling sound fills the air first, and then the smell. I'm not wild about the taste of fried onions with eggs, but love the smell of them cooking. She stirs the onions, stopping to wipe a drip from under her eye.

Fredrick burp-woofs, and she tosses him an onion. He sniffs at it and then runs from the kitchen while she and I both laugh.

She chops up more onions on the cutting board, banging at them like she really means it. "I'd like to kill your dad for keeping me away so long." She frowns and puts down the knife. "Well, not literally kill him."

A tear drips down her cheek, and she lifts her arm and uses her sleeve to wipe it away.

"Me too." I get up and fill a glass with juice. I down it in one gulp and then open the dishwasher and put the glass on the top rack. "Can we talk about my mom?"

Instead of frowning, she smiles. "Your mom?" She adds salt to her concoction on the stove. "She was a good person." She pats her heart and plunks the salt shaker down. "Inside. Where it counts."

She takes a plate from the cupboard and scoops some eggs and onions out of the pan. "In some ways, she had incredible strength. In the pool, for example. I never completely understood how she could be so great at something but so unsure of herself in other ways."

She removes more eggs from a carton on the counter and adds them to the sizzling pan, stirring them as she stares off, thinking. "She was hard to get to know in many ways. But I liked her." She frowns. "No. I loved her. She was like a little sister to me. Cheese?"

I nod, and she turns from the stove, grabs the parmesan cheese from the counter, sprinkles some on the eggs, and hands me the plate.

I smile my thanks, balancing it on my hand. "Do you think… was her death an accident?"

"Yes. It was. I believe that with every ounce of my being. She would never have left you on purpose." She reaches across, pulls open the cutlery drawer, hands me a fork, wipes her hands on her apron, and serves herself a plate of food.

I lean against the sink counter and stick a forkful of eggs in my mouth.

We eat our dinner standing and in silence, and afterward she disappears downstairs for a moment and then comes up wearing a black dress and purple witch hat. Fredrick follows her, prancing in a black bat costume with a look that dares me to make fun of him.

"You have to keep me company," she insists and perches herself on the living room couch before it's even dark, waiting for kids to come to the door. Fredrick crawls into her lap to wait.

On a TV table by the front door, a bowl overflows with oversized chocolate bars and full cans of pop that Aunt Allie bought. Much more extravagant than the fun-sized Skittles Dad picked up, which are pretty much there so he and I can nibble on them.

When Dad gets home from work, he changes and goes to the

kitchen for dinner and Aunt Allie moves to the chair closer to the door. She races Dad every time the bell rings or a tiny voice shouts out "trick or treat," and Fredrick breaks out into a chorus of cough-barks and jumps around in his bat costume. The kids *ohh* and *ahh* over him, and he looks at them with disdain. After the first couple of kids, Dad gives up trying to get to the door and rolls his eyes at his sister. I know him well enough to know he's a little disappointed. After all, I got my love for Halloween from him. But we both know it's been a few years since Aunt Allie had a house to sit in and children to hand out candy to. He's letting her have it.

My cell phone cheers, and I take it from my pocket to see a text from Taylor telling me that people are asking for me. I know she's lying and can't bear the thought of facing anyone at the place where Alex died.

As the parade of children starts to die down, Dad excuses himself and goes up to his room to watch TV in private. I put down the book I've been trying to read.

"I'd really like to do an angel reading," I tell Aunt Allie as soon as Dad's out of earshot. "Halloween feels appropriate."

"I find that a little insulting," she says and cackles at me.

"I don't mean it that way."

"I know." She stands up, grabs a chocolate bar, throws it to me, and takes one for herself and opens the wrapper. "The question is, have you written your letter to Alex?"

"Not yet." I hold the chocolate bar up and squint to read the list of ingredients on the back.

"Well. It's the stipulation. No self-respecting angel is going to provide guidance until it's done." She sinks her teeth into the chocolate. "Mmmm," she says and happy-sighs.

"You're making that up," I tell her.

"My angels, my rules."

I glare at her and hold out my chocolate bar. "This says it may contain peanuts."

Aunt Allie is about to bite her bar again but stops. "Okay?" Her voice is softer.

"Kids with peanut allergies can't eat them," I tell her.

She brings the bar away from her mouth. Her hand twitches and she brings it to her lap.

"We should have bought peanut-free candy. Just in case. More and more kids have nut allergies these days."

"But it's a small percentage, butterfly. Isn't it like one percent or something?"

"It's more like three or four percent. And what if one of them comes to our house?"

"Then they won't eat our candy?" She lifts her eyebrows.

I squish up my nose with distaste, and she nods.

"Okay. You're right. It would have been an easy thing to do. Next year I'll make sure."

I smile, happy that she hopes to be here next year at Halloween and that she'll go peanut-free with me.

"I'd really like to do the angel reading ," I say again. "I feel like I need to know from a higher power that things are going to turn out okay. Or not."

"You need to write your letter," she says. "Until you can deal with Alex in that form, there is nothing the angels can tell you."

"Hmm." I unwrap the chocolate bar she gave me and stare at the brown hunk. It looks harmless. My mouth can recall the smooth texture. The sweet, creamy flavor.

Aunt Allie pops the rest of her bar in her mouth. She has a look of rapture on her face.

"Catch," I call and throw my bar at her.

She reaches for it, but her hand twitches and she misses it. She grabs it quickly before Fredrick can get it. "Ten-second rule," I say.

She nods and smiles. "I shouldn't have another," she says and takes a bite. "But I will. We only live once. Well. Maybe." She points to the living room doorway. "Now go. Write."

I stand and take a deep breath. I can write a letter, even if it's not the one she wants.

• • •

Dear Chloe,

I type into my laptop. I'm not ready to talk to Alex. Not yet.

I push him out of my mind and concentrate instead on his sister. I don't know what to say to her. Sorry I kissed your brother? Sorry I have the equivalent of a tape worm in my belly and feel compelled to eat every five minutes. Sorry I chose peanut butter. Clair recommended it as good protein since I'm not much of a red-meat lover.

It was an accident. I feel so bad. Awful.

No.

That's all me. Me. Me. Me. It sounds trite and insincere even in my head. How do I convey my feelings without making it sound like I'm only feeling sorry for myself? My pain is nothing compared to losing a brother. I have no idea how that feels.

I close my eyes and type, letting thoughts flow from my brain straight through my fingers.

Chloe:

I have no idea how you must feel. I am so sorry about the loss of your brother. From everything I've heard, Alex was a wonderful guy. A great guy. I wish I'd known him better. Much longer.

I'm sure you've wondered what made me kiss him. I didn't know him well. Why did I kiss him despite that? Honestly, Alex was being kind. Trust me, I'm not usually the type of person who kisses boys I don't know. I wasn't. Until Alex, well, I'd never done that before.

He was trying to make me feel less sad and lonely that night. He was wonderful, trying to make me feel good about myself. He was a very nice person.

I can't blame my behavior on alcohol. I wouldn't even if I had been drinking. But I wasn't. No, the impulsiveness and the absolute carelessness of my actions were my own, and for that I am so, so sorry.

I know about peanut allergies. I should have thought about what I'd eaten before I kissed someone. Even though I didn't know Alex had the allergy, in this day and age, it should have been on my radar. My selfishness harmed someone you loved very much and for that I will always be very sorry.

I know it sounds trite. It is hard to even try to apologize. I would do anything to take it all back, but of course that isn't possible.

If there is anything, anything at all that I could ever do for you, please don't hesitate to ask.

I hope that you are managing to deal with your grief and that in time you will only remember Alex with good thoughts. I wish I could do something to help you get there.

Always and forever remorseful,
Samantha Waxman

It's honest. It's all I can do. I print the pages and carry them to the living room.

It's not even seven o'clock yet, but the trick-or-treaters in the neighborhood are already trickling down. Aunt Allie is watching a movie on TV, with costumed Fredrick curled up on her lap. She sees me holding up the pages. "For Alex?" she asks.

I shake my head. "No. Chloe."

"Hmm. Well. That's a start. I don't need to see what you wrote, though. It's between you and her."

Fredrick lifts his head and woofs his agreement.

"I'm proud of you, butterfly." Her eyes go back to the television, and I recognize Jack Nicholson on the screen.

"*Witches of Eastwick*," she tells me. "Jack is so delicious in this. Want to watch?"

"No, thanks." The ache in my bones hasn't gone away. I carry the pages back to my bedroom and sit on my bed, reading the letter over and over.

Finally, I reach across the bed and pick up the phone on my nightstand. It's time to make the call.

chapter eighteen

My brain is slodgy, and I cough to clear my throat. I push out a breath and punch in the numbers.

The phone rings.

"Hello?" A voice picks up on the second ring, and my heart stops. I'd been hoping for an answering machine or at least a couple more rings.

"May I speak with Chloe, please?"

"Speaking," she says, her overly polite tone matching mine.

I pause. We both know who's on the other end.

"It's Sam. Samantha Waxman." Recipient of the lame-o of the year award.

There's no response.

"Uh," I say. Brilliant. All the things I rehearsed evaporate from my head. My mind is blank. I squeeze my eyes tight. "I was wondering if we could talk."

I hear nothing. No breathing. No background noise. I wonder if she hung up on me.

"Hello?" I say.

"I'm here," she answers, her voice quiet and hesitant.

I inhale deeply, pant loudly, and then plunge back in. "So. I know this is awkward, but I was hoping we could talk sometime. Not on the phone. I suck on the phone." I close my eyes again and shake my head at myself. "As you can tell. Anyways. God, Chloe. I'm sorry. I'm not good at this. Do you think we could maybe meet in person? Sometime? For coffee or something?"

"Okay." Her voice is quiet.

"Really?" I stumble for more but clearly, I haven't thought this all through. "How about now?"

She doesn't answer, and I curse myself and hurry to fill the silence. "Of course not. It's Halloween. I'm sorry. Another time."

"I could meet you now," she says.

"Really?"

"It's okay, Samantha. It's not like I'm busy trick-or-treating. Or going to Taylor's party or anything." My cheeks flush. I want to melt away.

"I want to talk to you too," Chloe says.

My heart pitter-patters. Fear. "Uh. Good." I try to think of somewhere to meet her. Why did I not plan this better? I don't know many coffee shops in town.

"How about at Good Earth?" she says. "Fifth Avenue and Twenty-Fourth Street. On the corner. Not far from either of us."

Neither one of us says anything about how we each know where the other lives. I googled her house online. I've seen pictures of it from different street angles.

"Good Earth," I say. "Okay. What time?" It's far enough away from the high school that it's not likely we'll run into anyone. A good choice.

We agree to meet in a half an hour, and both of us hang up.

• • •

200

The streets are still vibrant with Halloween when I leave the house. Little kids with costumes over winter coats are being replaced by older kids. Younger than me, but not old enough for house parties, they wander around in groups. The girls are underdressed, and the boys jump around and whoop it up. Some trick-or-treat, some just hang out.

When I walk into the coffee shop, Chloe is the only customer at a booth. She's facing the door, but her head is down and her long, dark hair hangs to her shoulders. She glances around when the bell above the door rings. She's beautiful. Her thin fragility is emphasized by a black turtleneck sweater that brings out her pale complexion.

The scent of freshly brewed coffee wafts in the air. I lift my hand and slowly walk toward her. "I'm going to grab a tea. Do you want one?" I ask.

She points to a mug in front of her. "I already got coffee." Halloween music plays quietly in the background. A rapped-up version of "Monster Mash."

I head to the counter, where a girl about my age is wearing a trampy zombie costume. Like a French maid zombie. I interrupt her mad texting, but she serves up my mint tea quickly. She goes back to her phone as soon as she hands me my change. I wrap my hands around the steaming hot mug, carry it over to the table, and slide into the booth, opposite Chloe.

We stare at each other for a moment.

Chloe's eyes reflect everything I've dreaded seeing. They're shiny with sadness. Dark brown shades of sorrow. "Did you walk?" I ask.

"No. I took my mom's car."

"I ran here." As if it matters. I sound stupid.

We're both quiet for a minute. "Thanks for meeting me," I manage. It feels like we're on a blind date. There's familiarity, but a huge dose of awkward. I suck at small talk.

"I am *so* sorry," I blurt out, and my voice catches. I reach into my coat pocket, take out the folded note, put it on the table, and slide it toward her. "I said it better here," I whisper.

She stares down at the paper. Tears rim her eyes, and I blink quickly. *Stay strong. Stay strong. No crying.*

She picks the paper up by the corner. Holds it a moment and then opens it. Looks at me and then down, and her eyes dart back and forth over the words. She reads quickly. She stops. Blinks.

"He was," she says. "Alex was a great guy. He could also be a pain, but…" She folds the note back into squares. "I loved him."

She closes her eyes and inhales deeply through her nose, holding the breath in and then letting it go. "No one wants to talk about him," she says. "At school. Except Zee and Casper. Everyone else avoids saying his name. You know. Like they're trying to pretend he never existed."

My lips press together tight, but I force myself to speak. "I guess people don't want to make you sad."

She lifts a shoulder but doesn't look at me. "I don't want to forget him."

I lower my eyes and study the wisps of steam coming up from my tea. The scent of mint reaches my nose. "You won't."

"I'm afraid," she says. And I know that she means so many things. A phone starts ringing from the bench beside her. She reaches for her purse, digs around, pulls out a phone, and checks the screen. I wait for her to answer it, but she puts it down and ignores the next ring.

"It's okay. I don't need to get it."

"I don't want to make things worse. Being around," I tell her. "I've wanted to say I'm sorry. But…I didn't know how."

She lifts up the paper. "You did okay here."

We're both quiet.

"I know you feel terrible," she says.

I try to swallow away the lump in my throat. "Your family…I can't imagine."

She frowns and looks down again. "No. You can't." She lifts her cup and sips at her coffee. "My mom cried so hard when she got the flowers and note. That you and your dad sent."

My head snaps up, and I frown, but she's staring into her coffee, as if looking for answers inside of it.

"My dad cried too. I never saw him cry before Alex died."

If I could take a pill to suck out my insides, shrivel me up into dried-out bones for dogs to cart away, I would do it. Right there.

"There's more to that night than you know," she whispers, and then she looks at me and I see something else in her eyes. It looks like fear. "I haven't told them." She wipes under her eyes and takes another long sip of coffee. "But you deserve to know."

"What?" I watch her swallow her coffee and glance around the empty shop. She follows my gaze. It's all so surreal. Like a movie set. Decorations above the door. Skeletons made of paper. Ghosts. All of it rather amateur. Homemade. I wonder if the zombie French maid did it herself.

"There were a bunch of people at Casper's house before the party."

I turn back to Chloe. Watch her mouth move. I can't shake the sensation that I'm dreaming. That this isn't really happening to me.

"I had soccer practice and needed to shower and stuff, so I didn't go. Alex was pissed off at me anyway." She talks slowly and pauses between sentences. "It's a long story. He was usually cool with me hanging with them."

She tucks her hair behind her ear. "Anyhow, I met them at Taylor's. At least they didn't drive. They walked there. Alex, stupid drunk Alex, left his backpack at Casper's. All his meds were inside." She studies her nails. "He never usually went anywhere without them. But that night…" She shakes her head, glances over at the zombie French maid. "If I'd been there, I would have remembered."

Her hair flops out from her ear, and she tucks it back again and sighs.

"When I got to Taylor's, Alex was downstairs. They were smoking pot down there. I was looking for someone, but when I saw Alex, I was so pissed off. Instead of dragging him out, I thought, you know, it would serve him right, for being so stupid. It would throw him off for the next few days, and maybe he'd learn a lesson."

My memory is tweaked to the sweetish scent of smoke on Alex. Him saying he was on the deck to get some fresh air. The image makes me uncomfortable.

Behind me, the chime tinkles over the door. Chloe glances over and frowns at whoever walked in.

"Chloe!" a high-pitched male voice calls. "Your mom said you were here."

Casper is standing in the entrance way, dressed in a pirate costume. A skull headband, a big fake hoop earring. Tight striped pants and a vest that shows off his bare chest. I cringe inside a little. It's the male equivalent of a skanky girl Halloween costume. His head tilts, and he blinks when he sees it's me sitting across from Chloe.

"Hey, Sam," he says. His eyes dart from her face to mine and back. "What's up?"

Chloe reaches for the paper on the table in front of us and puts her hands over it.

"Kind of obvious, isn't it? We're talking," Chloe says. Her tone is a little rude, but they've known each other a lot longer than I have.

"Cool." He takes a step toward us and glances at the girl behind the counter and then back to us. "I stopped by your house before going to Taylor's. Your mom asked me to make sure you're okay, and you weren't answering your phone."

"I'm fine." She makes a face and takes a sip of coffee.

It's obvious we all know what's going on. What Chloe and I are doing. "You want to join us?" I ask and start scooting my butt along the booth.

"No!" Chloe says, her voice loud and firm. I stop sliding. Chloe frowns, her lips pressed tightly together, and it's clear she's not happy with him. Not at all.

It's kind of uncomfortable to be in the middle of whatever is going on between them. Like having someone's parents argue in front of me at their house. "I'm fine," she says. "And you're on your way to Taylor's. So don't let us stop you. You can tell my mom I'm fine."

He crosses his arms in front of our table, not appearing upset at Chloe's behavior. "You two having a good talk?"

"Fine, Casper," Chloe says and picks up her mug. "God. I need a refill." She glances at me. "I'll be right back." She slips out to the counter.

Casper and I watch the zombie barista put down her phone, pick up a coffeepot, and walk over to Chloe to refill it.

"How's it going?" Casper asks. His voice is casual, not giving away the intimacy we've shared or the tension that tangles between him and Chloe. I bet he'll be a politician someday.

"Fine." I force a smile. "Everything okay with you and Chloe?"

"Yeah. She's pissed at me." He doesn't offer an explanation and doesn't seem terribly fazed. "Her mom is using me to check up on her." He smiles and lowers his voice. "I'm glad you're talking." He gives me a sexy smile, and I imagine him at home practicing it in his mirror. "I wish you'd come to the party, but I get it. I can't wait until the festival."

I lift my eyebrow and watch Chloe stride back to the table, her coffee cup in her hand and a sour look on her face.

"Okay," she says when she reaches us. She puts down the mug and slides back into the booth. "You can report to my mom that I'm fine, Jack Sparrow," she says to Casper.

"I'm Captain Hook," he says.

She lifts her chin. "Whatever, pirate." She takes a sip of coffee and contemplates him over the top of the mug. "Either way, I'm sure you can't stop thinking about sailing."

"Why?" he asks.

"You have ship for brains."

A snort escapes my mouth. I laugh out loud.

Casper rolls his eyes at her. "Chloe. As always, you drip with charm."

He tips his fake sword at us, but his expression suggests he might actually be hurt. "Arrrrgh. Didn't know we were anti-pirate at this table."

Her scowl softens. "Casper, Samantha and I are in the middle of a conversation and it's kind of intense. You get that, right?"

He shrugs and smiles at us both. "Of course. I didn't mean to interrupt. Doing my duty for mama bear. I'll see you two later."

"See you, me matey," I call, trying to keep things light.

"Arrrrghhhh. By hook or by crook," he calls.

The bell dings as he leaves.

Chloe shakes her head when he's gone. She takes a big sip of coffee and stares at the door. "I think he's around so much because he's in love with my mom."

She glances at me. "Not in a creepy way. Parents love Casper, he's that kind of guy. My mom likes having him around. It makes her feel closer to Alex. She doesn't know they were kind of…" She puts her mug down and traces her finger around the rim. "Zee, on the other hand, finds it hard to talk to her right now. He feels guilty or something."

I bite my lip and glance away.

"I guess I was kind of rude to Casper." She sighs. "It's complicated. Everything is."

The phone rings again, but she doesn't even seem to notice. "He was there that night," she says.

I flinch and wonder if I'll ever be able to talk about that night without wanting to cry. "Casper? Yeah. I know. I saw him."

"I mean downstairs. With Alex. Casper was smoking the joint with Alex."

I open my mouth. Shocked. "Casper smokes weed?" Mr. Perfect Grades, Ivy League–bound Casper Cooper and illegal drugs. He'll have to say he didn't inhale.

She glances up. "Well. Not all the time or anything. Same with Alex. I mean. We've all kind of experimented." She sighs and waves at the letter I wrote. "You don't. Drink. Or smoke, or anything."

I shake my head. "Swimming." And then I remember I don't swim anymore and take a sip of the tea that's pretty much cold.

"Zee swims too," Chloe says and her voice quavers. "We're not bad. Not really." She sniffles and wipes a tear from her eye. "It's not like we do stuff like that all the time."

"I'm not judging anyone," I tell her softly. Me. Judging. After what happened. As if.

"Well. Maybe I am," she says. "Judging us, I mean. I was drinking too, and I was mad at Alex. I should have made sure he had his meds. Especially after I saw him downstairs. But instead of going to Casper's to get his stuff…" She drops her head and her shoulders shake, but she's silent.

I reach across the table and squeeze her hand. "It wasn't your fault, Chloe." I can't believe I'm offering her comfort. That she feels like she had a part in it. She's taking on guilt that clearly belongs to me.

"It was me who kissed him," I remind her. "I had the peanut

butter sandwich, and I barely knew him. I mean. He was a great guy, but…"

"No," she interrupts. "Everyone heard what people used to say about you at your old school." She drops her eyes. "That you liked girls. You probably wanted to start fresh."

It's an interesting theory. I only wish it were true.

"I kind of thought you had a thing for Zee. But I guess we were all trying to act more sophisticated. Sex. Drugs. Drinking. We're just a bunch of stupid kids."

She's sobbing softly now. I'm shocked that she seems to forget that I'm the one who caused her brother's death. Nobody else.

She looks up and sniffles. "We all had a role that night. Zee feels bad too," she says. "He always made sure Alex had his meds and stuff."

A tear slips from her eye and splashes on the table.

I wiggle on my seat, and the leather groans. "No." I glance around the empty restaurant. The coffee barista is sitting on a stool, still tapping at her phone. I hope she has unlimited texting. She's probably complaining about working Halloween night and being stuck with two losers. Or maybe she recognized us and is telling friends that the peanut killer and the dead boy's sister are having coffee. "It was my fault."

"Yeah? Tell Zee that. He's furious he got drunk. He doesn't usually. And he was with Kaitlin again, which he also feels bad about." She makes a face and then looks up, and the pity shines through the tears rimming her eyes. She wipes them away, but the pity stays.

I shake my head. I don't want to talk about Zee and Kaitlin with her. I don't want to hear that she knows how much I liked Zee. I kissed her brother. Killed him. I chew my lip, but she keeps talking.

"Zee thinks if he hadn't made out with Kaitlin, you might not have kissed Alex," she whispers.

I blink and blink and blink. Shake my head. I don't want her to think that. Alex was her brother. "Please don't, Chloe."

I push the tea away. So much for the soothing qualities of mint. The smell is making me sick.

"How's your family doing?" I ask softly to change the topic.

She sniffs and then chuckles, but it's not happy. "My mom is a mess. She cries all the time. Especially when she thinks I can't hear her. My dad has stopped crying, but he's sad. They're both messed up."

"You are too," I say.

"Yeah." She digs inside her purse and pulls out a package of Kleenex. Wipes her nose.

"I miss the weirdest things about him. The way he would always pull my hair to get my attention. The way he would laugh obnoxiously at jokes. The way he read my *People* magazines and pretended not to. He knew all the celebrity gossip. And the stupid Hot Wheels collection that's still in his room. I keep waiting for it to seem normal. That's he's gone. But it doesn't."

We stare at each other, and I don't think I've ever looked so deeply inside someone's soul. Felt such a connection to someone else's inner pain.

"I didn't tell my mom I was meeting you," she says.

My hand automatically reaches for the locket around my neck. Chloe's eyes go to it, but she doesn't comment. "I understand that," I tell her.

"Are you going back to swimming?" Her question takes me by surprise. I expect it from everyone else. Not her.

My hand moves to my braid. I twist it around my finger as I shake my head, to tell her no.

"You should," she says. The door chimes, and she watches as someone walks in, but there's no recognition on her face. I turn and see an older woman with frothy white hair. A black poncho is wrapped around her frail little body. She bows her head and hobbles toward the coffee counter.

"If I quit sports, I'd be lost," Chloe tells me. "It's the only thing that keeps me sane."

I watch the woman at the counter, her hands shaking as she opens her purse and slowly takes out coins. I wonder why she's having coffee alone, if someone will be meeting up with her. I hope so. As if she senses me watching, she turns, and her eyes sparkle and seem to see more than most. She smiles at me, nods her head formally, and then turns back to the zombie maid.

I turn my focus back on Chloe. Take a deep breath. "I've been looking into something. And I wondered if you might want to get involved. Kind of in Alex's memory. There's a group. NAAN. The Nut Allergy Awareness Network. They have teen chapters, but there isn't one in our part of Washington. I've been looking at starting a chapter. Here. In Tadita. There's a national walk coming up. The chapter could do lots to help raise awareness in schools.

Sponsor speakers. Maybe if we put together a team, we could raise more. All of us could walk in Alex's name? Use the money to start a website for kids with allergies. For friends and families?"

Chloe picks up her purse and clutches it tight to her chest. She shakes her head back and forth. "No. No. I can't do that."

The purse makes her appear even tinier. She glances around the coffee shop, and her gaze moves to the woman at the counter. "I should get going." She glances back at me and slides out of the booth. She stands up and tucks her hair behind her ear. "Thank you for the note. I'll see you around."

With that she hurries toward the door.

The bell sounds as she leaves.

I stare down at the table for a moment. The bell jingles again. I glance up quickly, but it's an older man walking through the door. He glances at me and then at the counter, and his eyes light up when he spots the woman. I smile to myself, pull on my skull cap, and head past him for the door. When I hit the pavement I start to jog. I don't care that I'm wearing jeans and a hoodie. My body wants to move. Running helps clear my head.

I don't think about it, but I find myself heading toward the recreation center. There are only a couple of cars in the parking lot. I decelerate down to walking and creep past the windows of the pool. The blinds are drawn and I can't see inside, so I head toward the entrance. When my feet touch the mat the automatic doors slide open. I step through and walk past the second set of doors. The aquatic centre is to the left, the ice rinks past the reception area directly in front of me. At the registration desk, a woman is sitting on a stool in front of a computer screen. She's wearing a sparkly orange witch hat over a long blue wig with a long black dress. She glances up and smiles. "Hey, Sam. Long time no see."

Her name comes to me. Dawn. She's a lifeguard and a swimmer and knows the whole Titans team by name. She fills in at the front when no one else can work. I approach the counter.

"I wasn't sure if the place was open," I say. There's a gold name tag pinned to her witch costume. Dawn Murray.

"Usual hours, but since it's Halloween, there's no one here." She gestures to the pool. "Titans have the pool booked, but Clair let everyone out early. There is a group of old timers playing hockey, but that's about it."

I smile politely.

"I've missed you, honey. How are you doing?" Her voice has the recognizable inflection. Concern. I guess it's better than an accusatory glare with no comment at all.

"I'm okay, thanks."

"You're not swimming." It's not a question. She knows.

I glance at the clock on the wall above her. It's a little past eight. It feels like it should be one o' clock in the morning.

"You must miss it," she says. I don't answer.

"You can take a girl out of the water, but you can't take the water out of the girl," she says. "I know. I used to swim competitively."

"That's not even close to the saying," I tell her.

She laughs. "I know." She cocks her head to the side. "You wanna go in?"

My body involuntarily jumps. My cheeks flush and my heart

races. I do. I want to go in. I shake my head back and forth. No. Of course I can't go in.

"What are you doing here if you don't want to swim?" Her voice is gentle, and I have an urge to crawl over the counter and make her hug me. I am officially pro-hugs.

"No one's there. Marcus is lifeguarding, and he's bored out of his mind. You'll give him something to do. I won't even charge you," she says and laughs. The phone rings, and she leans over to pick it up.

The clock ticks loudly. I watch the second hand noisily move and match my breath to its beat. I think of Aunt Allie and the angels guiding her. Talk to them in your head, she's always told me. They will hear you.

Please, angels, show me what to do.

"Samantha, you okay?" Dawn asks when she hangs up the phone.

"I don't have my stuff," I tell her.

"The new club suits came in a few days ago. Clair left the box in the office. I just happen to have access. And I have goggles and a cap I can lend you."

The only person stopping me is me. I close my eyes. I imagine my dad at home and the pictures he keeps on his dresser. I think of the hours he's volunteered at pools over the years. Driving me to early practices without complaining. Moving to a new city so I could have a better coach. And to repay him, I scrunched up his efforts and threw them away like crumpled balls of paper.

"Go on, Sam. You wandered in here for a reason. And I don't think it was to see me. Or get a free candy." She nods her head toward a black bowl on the counter. It's half filled with candy. "But help yourself." She smiles.

I hear my dad cheering in the stands. I remember him wiping away tears when I was seven and fell off the block and got my first DQ. Telling me he was proud of me for getting up there in the first place. How many thumbs-ups has he given me over the years?

Dawn jumps off her stool and disappears into the office. I think about sneaking away, but I don't move. She pops back out and throws a blue suit at me. I reach out and grab it. There's a white moon in the middle. I grip the fabric in my hand. Bring it up to my nose and sniff the new suit smell. A sticker on the tag says "Samantha Waxman."

She opens a drawer by her desk and pulls out a pair of goggles and a cap. I shake my head, but she hands me the gear. Then she walks to a nearby vertical cupboard, pulls out a plain white towel, and tosses that at me too.

"Go," she says. "Get wet. You'll feel better."

I don't move.

chapter nineteen

The cap is bright pink, but I tuck my hair under it anyway and dip my toe in the water. Cold. Perfect for laps. I hope the water will thaw out the ice that lives in me. My heart pounds, as if I've already done a set of sprints.

Part of me is terrified. The other part wants to dive in, feel the water flow. Pull through it. Breathe. In. Out. Head down. No thoughts but a checklist of technical tasks. The sound of Clair's voice echoes in my head. Kick. Kick. Kick.

Marcus is in the office facing the pool. He can see me through the window. He lifts his hand. Waves. I force a smile and then raise my hands over my head and leap.

I'm in.

I streamline and kick, easing into a freestyle stroke. Then I sprint to the opposite end of the pool. Feeling good, I flip-turn and push off the wall. Too soon, my body slows and struggles to find a rhythm.

I slow my pace to about fifty percent and swim another two hundred yards. My body feels like ass. It's dragging. I'm forced to breathe every stroke. Diagnosis: officially out of shape.

My belly burns, and a rush of fear mixes with frustration. I can't tell which is which. I've never been afraid of the water before.

Never. I tap the end of the pool and pull myself out, tugging off the pink cap and goggles. Without a word to Marcus, I march off the pool deck, back to the locker room.

I step into the shower, turn on the water, and shiver under a blast of ice cold. It hurts, but the sensation is a familiar manifestation of my emotions. I tug the new tight suit down and drop it on the shower floor, staring at it as icy water pelts down on my head. I have to give it back to Dawn wet. Clair will know I used it. I didn't think this through. I don't want her to believe it's a sign of intent.

Instead of relief or even sorrow for returning to the water, I'm brewing with anger at the way my body performed. Betrayed me, really. But fear has sunk its teeth into me too. For losing my edge. I don't know what I expected. But it wasn't that.

When I skulk back to the front desk, Dawn is tapping something on the computer. "So?"

I hand her the pile of wet supplies and lift my shoulders.

"It sucked, right?" she says.

"Totally sucked," I tell her.

"It'll take a few weeks to get it back."

I don't say anything to that.

"You were dragging your ass," a voice says from behind me. I almost jump out of my skin.

"Zee," I say. Nothing further comes to mind. He's staring past me.

"I heard you had coffee with Chloe," he says. As if it's no big deal that I was swimming.

"What are you doing here? I thought you'd be at Taylor's." I wonder if anyone is showing up to her house.

Zee glances at Dawn, and she stands up. "I have to get something out of the office," she says and disappears through the door.

"I don't know," he tells me. "I couldn't go to Taylor's. It's weird." He looks away. "I was in the skate park doing Parkour. But it got cold. So I came inside to warm up."

Above us, the clock ticks even louder. The whir from vending machines is suddenly deafening.

"I'm glad you swam," he says. "That's good."

I press my lips tight and stare at the Halloween decorations instead of him. "It sucked. I sucked."

"Yeah, well. You haven't been training. What'd you expect?" He walks to the counter and dips his hand in the bowl of candy.

"It doesn't mean anything."

"No? What about Casper, he mean anything?" He pulls a wrapper off the candy and pops the whole thing in his mouth.

There's a shout of laughter down the hall, and I see a couple of old guys in hockey skates march out of the arena into the main area, hockey sticks in their hands. They wobble on their skates to the vending machines in the hallway.

"What do you mean about Casper?" I ask cautiously, watching the guys purchase Gatorades instead of looking at Zee.

"You like him, right?"

I lift my shoulder and push my braid from my eyes. "He's been nice to me." The old guys open the arena door and disappear with their sports drinks.

"I guess not everyone is," Zee says.

I turn to him. He's got on a ball cap. A sweatshirt over his jeans.

Skater shoes. It's a basic outfit, but he makes it work better than most. Too well.

"You think?" I ask, regretting the words as soon as they come from my lips, but I can't pluck them out of the air now.

He cracks his knuckles and grabs another candy. "But I mean, you like him, right?"

"Casper?" I shrug. "He's okay."

"Chloe doesn't know about you and Casper, does she?"

I'm weirded out by this conversation. "When were you talking to Chloe?"

"She texted me. Told me you had coffee. She doesn't know you're going to the festival with Casper."

"I can't imagine why she would care." I blink at him, not surprised he knows. Everyone knows everyone's business in this town. "You're going with Chloe," I say to show him I know things too.

"Chloe and I are tight," he says. "Because of Alex."

His words cut deep. Neither of us says anything for a minute. I shift from foot to foot, feeling stupid and ashamed.

"Well, I should get going." I pull my skull cap from my pocket. Tug it onto my head.

He doesn't answer, but I start walking. The first set of doors slides open.

"Sam?" Zee calls.

I turn around.

"You got the Jelly Bellys?"

Despite everything, I smile. "It *was* you."

He grins and then ducks his head so he's hiding beneath the ball cap. "I really am sorry," he says. "About everything."

"Yeah, Zee, me too."

The doors slide closed behind me. A whole pile of "what ifs" float in the air.

chapter twenty

My hair is wet and sticks to my head under my cap, forming icicles in the chilly night air. I'm running up the street on the sidewalk opposite our house. My mind is full. Chloe. Casper. Zee. I need to process it all.

At our house the porch light is on, and I see Aunt Allie at the front door. Her laughter carries across the street, and a couple of extremely tall trick-or-treaters stand in front with her. Teenagers in costume. I left the pool at almost nine, so they're definitely pushing their luck collecting leftovers this late. Every older kid knows the trick. People dump whatever's left in the bowl to get the last of the candy out of the house. They're lucky Aunt Allie is answering the door, not Dad.

As if she senses me, Aunt Allie looks across the street and waves. "Hi, Sam!"

Fredrick barks his raspy little woof. I see his little body as he takes off out the front door. The black wings on his bat costume flop from side to side. I can almost see a tiny grin on his face and hear his snort as he charges toward me, faster than his little pencil legs look capable of carrying him.

Behind me, a car engine roars.

"Fredrick!" Aunt Allie screams. "Come here. Come."

"No," I echo from the opposite end of the street. Everything slows. I turn to see a silver hatchback driving forward. Fredrick charges onward, unaware. His nails click-click on the pavement.

"Noooooooooo," I cry again.

"Freeeeeeeeedrrrrriiickkkk!" Aunt Allie's voice floats above the other sounds.

The driver spots the little black blur running straight for the car wheels and slams the breaks. The sound of squealing tires joins in with the voices. In stereo. A capella.

"Fredrick!" *Scrrreeeeeeeeech*. "Nooooooooooooo!"

And then there's a tiny thwap. And silence. Fredrick's little body hits the car, and he flops down on his side on the road. Not moving.

I run at the car, which is now spun sideways on the street, stopped. Aunt Allie races up the driveway. Teens dressed as zombies follow her but run more slowly, fueled by curiosity, not panic. I reach him first, as the front door of the car is opening.

"Fredrick?" Tears and panic mix and contort my face.

"No! No! No!" Aunt Allie is running toward us. The teenagers gawk.

I kneel down. Fredrick's eyes are closed. He's not budging.

"Oh, Fredrick," I moan.

I blink, trying to process it. A feeling of déjà vu creeps into my head.

"Oh my God!" A female voice shouts. "Samantha? I didn't see him. Is he okay?"

The voice registers in my brain, but Aunt Allie's voice fills my ears. "Oh, Sam," she cries. "How is he?" I reach down. Put my hand on his bulging stomach.

Cold sweat forms on my head, making icicles to match the ones in my hair.

"Fredrick?" I put my other hand on him. "Fredrick?"

The girl bends down beside me. She's crying. "Oh my God. Is he your dog? I didn't see him. I swear. Is he—"

"No," Aunt Allie cries. Her hand covers her mouth. "No," she repeats. "He can't be dead. He can't be."

"I'm so sorry. I didn't see him," she says over and over. Her eyes are teary and wide.

"Quiet!" I yell at her. "Chloe. Please."

She immediately clamps her hand over her mouth. Aunt Allie kneels beside me. The teens creep forward, but they don't come closer and don't say a word.

Tears stream down my cheeks. Not Fredrick. Aunt Allie's baby. He's so little. So good. He's never hurt a fly, never done anything except bring joy and happiness to everyone around him. He doesn't deserve this. It can't be happening.

His chest moves under my hand. "He moved!" I shout.

Aunt Allie and I stare at each other and then back at him.

"He's breathing," I confirm, my hand still on his belly. "He's breathing."

Her hands fly to her mouth. She stares at him with wide eyes.

I slip both hands under his tiny body, and he lets out a whimper. I'm so relieved to hear it that I giggle.

Chloe stares down at me, her eyes widening. "He's alive," I assure her.

"Thank God," she says.

My brain kind of registers how strange and horrible this is, but I can't think about that yet. Other thoughts have prominence. Keep Fredrick still. Don't move him around needlessly. I need to let Aunt Allie hold him, though. His mommy.

"Put out your arms," I tell Aunt Allie. "Keep him still." I gently lay Fredrick over her outstretched arms, pull off my hoodie, and tuck it around his little body. His eyes open for a second and he looks at Aunt Allie and then at me. There's pain in his eyes but also trust that we're going to look after him. He whimpers again.

Chloe wrings her hands. "What can I do to help?"

"I'm sorry," Aunt Allie says. "But I can't deal with you right now."

Chloe looks broken. My heart goes out to her. She didn't mean to hit Fredrick. It was bad timing. A horrible accident.

Aunt Allie whispers soothing words to Fredrick.

"There's a twenty-four-hour vet clinic downtown," Chloe says.

"We have to take him," Aunt Allie says. "Now."

"I'll drive," Chloe shouts. "I'll take you."

Part of me wants to send her away. She hit Fredrick. She should bask in guilt. Not be a part of the rescue. Her expression is part terror and pure remorse. It's all too familiar.

"Come on," she begs.

"Let's go," Aunt Allie cries, and it's decided. I open the back door and help her inside without disturbing Fredrick, and then I jump in the passenger seat. Chloe floors it, speeding all the way to the pet hospital. No one talks except Aunt Allie, who whispers comfort and encouragement to Fredrick in the back.

When we pull up to the front door of the vet clinic, Chloe turns to the backseat and then glances sideways at me. "I'm Chloe," she says to Aunt Allie.

"I know who you are," Aunt Allie says.

I help her get Fredrick inside, and Chloe parks the car. When she rushes into the check-in area, Aunt Allie is already in a private room waiting for a doctor. I'm giving the receptionist our address details. Chloe walks up beside me and offers to pay the medical fees, which I imagine will be pretty enormous despite Fredrick being such a tiny dog.

I shake my head no. Aunt Allie can more than take care of it.

"It was an accident," I tell her.

We stare at each other. She said the same words to me earlier in the night.

"I'm so sorry," she says.

We go to the waiting room and sit side by side. Neither of us talks. Time whirs by, and then Aunt Allie comes out and tells us Fredrick is being rushed into surgery.

Aunt Allie takes her hand, and Chloe starts to cry. I watch the two of them. Fascinated. Sad. Envious. Guilt is written all over Chloe's face. Her remorse is clear. But Aunt Allie isn't blaming her. She's being kind. She knows it was an accident. Chloe didn't mean to hurt Fredrick. She is already forgiven.

I wonder if I ever will be.

chapter twenty-one

I make it through another week like I'm hanging from my life on a fishing line. Waiting for something to snatch me up, and bored with waiting. I try to function with the lowest level of involvement. I have a session with Bob, but even he seems frustrated with me. He tells me I'm not trying hard enough, but I don't react. On some level, I know he's right. I just don't care.

Only Casper and Taylor talk to me at school. Taylor is busy with swimming and Justin, but she texts me several times a day. Casper's interaction has kind of dribbled down to quoting Dr. Seuss to me in English class. Chloe and I smile and acknowledge each other in the halls, connected but staying apart, like opposing magnets. I rarely catch a glimpse of Zee, which means he's successfully avoiding me.

Aunt Allie watches me with knowing eyes. After school one day, she catches up to me in the kitchen while I'm making a grilled cheese.

"How are things?" she asks.

"Great," I tell her. I take the sandwich off the grill and put it on a plate. I cut it in half and hold out the plate.

"Liar." She smiles and reaches for it. "You know, when I was downsized from my job, I thought it was the worst thing that could happen to me. I didn't have a family of my own. Your dad didn't want me in your life. My parents and I were estranged. My job was the only thing I had. It felt personal. Really personal. I was lower than I'd ever been in my life."

She takes a bite of the sandwich and pauses to chew.

"But in the end, it was the best thing that ever happened to me. Not that this will ever be the best thing that happened to you. But my point is you can get through and make your life better because of it." She takes another bite.

"So what can you do to make things better, Sam?"

Tentatively, I tell her about my plans, and she smiles as she listens. When I'm finished, she kisses my cheek. "You might not know it yet, but God works in mysterious ways."

"I thought you didn't believe in God," I say, as I put another sandwich on the grill.

"Of course I do. Who do you think angels are working for, butterfly? It's not the bad guys. Write the letter," she tells me. "I think you're ready."

I want to, but I'm not quite there.

• • •

The night of the festival, Aunt Allie and Dad are acting weird and dying to chat about my date, so I go to my room to hide from them and wait for Casper to come pick me up. They're trying not to make big a deal out of it, but they seem to think it's my grand re-entry into society or something. Like I should wear a ball gown and glass slippers to sidestep horse and cow patties on the fairground.

I log onto my computer, click on Facebook, and go to my wall.

> Reason # 1,200,334 never to kiss Samantha Waxman.
> Peanut Butter Breath.

Beside the comment is a picture of Kaitlin. In a bikini. Her profile picture. Her comment already has 52 likes.

"I hear she spreads it like PB and J," a girl commented below it. I don't recognize her name or picture. There are more comments underneath. I see the words slut and whore.

I click the computer off without logging out. Something Dad always warns me not to do.

The bandages of self-preservation I've wrapped around my heart tear a little. I close my eyes, trying to close the hole the post ripped into me. As if I'm right back where I started. I lie on my bed and stare up at the ceiling, but tears threaten to spill, and I actually took the time to put on makeup. Determined not to let the nasty comments undo me, I hurry to the living room and sit stiffly on the couch beside Aunt Allie.

Aunt Allie clucks her tongue. "Don't be nervous," she says. "We promise not to embarrass you." Fredrick glances up at me from her lap but closes his eyes again as if my mood bores him. He's recovered nicely from his accident, didn't even have to stay at the vet hospital overnight. If anything, he's milking the little cast he's wearing on his leg. He hardly has to walk anywhere anymore. Aunt Allie and even Dad carry him everywhere. His expression when he's being carried is one of bliss.

"You look nice. I love that sweater on you." She sighs. "I barely remember being able to look cute wearing jeans."

"You're built like Mom's side of the family," Dad says. The two of them are sitting quietly drinking wine.

"So you're saying my butt has its own time zone?"

"I think you look great," I tell Aunt Allie softly. I mean it. She's sturdy and as colorful as a fall day, perfect the way she is. I couldn't imagine her being thin and wearing trendy jeans, trying to look younger.

She smiles and lifts her wine glass in a toast. "Thank you. And I think you're gorgeous. Are you actually wearing makeup?"

"You look beautiful," Dad says, saving me from answering. "You look like your mom."

My hand goes to the necklace tucked inside my sweater. Thankfully, the doorbell rings, and I jump up, glad he arrived before the conversation got any more embarrassing.

Dad is already standing and waves his hand at me to sit. "I got it," he tells me.

I plop down and try to keep the swirling in my belly under the surface.

"He's more nervous than you are," Aunt Allie whispers.

Fredrick's head perks up, and his ears point straight up. Tiny burp-growls erupt from his throat. He doesn't move from Aunt Allie's lap, though. Aunt Allie speaks for him in her fake Spanish accent.

"Aye, Chihuahua. I cannot get up. Bring me the visitor."

She smiles at me, but I don't smile back, and she frowns. "You okay?"

I don't answer her.

"Sam?" Aunt Allie says in a quiet voice. "You'll make sure this boy treats you right?"

"It's just a festival," I mumble. "He's just a boy." I want to tell her about the comments on the computer, but there's no time to get into it now.

"Hmm," she says under her breath.

I want to tell her people think I'm a whore.

"Come in," Dad's voice booms out from the front door. From the living room, I see Casper step into the house. He looks like an ad for Guess, in jeans and a corduroy jacket with a scarf draped around his neck. I stand but don't go to him yet.

"So. You're here to take out my daughter?" Dad says in an overly loud and unnatural voice.

It feels like I'm watching a TV show about a girl going on a date.

"I am, sir. I'm a lucky guy," Casper tells him.

"I'm a great believer in luck. I find the harder I work, the more I have," Dad says.

"Thomas Jefferson," Casper says without missing a beat.

"Nice," Dad says. "Sam said you were smart."

"But not as smart as your daughter."

I walk out of the living room toward the front hallway. Casper winks at me.

"Liar," Dad and I say at the same time.

Casper laughs. "I'm always sincere, even if I don't mean it."

I imagine a studio audience with canned laughter and clapping.

Dad chuckles. Casper does handle parents like a pro.

"Taurus," Aunt Allie calls.

Casper stands on his toes to see inside the living room. He waves at me when I get closer and nods at Aunt Allie. Polite but puzzled. "Pardon me?"

"When's your birthday?" she calls.

"Hi, Casper," I say. "That's my Aunt Allie."

"Nice to meet you," he calls.

"I'm just asking," she says to me. Fredrick burp-growls but doesn't move. "I'd get up, but Fredrick has a broken leg and I don't want to jostle him."

"May sixth," Casper says. "My birthday. Cute dog. I heard about the accident. Glad he's okay."

I glance back at Aunt Allie. "Thank you." She nods thoughtfully. "Same birthday as George Clooney. I was right. Taurus." She runs her hand along Fredrick's back. He lets out a sharp bark.

"You want to come in?" Dad asks.

"No," I say and give my dad a look as I open the front closet to get a cardigan.

Casper smiles and helps me put the sweater on while asking Dad if he follows Washington State football. They chat a little about his injury and college football while I shift from foot to foot.

"Okay. Interrogation over," I tell Casper. "We can go."

"It's okay, Sam," he says.

"Not by me." I make another face at my dad and he grins. Casper passed the test.

"Fine. You kids have fun at the festival."

"You're not going?" Casper asks him.

"My sister can't leave her dog for longer than five minutes. I don't want to leave her alone."

"What that really means is that unlike Sam, he couldn't get a date," Aunt Allie says.

I shake my head.

"I could get a date. I just didn't want one," Dad calls back. He winks at Casper, and I cringe on Dad's behalf.

"We're watching a movie instead," he over-shares.

"Romantic comedy," Aunt Allie calls.

"More information than the boy needed," Dad tells her and smiles at Casper. "I was hoping for something with a little more action."

"You were not," Aunt Allie calls. "He's mushier than I am."

Dad's face reddens.

"I'm partial to romantic comedies myself, sir," Casper assures him.

I blink at him. Sir? Partial to romantic comedies?

"Let's just not repeat this conversation to any other guys," Dad says.

I silently agree, as Casper laughs and I roll my eyes and gesture toward the door. Let's not repeat it, period.

"Come on, Casper. Seriously, we should go."

Casper sticks out his hand and Dad shakes it vigorously. "Nice to meet you, Mr. Waxman. Nice meeting you too," he calls to Aunt Allie. "Hope your dog feels better."

Fredrick growls.

I slip on my boots while Casper winds down the small talk with Dad.

"Not too late, okay, Sam?" Dad says. He leans over and kisses my cheek, not a normal thing for him to do. It leaves a hot mark but surprisingly doesn't embarrass me. I touch my fingers to the spot and tell him and Aunt Allie good night.

"Wow. I'm sorry about that," I say as soon as we're outside.

"No big deal. I specialize in parents. And your aunt is funny." Casper opens his car door for me and tucks me inside. As soon as he's in the driver's seat he leans over and gives me a long, hot kiss on the lips.

I glance sideways at him when he pulls away. Where's all this passion coming from? We've hardly spoken at school all week, unless it was for class. I wonder if he saw my Facebook wall. I wonder if he ever thinks about me as a person. If I even deserve that.

"My aunt's an individual, that's for sure." I scoot a little closer to the door and sit straight. She'd kick his butt if she saw the way he just kissed me. I watch out the window as Casper drives and chatters incessantly without needing much input from me. I'm glad he doesn't bring up Chloe or the accident with Fredrick. I'm not in the mood to talk about that. I'm not in the mood to talk about much.

I notice the houses getting bigger and see that we've turned onto his street. He pulls into his driveway and leans over and kisses me again. It makes me feel strange, this intimacy. "Want to go inside?" He puts the car in park.

"Uh." I want to say no. I want to tell him I'm not that kind of girl. "What about the festival?"

What about the eyeliner I had to trace on and wipe off four times to get right? And the Plum Perfect lipstick, and the new jeans I bought for the occasion with the little spending money I actually have? I ignore the little voice in my head telling me I want to impress a different guy. Who is probably at the festival already.

I wasn't expecting this. It's such a one-eighty from the old me. I fight a desire to laugh because if I start, it'll turn to tears that might never stop.

"We have plenty of time. My parents sponsor the rodeo, so they had to show up early. Theresa went with them. I told them I'd be by later." He turns the ignition off and leans back, with a smug smile on his face.

"Won't they be suspicious about what we're doing? Don't they know you already picked me up?"

He shakes his head and looks toward his house. It's lit up with flood lights.

I almost let it go. But I need to know. "Did you tell them you were taking me to the festival?"

"I told them a bunch of us were going together." He leans over and puts his hand on my knee. "Which is true. Only you're the most special one."

I lean my head back against the seat. "You didn't want them to know it was with me." I don't ask it as a question. I should have known his parents wouldn't want to hear that he's with me. We've never met, but of course they know who I am. Being associated with me might ruin his chance to get into his first-choice university or something.

"God, Sam. No. I'll introduce you to them when we get there. It's not that. I just wanted to have some time alone with you before I have to share you." He pats my leg. Rubs his hand over my jeans. "You want that too, don't you?"

I don't answer. He lied by omission to his parents and pre-planned private time at his house. Is that something you do with a girl you're taking on a date? He traces his fingers over my leg, spelling out my name. "You know I've been dying to spend time with you. Don't you?"

I glance at his huge house. "I don't know. I told Taylor we'd be there soon."

"Taylor will be fine for an hour or so. She's with Justin." He opens his door, climbs out, hurries to my side, and opens the door. He holds out his hand. I take a deep breath. "Come on," he whispers. "You know you want this."

I do?

I feel nauseous. Helpless. Like I don't have the right to say no.

Zee is taking Chloe to the festival, I remind myself. Not me.

I take his hand, and Casper pulls me up. I take a deep breath and convince myself it's what I want too. I follow him into the house.

He tickles me and pulls me down the hallway. As if I've left my body, I watch him. I pretend to laugh. He doesn't notice that I'm faking it. Or he doesn't care.

I follow him up the spiral staircase, hanging back, but he tugs me along and tells me not to be shy. This isn't shy. This is dread. I imagine Alex again, and when Casper turns me around and kisses me, I'm so relieved that he doesn't fall down and struggle for breath that I let him lead me to his room. He takes me to his bed.

I wait to lose myself in him. I want to forget everything else. Before, when Casper kissed me, I got lost in it. I didn't have to think about anything. But I wait. And wait. And it doesn't happen. The whole time he touches me, taking off my clothes, I wait. But instead, I feel removed. I think of Alex and close my eyes tight. I want to forget, but it doesn't happen. And then it's too late. I want to explain myself. But I can't.

• • •

"So? How was it?" Casper is stroking my back.

I guess he didn't notice my clenched teeth or the way I'd scrunched up my eyes. I'm rolled on my side, not facing him. He's finally rolled off me. Done. And now, curled up in a ball of nakedness, I'm strangely empty despite the fact I've just done the most intimate thing possible with another human being.

"I didn't know I was your first. But I'm glad." He sounds proud. I want to ask him why he's glad. For me or for himself?

"I know the first time isn't supposed to be very good for a girl." He traces a finger along my backbone. "It'll get better, I promise."

I want to roll over and punch him in the gut. How does he know about a girl's first time? How does he know whether I want it to get better, or to do that with him ever again in my life? Because I don't. I won't. I wanted him to help me escape my head. But the truth is there's no escaping. Not with Casper.

I don't say anything.

"Sam?" He sighs. "It was great, right?" His finger moves up to my shoulder. I use all my remaining self-restraint not to swat him away.

Not for me, I want to snap. It wasn't great for me.

"Sam?" he asks in a quieter voice. "Is everything okay?" There's compassion in his voice now. Less boasty pride.

239

I close my eyes. I made my own bed. In every sense of the phrase. I roll over and grab the sheets and pull them up to cover me.

He leans over then and kisses me on the lips, and I kiss him back, trying to feel something. Anything but the numbness that is me. His lips don't thaw me, and he pulls them away. My body has become a hollow vessel.

And then Casper wraps his arms around me and snuggles into my back. I don't move, but the warmth is better. His heat soothes the coldness of my skin. I wiggle closer, trying to fill myself with his essence, become a whole person. Borrow his body temperature.

He gently slides his arm away.

"Okay. I have to get this condom off."

I close my eyes and shudder at the casual way he says it.

He leans over me and kisses my nose. "And we should get going." His high-pitched voice squeaks at the end of the sentence. "My parents will be expecting me soon."

I want to snatch his arm back. Force him to stay with me in his bed, not shove me back into the world. The world where I killed an innocent boy. The world where I'm no longer a virgin.

He slides out of bed and puts his hand over his private parts. Truthfully, I wouldn't look anyhow. I have no desire to gawk at him.

"I'm going to have a quick shower." He doesn't ask if I want one too. Or if I feel horribly filthy. I want to shower. Erase his fingerprints from almost every inch of my body.

He disappears into his bathroom. When he closes the door, I lean over the bed and locate my clothes. I pull them all on and sit fully clothed on his bed until he returns.

He is clean. I am not.

I ask to use his washroom and clean myself up as best I can. I'm tender and sore, and I definitely feel different now. But not in the ways I thought.

• • •

Casper finds a parking spot in the open field. It's packed with cars already and is separated from the fairgrounds by a thick strip of fir trees.

I step out of the car and immediately get blasted by the atmosphere of the fair. The sky is lit up with midway lights, and music drifts over along with laughter and screams. Smells drift in the air, crawling over each other, competing for prominence, from the pleasant scent of greasy foods cooking to the stench of horse poop on the ground.

Casper comes round and puts an arm around my shoulder. I cross my arms but lean awkwardly closer to him, wanting to feel special and connected to him instead of lonely and shamed. He starts in with a story about his dad and him and the first horse they ever entered in a rodeo as we walk toward the fair entrance.

When we pass the trees, someone calls his name. Casper immediately drops his arm from my shoulder. He waves at some guy I don't recognize. I shiver and pull my sweater tighter around me, trying to pretend it doesn't matter. He calls to the boy but doesn't introduce me, even when he catches up and walks on Casper's other side.

I shrink into myself a bit. When we reach the front gates, Casper is still deep in conversation and isn't acknowledging me.

Don't mind me. I just lost my virginity with you, no big deal.

I walk away from him, find an open kiosk window, and buy myself a ticket to get in.

"Hey." Casper walks up behind me as the women hands me change.

"I was going to pay for you." He buys a ticket for himself but doesn't offer to pay me back.

I walk ahead of him inside the gate, and he follows me. In a few more steps, I find out that almost every person in Tadita is packed onto the grounds. It's already dark, and lights flare out and sparkle from rides and food stands and game booths. Bodies swarm everywhere. Loud voices compete with music from rides and the calls of carnies. We walk into a swarm of people scurrying around game and food vendors.

A bell starts ringing behind me, and I swivel for a minute to watch a man hold up his hands in victory. When I turn back, Casper is gone. I stand on my tiptoes, looking around to see if I can spot him. There are crowds of people moving in and out, but no white-blond hair and skinny jeans.

"Great," I mumble to myself. My phone is in my pocket and I know I can text him, but I take a quick look around, searching first.

I'm jolted by a body slamming into the side of me and grunt out as an elbow pokes me in the ribs.

"Well look who's here all by herself. What's the matter, you kill off all your friends?" Kaitlin stands in front of me, her hip jutted out, flanked by two equally tall girlfriends. They're all wearing short skirts with black tights and tall black boots. She's holding a stick with a big puff of pink cotton candy on it.

She flips her curly hair over her shoulder, looking down her nose at me like I'm the grease on the bottom of the corndog fryer and nibbles at her frothy pink candy. The way her tongue darts out reminds me of Fredrick.

"Oh, oops, do you even have friends? You here with your daddy?" She glances around, more than likely to see if she needs to back off due to parental protection.

"I'm here with Casper," I say, and even the words sound wrong on my lips. I glance around, hoping he'll magically materialize.

"Casper?" She stops pulling pieces off her cotton candy, looks around, and then stares at me, her eyes wide open. "He ditch you already?" She starts to laugh, and her friends join in, but then she narrows her eyes. "You'd think that you'd learn to leave guys alone. But, no. First you off Alex, now you're with Casper? And yet somehow you still feel the need to keep trying to mess with Zee?"

Behind me, someone's balloon pops, and it sounds like a shotgun. I flinch, but it's her words, not the sound that I react to. The words dangle in the fragrant air. I wish the fairground would open under my feet and swallow me up like in a good horror movie. Suck me down into the dirt and fill and reclose over me.

"I'm not messing with Zee," I say quietly. I can't defend myself about Casper.

Kaitlin nibbles at her cotton candy and glares at me. "No? Well you certainly messed things up by killing his best friend." She rolls her eyes. "I'm so sick of Zee going on and on about how much Chloe needs him. God knows she's been waiting for a chance to get to Zee, and now the little bitch has the perfect excuse."

I take a small step back from her and shake my head. "You honestly think she'd use her brother's death to get a guy?"

Cutting me down is one thing, but is she for real about Chloe? Behind me I hear the clicking of a game wheel slow down and come to a stop. "Be mad at me if that makes you feel better, but show Chloe some respect."

"Whatever." Kaitlin narrows her eyes. "I know it bugs you too. I've seen the way you look at Zee. Even that night. You kissed Alex, but you wanted Zee." Her friends bob their heads in agreement, as if they had been there. My hands clench into fists. It may hurt, but I would never blame Chloe for being with Zee. "Shut up, Kaitlin," I tell her.

She steps forward and shoves me with her free hand. Hard.

I stumble back and almost land on top of a little boy standing with his mom, clutching a tiny stuffed animal. He starts to cry, and I apologize profusely to him and his mom while Kaitlin and her friends laugh in the background.

"Klutz," one of the girls calls. The mother shoots her a dirty look, bends down to pick up her little boy, and turns away from us.

"What's going on?" says a deep voice behind me.

Kaitlin's face changes. I glance back and Zee is right behind me. He's holding a white bag filled with little doughnuts. He's got on his Titans jacket, and the black and blue makes his hair shine and his eyes light up.

"I saw you shove Sam. What's up, Kaitlin?"

She bats her eyes at him. "Nothing."

She turns to me and glares, but when she looks at Zee she smiles and flutters her eyes again. "She was saying some rude stuff about Alex and Chloe. I got mad so I pushed her. Not hard. She's not very coordinated."

She shrugs, and my mouth opens, but before I form any words, Zee says, "Bullshit. Why don't you and your friends go and leave Sam alone."

Her flirty look disappears, and she scowls at him. "Whatever." She glances at me, and I see in her eyes that she knows she blew it. And that she blames me again. She tosses her cotton candy at my feet. "You're both losers." She stalks away, her friends close behind her, and quickly get swallowed up by the crowd.

"You okay?" Zee asks, popping an entire little doughnut in his mouth. A flashing light from a ride makes his face blue.

"I'm fine." I look down at my boots and step off the cotton candy that's already picked up torn tickets and bits of popcorn from the pavement.

He glances around. "Where's Casper?"

"Uh. I lost him. Where's Chloe?"

"She's in the bathroom." His expression changes to a scowl. "You should stay lost. From Casper."

I frown and look around. "Didn't you used to be friends?"

"He was always more Alex's friend than mine. He's a little too much for me. Alex never saw it."

I search the crowd, but with all the lights and people it's blurry and overpowering. Hawkers call out for gamers, change rattles, and lights flash. My senses are going into overload.

"Kaitlin's got issues. Don't let her get to you." He holds out his bag to offer me a doughnut, but I shake my head. The thought of the grease and sugar make my stomach squirm.

I stick my hand in my sweater pocket for my cell phone and pull it out. I need to text Casper. Get out of here.

"I wish you'd stay away from Casper," he says again. He pops another doughnut in his mouth, watching my face as he chews.

"It's not really your business," I say, keeping my eyes on my phone. "Those doughnuts part of your nutritional plan for the state finals?" The whole night has turned into one big mistake. I'm here with a guy I don't want to be with. I did something with him I shouldn't have done. Nothing feels right. I want to go home.

"At least I'm on a plan. And you're right," Zee answers. "It isn't my business." He looks like he's about to say more, but a little girl starts tugging on his jacket.

"Hi!" she says. She's about six, and there are two other little girls with her, holding her hand. They're all staring up at Zee with nothing short of worship.

His features soften, and he smiles. It lights up his whole face. His entire body changes. "Hey!" he says. "Ciara, Carly, and Cede. My favorite swimmers." He rumples the hair of one girl, and then he holds up his fist and another girl pounds it and giggles hard. My heart melts as they smile and wiggle happily while Zee makes a fuss over them. A woman walks up beside us. She glances at me and smiles and then focuses on Zee.

"Hi, Zee. The girls spotted you and insisted on coming over to say hi." She glances at me again, as if she thinks she knows me from somewhere but isn't sure where.

"Hey, Mrs. MacLeod." He charms the little girls until the mom shoos them off and pushes them the other way.

Zee bends at the waist with an elaborate bow as they leave. I recognize the smile. He used to smile at me like that. The girls skip happily off, still holding hands and full of excitement about their Zee spotting.

"Zee?" Chloe comes up beside him. "Hey, Sam." She smiles. I kind of want to hate her for being with Zee. But I can't. Chloe glances at Zee and then at me with an unasked question on her face.

"Hi," I say.

"There you are!" Casper runs up from the other side and puts a hand on my waist. "Guess who I found?" He spots Zee and Chloe standing with me and drops his hand faster than a photo-finish swim race.

"Zee," he says but he's looking at Chloe. "How you doing?" he asks in a softer voice.

Taylor clomps up behind Casper and squeals. She's dragging Justin by the hand, and he grins at all of us good naturedly.

"Finally!" Taylor shouts. "Where the heck were you kids earlier?"

My face burns, but it's dark enough I hope no one notices.

Casper clears his throat, and Chloe glances around like she wants to leave. Zee is watching me.

"Yay! The gang's all here!" Taylor shouts.

Chloe spins then and whizzes off into the crowd. Zee glances at me for another split second and then takes off after her.

Taylor stares at the spot they just left. "What?"

I twist my braid, watching them go. I can guess Chloe's reaction. Her brother was part of the gang. But he's not here anymore.

"Taylor," Casper says. "Just once you should try thinking before you talk."

"Hey," Justin says. "Back off. She didn't mean anything."

Taylor's expression drops as she rethinks her words, and then she thumps her forehead with her hand. "Crap. I did not mean to upset her."

Casper stares off in the direction Zee and Chloe took. But then he turns to me, glances at Taylor, and shrugs. "Sorry," he says to her. "I know you didn't mean anything."

Justin pulls Taylor in, gives her a big hug, and then spins her around in a circle by her hand. "Okay! Let's get this party started. You want to go on some rides?"

Taylor giggles. "*No!* Justin you have the stomach of a two-year-old." She grins at me. "He'll throw up all over me."

"I will not!" The two of them wrestle and fake argue and then link hands.

"Come on!" Taylor calls, and they start walking.

They're so cute and affectionate. Casper and I follow silently behind them. He sticks his hands in his front pockets. I don't really want him to hold my hand but wonder why he doesn't even try. Is that too intimate for him? Never mind what happened between us earlier? PDA is unacceptable?

Taylor stops, and we catch up to them. "Why don't you two go try to win us a stuffed animal at that ball-throwing game?" she says to Justin and Casper. "Sam and I can get some drinks. Hot chocolate?"

Justin drops her hand, pulls out his wallet, and hands her a twenty. "Sure. Or a Coke if they don't have hot chocolate." He turns to Casper. "You want one?" Casper nods.

"I'm all over this," Justin says and points at a booth. "Meet us over there." The two boys race off.

Taylor watches them go and then turns to me. "God. I can't believe I said that to Chloe. Sometimes I say the stupidest things."

"It's okay. Most of the time I do really stupid things," I tell her.

She takes my hand and squeezes it. "You okay?"

I nod as we step into a line for drinks.

A group of preteen girls runs by us screaming at the top of their lungs. A group of boys follow. She watches them for a moment. "We all just miss you at swimming. Finals are coming up."

"I heard you were kicking ass."

A drunk old man bumps into me, and I push him aside and step out of his way.

Taylor makes a face at him as he mumbles to himself and stumbles off, and then she looks at me. "I'm doing okay."

I turn my attention on her. I poke my finger into her arm. "You always do that."

She blinks. "What?"

"Downplay yourself. Pretend you don't want to win. It's okay, you know. We're competitive. I have no problem with you kicking my ass."

Or at least trying to, pops into my head. I stand a little straighter, surprised at myself.

Taylor chews her bottom lip. "It's habit, I guess. My mom doesn't think it's dignified. To be competitive. She'd rather see me in a bikini, strutting across a stage with a spray tan and a sash across my chest."

"Are you serious?" I ask.

"My mom did the pageant circuit. She'd love if I did too. Became more of a lady."

"For real?" It sounds archaic and foreign.

She laughs. "I know, right? I fought hard to get her to let me swim. I have to get her out of my head."

I bump her hip with mine. "You are totally good enough to win," I tell her.

She shrugs again. "Not compared to you. I'm second best."

"You're not, Taylor."

"Tell that to my mother."

"Tell that to yourself," I say.

She rolls her eyes. "Okay, Dr. Phil. I got your point."

"I heard you were at the pool last week," Taylor says in a low voice.

"It's kind of hard to keep secrets in this town, isn't it?"

She laughs. "Depends what they are." She points at a balloon floating up in the air. "Look! A balloon!" I follow her gaze and watch it drift higher and away.

"Zee told me. That you were swimming. I'm glad," Taylor says. "I hope you come back soon. Even if you miss finals. It's who you are."

"Is it?"

It's who I used to be.

"How are you and Zee doing?"

"Zee and I? We're fine."

"Freaked out, Insecure, Neurotic, and Emotional?" she says and laughs.

I can't help but laugh with her. We step forward with only one person in line ahead of us. "Things are messed up," I admit.

Taylor nods. "I know, sweetie." She puts both arms around me. For a moment I stiffen, but it feels incredibly good. To have someone on my side.

I squeeze back.

"You're a good person, Sam."

"Not really," I say. "But thanks, for standing by me through, you know. Everything."

She pushes my braid behind my ear. "I know." Then she grins. "So. What's up with you and Casper? Why were you two so late?"

I swallow and squish up my nose and shake my head, fighting off an overwhelming urge to cry. I wish I could be happy and squeal about my first time like girls on TV who are sophisticated and tell each other everything and analyze every move. But I'm confused. And not terribly happy or proud.

I can't tell her I've lost my virginity to a guy who doesn't think it's a big deal. And that afterward he didn't even pay for me to get into the fair. Or offer to buy my drink, like Justin did. Even though he's richer than all of us. That he won't hold my hand in public, or introduce me to his parents. And it's a huge deal to me.

Instead I sigh. "It was nothing."

"Good," she says.

The lady in the food kiosk calls down to us. "Next! What'll you have?"

Taylor looks at me.

"I'll get my own," I tell her.

"Forget it. Justin's buying. Hot chocolate?"

I nod and she orders four. "Be careful with Casper," she says when she hands up the money. "I mean, you're not emotionally involved, right?"

My body sure got involved. But what about my mind?

"He's a good guy most of the time," Taylor says and hands me a styrofoam cup. "But I don't know. He's spoiled. Entitled."

She hands me another cup. "His house is huge," I say.

"I know. His family is loaded. Both of them. But it's more than that. Justin's family has money too. But he's more…respectful. Casper's dad…"

She stops to take two more cups and thanks the woman who sold us the drinks.

I glance across the crowd and spot the boys. She follows my gaze. "What about his dad?" I ask as we start toward the boys.

"He thinks Casper can do no wrong. You know? He encourages bad behavior."

I shrug. My dad certainly doesn't have the luxury of thinking I do nothing wrong anymore.

Taylor looks at me as we scoot around an old couple walking slowly. We start toward the boys as they hand bills to a guy holding baseballs. There are big baskets behind him. They have to throw the balls inside, without them bouncing out, to win.

"Look!" Taylor shouts. "Justin just won!" I look over as Casper throws a ball and it bounces out. He laughs along with Justin, but there's something about his smile that hints at anger.

252

The carnie hands Justin a huge stuffed toy.

He whoops as he holds up the huge Pokemon character. It's almost as big as him.

Taylor squeals and runs over and does a cute victory dance. Justin's grin is wide and proud, and he looks at her with so much happiness it makes my insides hurt. He puts the animal down, takes the drinks from her, and gives her a big smooch. "For you," he says, and she picks up the huge animal and hugs it.

I hand Casper a drink.

"Thanks."

I point at Justin. "Thank him."

Casper's lips smile, but his eyes don't crinkle in the corners. "Stupid game is rigged." He takes a long sip of the drink. "Justin got lucky. Hey. I have to use the bathroom." He points off to the right. "They're right over there." He takes off. "I'll be right back."

"He hates not winning," Taylor says.

"He's totally into scoring, though," Justin says.

I wince, and Taylor punches him in the arm.

I throw my cup in a nearby garbage, apologizing that the taste doesn't agree with my stomach. Casper returns, and we're both quiet. When I tell him I don't feel well, he seems relieved and agrees to take me home early.

"You'll miss everything," Taylor says, hugging her big plush toy.

But I feel like I missed out on a lot already.

I need to make changes.

chapter twenty-two

"Cut it all off," I say to the hairdresser.

Monday morning I walk into the first salon I see on the way home from school. The place is old and smells like cleaning supplies. There's only one customer besides me, an old woman with short white hair. She's getting it blow-dried by a young girl with tattoo sleeves on both her arms.

"Define 'all.'"

My hairdresser is middle-aged, in high heels and tight jeans that give her a definite muffin top. She snaps her gum as she runs her brush through my hair. She's looking at my reflection in the mirror. I stare back at hers.

I hold up a picture I found in an old magazine in the waiting area. It's Emma Watson, when she cut off her hair after the last Harry Potter movie. Cropped short. The hairdresser shakes her head and keeps brushing. "Boys don't love the short hair, you know."

I narrow my eyes at her reflection.

"All right," she says and snaps her gum. "If you're sure. It'll take a while to grow back. I'm warning you." She lifts the long, thin braid that's been my trademark for so long. "This too?"

I nod. "But can I take it with me?"

"Whatever floats your boat," she says. In a swift movement, she grabs a pair of scissors and snips it off, leaving a short piece at the top. She puts it in my lap. "It's all yours."

• • •

Aunt Allie is sitting in the living room reading when I walk through the front door. Her sweater is bulged in the front. Fredrick is burrowed inside.

"Wow," she says and puts her book down. Fredrick grumbles, sticks his head out of the top of her sweater, grunts, and snorts hello. He doesn't move, though.

"Your dad know you were going to do that?"

My neck feels vulnerable and exposed with no hair covering it. I'll need to borrow some of Aunt Allie's scarves. I shake my head, still clutching my braid in my hand.

Aunt Allie reaches inside the sweater, removes Fredrick, and puts him on the floor. He limps over to me and wiggles around, demanding to be picked up. I ignore him until he snorts indignantly and toddles out of the living room. No doubt going to his little house to pout.

"I like it," Aunt Allie declares. She stands and moves toward me and places a hand on each of my cheeks. "You look older. Wiser." She moves her hands down to my shoulders and pulls me in tight. "You're going to be all right, butterfly," she says.

I sniff in the familiar, comforting scent, and her sweater soaks up my tears.

It's a little different when Dad walks in and sees what I did to my hair, but I stand up to him.

• • •

Bob stands, watching me walk across his office to the chair I sit in for our visits. "New haircut," he says. His tone is noncommittal.

I shrug and sink down. "Why is everyone so worried about my hair? Dead, useless follicles on my head."

He sits down after I do. He's old-fashioned that way. "It's a big change. Usually something like this is symbolic."

He doesn't ask me of what. For that I'm grateful. The pit of anger in my belly eases a little. "I had sex," I blurt out.

He nods but doesn't comment. I'm getting used to his silences. He usually gives me time to find the courage to say what's in my heart, but today the whole story spills from me in a burst. I've been wanting to tell someone what happened. Someone who is paid to listen and stay nonjudgmental.

I tell him that I don't love Casper. I ask him if he thinks I'm a slut.

A small smile tugs at his lips before it disappears. "I don't think you're a slut," he tells me. "I think you're a smart and nice young woman who made a mistake." He stops when he sees my eyes fill with tears.

"Mistakes don't make us bad people, Sam. They make us human. You're in a vulnerable place. You're searching for meaning. But I want you to think about something." He leans forward and taps my knee with his pen.

"Why do you think you did what you did?"

I sniffle my nose. Sigh. "I wanted it to make me feel better. Or to make me forget everything. Maybe I wanted to feel loved." I stick out my tongue and make a face. "It's so cliché. It's embarrassing.

I thought it would make me feel good, but it made me feel worse later. More alone. Horrible about myself."

He nods and presses his lips tighter, watching me.

"Do you think you're worth loving, Sam?" he asks.

I can't answer him. I hold onto the necklace around my neck. It doesn't help me. Nothing can. I don't want to tell him what he already knows. The answer is no. I shake my head back and forth, but I don't look up.

"Well," he says. "I don't like to tell people this too often. But you're wrong. You're wrong, Sam." He stands up and I glance up, surprised. He has a strange expression on his face. Almost as if he's mad. I hunch my shoulders and look down.

"You are one hundred percent worth loving."

My cheeks warm then.

"What can you do now?" he says. "What can you do to start feeling like you are a good person again?"

"I don't know." I reach for my braid, to twirl it in my fingers, but it's gone. At home in a drawer. Put away. No longer my security blanket.

My hands go to my lap. I'm sick of myself and my feelings.

Bob sits back down. "Well. We're going to figure that out. If it's the last thing I do."

I don't want him to feel like he's failing me. "I went swimming," I tell him.

He nods. Sticks his pen in his mouth and leans back.

"I did it for my dad."

"And?" he prompts. "How did it feel?"

"It kind of sucked," I admit. "It pissed me off. I was in great shape. I was good. Really good. Before."

"You can be again."

"I know."

His lips turn up in the corners. "When you do it for yourself."

"There's something else too." My insides swirl with a little bit of excitement. I've been going ahead with my plans. With or without Chloe. "I'm starting a local chapter of NAAN. For kids with allergies. I'm raising money in a walk to build a website. And I put word out online that I need people to go into schools. To talk to kids about how they can help keep other kids safe."

He claps his hands together, and it's loud and sudden and startles me.

And then he smiles. "It's a start," he says. "Don't tell your dad, but I like your hair."

I smile back. "I've been thinking about what I can write to Alex."

chapter twenty-three

A few days later, Aunt Allie is pushing the grocery cart, grumbling that the store doesn't carry Fredrick's favorite treats. Which are human treats, of course. Fredrick doesn't eat dog food. He's in a baby sling around her chest, his little pencil leg still in a cast. He's fast asleep, and from the front it looks like she's carrying a baby, so no one bothers her about having a dog in the store.

"I'm going to go to the produce section to grab the peppers. Okay?" She nods once and wrinkles her nose, frowning at a bag of dried chicken treats. "Seventeen dollars for this? I thought this grocery store had competitive prices."

A woman wearing a tight skirt and blouse and tottering on high heels that make her legs look great gives Aunt Allie a side-eye. Smiling to myself, I push the cart around the corner and head toward the produce section.

My legs stop when I make it around the corner. My body freezes. Directly in front of me is a woman I feel like I know intimately. Better than my own mother. A woman whose face has spoken to me from television reports.

Alex's mom.

In person, she looks normal. You wouldn't know that she's

suffered a tragedy. From where I'm standing, she looks like a million other women her age shopping for groceries. Not someone who lost a child. She's wearing a pair of jeans tucked into a pair of tan boots and a floral blouse with a blazer. A thick gold necklace is wrapped around her throat, and her hair is up but kind of in wisps, the way women her age like to wear it. She lifts a honeydew melon to her nose, sniffs, and then places it in her cart. And then she must sense me, because her eyes look over and meet mine.

We stare at each other like deer looking into bright headlights, unable to look away. I see questions run through her mind. Why? Why a peanut butter sandwich? Why did I kiss her little boy after eating a peanut butter sandwich?

Part of me, most of me, wants to run. But Alex's mom is right there. Looking at me. And the thing is, she looks afraid. My eyes open wider as we peek inside each other's souls.

My heart beats faster than when I'm standing on a starting block, waiting for the horn to start a race. I step toward her. I won't run. I can't. I failed once when I didn't walk into the funeral home. She deserves to have her moment. To yell at me. Or cry. Or slap me for taking away her boy. Whatever she needs to give me, I prepare myself to take it.

Mrs. Waverly's lips turn slightly up, not quite a smile, and her features wobble. Slowly she pushes her cart toward me. Her heels clack on the floor. A tear rolls down my cheek, leaving a warm trail, and I reach to wipe it away, ashamed to have her see that. My sorrow. My guilt.

I want her to feel the freedom to spew any words at me she

needs to. The blacker the better. She's earned the right to hate me. "Samantha," she says simply. We stop with a short space between our carts. Of course we don't need to be introduced. "You cut off your hair."

I nod and try to smile, but I can't. "I'm sorry," I whisper. It sounds trite. I want to tell her it's okay to despise me. That I hate and I loathe myself too, almost as much as she does. That I'd shave myself bald if it would help.

She lifts her chin slightly, her jaw clenched. She moves her head down and then back up. A barely perceptible nod. Acknowledging the apology.

"He told me about you. He loved your long hair." Her voice is barely above a whisper, and she tucks her hands into her blazer sleeves, as if she's freezing.

My hand goes to my short hair. Have I offended her? By cutting it off?

A smile turns up her lips. Her eyes look off into the distance, and I realize she's remembering him. A lost conversation. It breaks my heart, because I hadn't even been aware that he'd noticed my hair. I barely noticed Alex until the day I killed him. With a kiss. Meant for someone else. Not him.

"He went to see you swim. He said you were good." Her mouth turns up again. "Better than me, he said. He likes to tease me." Her eyes widen. "Liked," she corrects herself automatically.

"You swam?" I ask in a soft voice.

"Swim," she says. "It's been years since I swam competitively, but when I was young—your age—I used to swim against your mother."

263

I inhale quickly. My hand goes to my necklace. I touch it but quickly let go.

"She was an amazing person," she says. "I'm sorry you never got a chance to know her."

"Thank you," I manage, but I'm dizzy as if I'm about to faint.

A tiny smile pulls up her lip on one side. A crooked, shaky smile. "Alex also said you were pretty." Her voice is tight, and it doesn't sound like a compliment.

"I'm not," I say automatically and immediately regret it, hoping she doesn't think I'm digging for compliments. My face burns and I look down, staring at bunches of unripe green bananas in a bin beside me. I wish so hard that Alex had never noticed me. And I know she does too.

"Smart too," she says, and I want to tell her to stop.

Someone coughs, and I step aside slightly as a woman pushes her cart around me with a dirty look. I move my cart to the side a little more.

"Chloe said she had coffee with you," Mrs. Waverly is saying.

I glance around at other people in the produce section. Shopping. Squeezing tomatoes and checking strawberries for mold, not aware that I'm talking to the mother of the boy I killed.

"She said you were nice." She's speaking quickly.

I blink. Shake my head. "She told me about your aunt's dog too. The accident. I'm glad it's okay."

"He's fine," I tell her. "He's doing good."

She nods. "I read your note. Chloe didn't tell me I could. But I found it and read it anyway."

I open my mouth, but nothing comes out.

"I think about you a lot," she says quietly, and she seems to run out of energy.

"I think about you too," I whisper back, and my voice cracks.

She blinks quickly and takes deep breaths through her nose and presses her lips together. "I've wondered how you're doing. We got the flowers and note from you and your dad."

She looks to me, as if it's my turn to say something.

I can only shrug and blink quickly. I can't tell her I didn't know he sent them. That I was not thoughtful enough to do anything but hide in my room for days.

She takes her hands out of her sleeves and places them back on the handle of the grocery cart, staring down. The moment drags on, and I wonder if I should walk away and leave her. Let her have privacy and dignity. Seeing me must stir up so many things.

"It must be so hard," I finally say. It's all I can force out.

"It is," she answers.

"I'd do anything to take it all back."

"I know." She's perfectly still, staring at her hands.

It's time for me to leave her, but then she looks up.

"I sleep in his room sometimes," she says softly. "It makes me feel close to him." She glances up at me with watery eyes. "My husband and daughter hate it. Chloe thinks it's creepy."

I chew my lip, wondering what I should say.

"His baseball uniform is still crumpled on the closet floor. Where he left it. I yelled at him that morning. For throwing it there. I told him he needed to learn to clean up after himself. For college."

My lips quiver. I try desperately to think of something to say.

"I feel like I can tell you these things," she says.

I nod and smile with as much understanding as I can inject into my lips.

"You might think I'm crazy, but sometimes I feel like he's still around. He's left signs."

"What do you mean?" I ask slowly, wondering if maybe she is going crazy.

"Alex loved Hot Wheels. He collected them. He had hundreds and kept them on display, even when he got older. He'd hate that I was telling you this. It was a family secret after his eighth birthday."

I don't remind her she talked about it on national TV. I know she's not trying to disrespect him, but trying to keep him alive.

She darts her head from side to side and then back to me. "Anyhow. A few nights ago, my husband and I took Chloe to a movie. It wasn't very good, but we wanted to get out of the house. As a family. At the theatre, I went to the washroom. It was empty. When I came out to wash my hands, there was a Hot Wheels car sitting by the sink. Just sitting there. It wasn't there went I went in. I'm positive of that."

"Wow." Goose bumps spread all over my body.

"You believe me," she says.

"You should meet my aunt."

She frowns and pushes back her bangs. "Chloe told me you stopped swimming."

I raise my chin and realize something I wasn't completely aware of until that moment. "Actually I think I'm going back," I tell her. "Soon."

I wince, wondering if she'll condemn me for going back when her son can't do the things he loves anymore.

She presses her lips tight and stares at me.

"Yes." She finally says, and her whispery voice is fierce. "You need to keep living, Samantha. For both of you. You're forever connected to Alex now. You need to do things bigger. For two people. You need to live for both of you."

I can't blink fast enough to keep the tears from spilling over, and a trail of warmth rolls down my cheeks. I reach up and wipe them away. There is a bond between her and me too. It will be there forever.

"I'm sorry," I repeat. The sadness in my heart travels to my throat and lodges itself, wanting to choke me. Her request circles through me, echoing in my head.

"I know," she says. "I know you are."

And then, in a swift movement, she pushes her cart away from me, click-clacking quickly as she disappears out of the produce section.

Aunt Allie comes around the corner where Mrs. Waverly disappeared. She's holding a box, smiling in victory. "Fredrick will like these." She stops, and the smile vanishes when she sees my face. She rushes toward me, tossing the box in our cart, and throws her arms around me. Fredrick squeaks from his sling, but she surrounds me with her arms and pulls me in. She doesn't even ask me what's wrong, she offers support unconditionally.

Aunt Allie holds me, but I'm stiff even when Fredrick sticks his head out and licks my face. She pushes me gently, taking an arm and wrapping it protectively around my shoulder. "We'll go, we'll leave."

"But…" I glance back at the grocery cart behind us, three-quarters full.

She doesn't look at it. "Forget about it," she says. "We'll come back for groceries later."

Aunt Allie is the kind of person who will abandon a cart full of groceries for me. We walk to the parking lot and she holds out her hands for the keys.

"I'll drive," she says.

I give them to her without a fight, even though she hates to drive. She climbs in the car, takes Fredrick out of his sling, hands him to me, and pulls on her seatbelt. I do the same. Fredrick circles in my lap until he's comfortable and then lies down.

"You want to talk?" she asks when we leave the parking lot.

I shake my head and she reaches over and pats my hand.

"When you're ready. You let me know." She puts in a CD she gave me. Burbling creeks in the mountains or something.

When we get home I head straight for my bedroom and dive under the covers. My body is weary and heavy, and all I can think about is sleep. My head spins when I lay down and, drugged by sorrow, I drift to sleep within minutes.

I don't know how much time's passed when there's an imprint on my bed and the weight shifts me toward it.

"Sam?" Dad shakes my shoulder.

I pull the covers down and see him staring at my hair, his eyes sad.

He hates my haircut, but he hasn't said much about it, other than dragging me to Bob for an emergency meeting.

"You sent flowers to the Waverlys," I say. "You never told me that."

He clears his throat. "I had to."

"Thank you," I interrupt before he says more.

He glances around my room instead of at me. It's messy and unorganized, but he doesn't comment on the clothes piled on the floor. "If anything like that ever happened to you. If I lost you. I don't know what I'd do."

He stands up and walks to my bulletin board and runs a red swimming ribbon through his fingers.

"You're the only thing that kept me going when I lost your mom. You're the most important thing in my life. And if I've done wrong by you by not telling you about the person she was, I'm sorry. It seemed easier. Not to talk about her at all. But Bob has helped me see that it's better to talk than to sweep things under the rug." He turns away from the board and faces me.

"Are you seeing Bob too?" I ask.

He walks back to the bed. "A couple times. I should have a long time ago. But as usual, I needed you to show me the way." He eyes my Michael Phelps poster. "I'm not perfect, Sam. I had no idea how to deal with this. All my life I've tried to keep you safe by hiding things from you."

He shrugs again, sits, and takes my hand. "It doesn't work." He squeezes and lets go, and then he runs his fingers over the top of my head. "What happened?" he asks.

Where do I start?

I scooch myself up to a sitting position and hug my knees, resting my head on top of them.

"I saw Mrs. Waverly. At Safeway."

He purses his lips and lets out a loud breath. He reaches for my hand again, but squeezes so hard it hurts.

I pull it away from him. "It's okay, Dad. She was nice. I mean, considering."

"Good," he says. "Good." His eyes go to a framed certificate above my bed. "I can't imagine how hard it must be for the family. When I lost your mom…" He pauses and stares down at the bed and then at me.

I reach for his hand to urge him to continue.

"I was terrified. I didn't know how to raise you alone. Allie wanted to help, but she'd already given up most of her childhood. She spent most of her free time looking after me. She sat through a lot of swim meets. Took me to school. Cooked."

"Where were your parents?"

"They traveled a lot. Business." He presses his lips tight. "Mom and Dad paid for things, but she's the one who showed up. She missed out on a lot because of me. I didn't want to do that to her again. But also, I think I wanted to do it myself."

I'm quiet, digesting that information. "I think she wanted to help with me, though," I say softly.

Outside my window, the wind blows and rattles the blinds. He glances at them and then at me.

"I know. I thought she needed to find her own family. I didn't realize she already had one. Us. She loves you so much."

It's the nicest thing I think I've ever heard him say about Aunt Allie.

The blinds rattle again, and Dad glances over. "When I lost your mom, it seemed like my fault. That I was being punished for not being able to help her more."

"Oh, Dad. It wasn't your fault."

"I know that now, butterfly. But it took me a long time to figure it out. The same way you'll figure out that what happened to Alex wasn't your fault either. Not really."

"Mrs. Waverly said she swam with Mom."

"I know. Your mom used to kick her ass in the pool." Something bangs against my window. A branch from a tree blowing in the wind.

Both of us laugh for a minute, and then his expression changes. "I don't think I handled any of this well. Or the rumors in Orlie. You don't know how much I wanted your mom to be here to deal with those things." He pretends to grab at his heart, and I smile but it fades quickly. "I know there'll be more boys, Sam. That Casper seemed like a decent boy."

I close my eyes and fight a sudden desire to throw up. For wasting my first time on Casper. I can never get that back. "Casper's not the right guy for me," I say softly.

He stiffens, and I practically see the hairs on his back rise. "Did something happen?"

"No, Dad. He's just not my type." Some things he doesn't need to know.

He presses his lips together. "Okay. But if you need to talk."

I hold up both hands to my neck and stick out my tongue, pretending to choke, and he laughs. "I've always regretted that your mom wasn't here with me to watch you grow up. To see the wonderful person you've become." He reaches over and lifts up the locket around my neck. "But maybe she's been watching out for you all along. Maybe Aunt Allie isn't as crazy as I think she is sometimes."

He lets the necklace go but runs his hand over my short hair and smiles.

"Don't give up on me, Sam. Crawl out. Fight to come back where you belong. With the living."

I can only nod. I think of Alex's mom. The look on her face when she pleads with me to go back to living. To live larger. For both of us.

chapter twenty-four

I time my arrival at the pool so that everyone is already on deck. My heart pounds as I hurry out of the locker room, trying not to think or plan ahead by more than five seconds. The familiar scent of chlorine is like sweet perfume in my nostrils. I quickly head toward the pool, hanging onto my swim bag for dear life. My nerves are far worse than they were on my first day with the club.

Clair spots me moving toward the team gathered around the white board and waves. I already spoke with her to tell her I was coming back, and she's ecstatic even though we both know I won't be in shape for the state finals. I give her a shaky smile and watch many pairs of eyes turn to look at me. Out of habit, I dip my toe into the water as I walk by. Cold. My heart thumps in my chest, on fast forward.

Taylor rushes forward, hugs me, and tugs my hand, pulling me to the team huddle. "It's great to have you back," she says.

There are a few friendly smiles and some not-so-friendly smiles. A couple of people clap, but it's not very enthusiastic.

Long legs step out of the group, and then a body whisks past, leaving a breeze in the air. Zee hurries away, toward the locker room.

"Zee?" Clair calls after him, but he doesn't turn back.

Taylor grabs my hand and squeezes it, and I close my eyes and concentrate on that and fight an urge to run away too. It's been weird between him and me for a while, but he's been mad at me since the festival. I remember the days when Zee and I would goof around on deck. I think of Bob's words. As much as I want to, I can't be responsible for other people's actions or feelings. Whatever he's mad at right now, he owns those feelings. Not me.

"Okay," Clair says. "We were just going over our drill. We're starting with butterfly off the block, 200, then 200 back, 200 free. We're warming up, so don't go hard yet. Especially you, Sam."

I step to the back of the lineup. Not the front, where the fast swimmers begin. Bodies start plunging in, and a splash of water wets my suit. I take equipment from my bag, stretch my cap down over my ears, and adjust my goggles. Clair steps to my side. "I didn't tell Zee you'd be back today," she says softly. "He needs to adjust is all. We're all glad you're back."

I jump in the water. "Go easy at first, Sam," she calls down. "You need to work your way back."

My arms itch, my legs eager to kick. The sensation is familiar, but I wait my turn and then push myself off the wall.

I pace myself way slower than normal, but my legs burn almost immediately. I struggle to get my natural rhythm. I struggle against myself. After my first lap someone passes me, but I let them go without trying to sprint ahead and catch them.

My breathing comes in fast bursts, and I swallow trying to catch up with it.

The drill seems endless, and when I finally touch the pool to end it, Clair bends over. "Not bad for almost two months out of the water," Clair says.

For the life of me, I can't remember why I missed this.

Taylor hangs over the lane rope and gives me a high five that I return without enthusiasm. Clair calls for a new drill, and I climb out of the water to grab fins and a paddle. My body actually hurts already, and not in an "I pushed myself hard and feel awesome about it" way. I suck hard.

I want to head straight for the locker room. Soak myself under the shower and then change and go home.

I pull on a fin. "You'll take a couple weeks to get it back, Sam," Clair says. "You've got time before nationals."

I bend over to put on my other fin. "It felt like ass."

"It's supposed to feel like ass. That's why we train every day."

I think of Alex's mom and how I'm supposed to do this for both of us. I wonder if he'd rather I quit to spare him the embarrassment. Clair keeps feeding me words as if she's searching for the right one to plant inside my head. I sit on the end of the pool, my fins in the water.

"Zee," she calls. "You're back. You want to pace Sam for a long slow swim?"

I glance up. He's looking down at me as if I'm a foreign substance that shouldn't be floating in the pool. I plop into the water, and Taylor grabs a spot on the wall beside me.

"I'll swim with Taylor," I tell Clair and glance over at Taylor. She nods.

"You okay?" she asks. I smile and hold up my thumb, and we take off from the side in silence.

After a few strokes, Zee passes me in my lane, and I ignore him but kick harder. I manage another half hour in the water without bawling or falling apart, and then, finally, it's done.

I pull myself out of the water and bend over to put my gear away.

"Your boyfriend know you're back to swimming?" Zee asks.

I stand, about to tell him Casper is not my boyfriend, when a girl interrupts us.

"Hey, Zee. What's up?" I glance over and see a slim girl with pink tips on the ends of her hair. She's wearing an old Titans swimsuit and is standing close to us, near the white board. I don't recognize her. Another pretty girl walks up behind her, and in her arms is the cutest little African American boy I've ever seen. He's got tight curls and crazy green eyes and every single one of his fingers are shoved in his drooling mouth.

"Ashley, how's it going?" Zee says. He nods at the friend with the baby.

"Taylor!" the girls says when Taylor walks up behind me.

"Hey Ashley," Taylor grins and points at me. "This is Samantha Waxman. The girl who has been all over your state records." I realize who she is. Ashley Anderson. She swam with the Titans last year but is in college now.

Ashley grins. "I heard all about you." Then her face kind of changes, and I see her remembering what else I'm known for. Outside the swimming pool. "Oh. I totally didn't mean it that way. I heard about your swimming." She pauses. "I'm sorry. About that boy."

There's genuine sympathy in her eyes. Not judgment or blame.

I nod my hello and acceptance of her words.

"Alex," Zee says. "His name was Alex."

The little boy shrieks at the top of his lungs.

"Joe," the girl holding him says, but she laughs. "Sorry. Joe likes to announce his presence if he feels like he's being ignored.

"This is my friend Jaz," Ashley says to all of us. "And her little brother with the lungs is Joe."

"Hi," I say.

Jaz smiles. Her smile gets wider, and I see she's looking behind me. I turn and spot a beautiful dark-haired boy in swim shorts walking toward us.

"Jackson," Jaz says when he reaches us. "This is Sam. And Zee. And you know Taylor." We all say hi, and Jaz transfers the little boy to him. Jackson kisses Jaz's cheek as he tucks little Joe under his arm.

"Hey, buddy. Let's go splash while your big sister and Ashley do laps, okay?" He smiles and swoops the baby up in the air, and the boy giggles. The laughter in his young voice is the best sound I've heard in a long, long time.

Taylor throws her gear over her shoulder and heads off with Ashley and Jaz toward the public swim lane. I overhear Taylor asking about the university team Ashley is swimming with.

"I gotta get going," Zee says with a wave to Jackson. He disappears toward the men's locker room.

Jackson and I are left alone. He smiles at me as he swirls a giggling Joe in the air. "I'm sorry about what happened," he says. "To that kid."

"Yeah. Me too."

"I saw his sister at Grinds the other night, the coffee shop where I work." Jackson swoops the little boy in the air but looks at me. "Her and her boyfriend."

"Zee?"

He glances off. "No. Her boyfriend. Um…Casper."

I frown.

"That's not her boyfriend."

"Really?" Jackson shrugs. "That's not what it looked like to me."

I pretend to smile and nod, and he excuses himself and takes Joe to the kiddie pool. I wrinkle my nose, not envying him getting inside that water.

I watch as he dips the little boy's toes in the water, wondering what made him think Casper was Chloe's boyfriend.

• • •

When I get to the parking lot, Zee's leaning against the driver's side of my dad's car. I walk slowly forward, as if I'm approaching a hangman with a noose.

"I'm sorry," he says when I'm closer. He pushes off the door. "For acting like a jerk in there. Taking off. I didn't know you were coming today. It took me by surprise."

I click the door open with my car starter. "It's okay."

"No. It's not." A horn honks, and Taylor waves from the passenger seat of Justin's truck as they drive by. Taylor mouths something, but I don't catch what it is. "It was stupid."

Zee ignores them and touches my arm for a second and then pulls back. "I just hate it so much that you're with Casper," he says. "It pisses me off."

I study my keys, ignoring the cars pulling in and out of the parking lot around us. "There's nothing between Casper and me." Not anymore. There won't be again. I want to forget him completely, but they say you never forget your first.

"Good," Zee says

"Good?"

"Good. At least Alex was a good guy. Casper doesn't deserve you." He takes a step closer to me.

I think about what Jackson said. "Are you and Chloe doing okay?" I ask him. Behind us, two boys, about thirteen, rattle the chain-link fence that separates the parking lot from the field. They leap over it and head toward the graffiti-covered mini skate park.

"Chloe and me?" He tilts his head. "What do you mean?"

I bite my bottom lip. "Well. You're together, right?"

"Together? You mean *together*-together? No. Who said that?" His eyes narrow. "Don't tell me. Casper." It looks like steam's about to blow from his nose.

"Actually, it was Kaitlin."

"Well. Consider the source. Alex's been my best friend since we were twelve." He pauses. "He was my best friend. Chloe's part of the package."

I watch the boys race each other to a concrete bike jump. "You're not together?"

"Friends."

I nod. Pretending this isn't pretty awesome news in my world. "Well. Good. Jackson just told me he saw her with Casper. As in making out."

In the field, one boy falls to his knees, and the other bends over laughing.

"Asshole." Zee whistles under his breath. "He can't leave anyone alone."

He glances over to the field, at the boys I'm watching. We both stare at them as they goof around, hurdling steel ramps.

Zee kicks his foot at the ground. "I'm still so messed up." He runs his hands over his hair and tugs on the ends. "About Alex…I miss him."

"I know."

He glances out at the boys, but they disappear behind a half-pipe.

"I always thought it was supposed to be us, Sam. Me and you. I thought we were the ones who were supposed to be together." He turns to me then and I open my mouth, struggling to think of something to say.

My cheeks flare, and some ice slides off my heart and melts into my belly. "Really?"

"Really."

"Me too," I admit.

With a graceful swoop, he slips a hand onto my back and then pulls me toward him by my waist. Our faces are less than an inch apart. Zee smells like chlorine and promises.

My mind spins, but all I can think of is how delicious he is. His hair curls up on the ends from the cold. Our hips bones crush together.

"But it got ruined," I say softly.

"So I totally messed it up?" he whispers.

A horn blares, but neither one of us looks toward the car. "What about me? I messed up worse."

"I want to kiss you," he whispers. "More than I've wanted to kiss anyone in my whole life."

I shiver and hold my breath. Waiting. But then he lets me go, and I stumble before regaining my balance. The disappointment is familiar. It's Alex, I guess. His ghost will always be around us.

"I have to get to Chloe's," Zee says. "She texted while we were swimming. She wants me there right away. Her mom wants to talk to us. Casper too, I guess." He reaches for my hair, brushes his hand over it. "Can we talk later? Can I text you? Is that okay?"

I pause for a second. Is it? After everything? I nod, and when Zee smiles it lights up his whole face. He waves and runs off, leaping over the chain-link fence.

He stops and swivels around. Waves again. I watch him go. Sad. Confused. But slightly, ever so slightly hopeful.

chapter twenty-five

"Did Chloe ask you to come?" Casper asks. Leaves crunch under our feet as we walk down the long driveway in front of his house.

After texting him and finding out he was home, I showed up at his door, shaking with anger, demanding to talk to him. He slid his shoes on and walked outside with me without a coat instead of inviting me in. As if I'm that offensive.

"Why would Chloe ask me to come here?" I spit. "Because she's your *girlfriend*?"

"She's not my girlfriend," he says and glances over his shoulder at the house. I think a curtain moves in the huge window in the front room.

"Her mom asked me to go to her house earlier. But I couldn't." He glances at the house again. "I have some family stuff going on."

"Does Chloe know? About us?" I ask. Casper stops and leans against the grille of my car. He glances at his house again as if he's worried that the windows have ears, and then he turns back to me.

"I never said anything to Chloe. Why would I?" He seems calm and collected. He doesn't even shiver in the cold in the thin T-shirt he's wearing.

"Well. Maybe because you were *sleeping* with her too," I spit out.

"I never said we were exclusive, Sam. You knew I was seeing other girls," he says in a soft voice.

I cross my arms and glare at him. "No, actually I didn't know. And Chloe? That's kind of taking advantage of someone who's grieving. Don't you think?"

"We were together before Alex." He stops, and I close my eyes and breathe in deep, fighting a desire to fire my fist into his midsection.

"So why on earth did you bother hooking up with me?" I ask. *Someone else who was grieving,* I silently add.

"I never meant to hurt you," he says, and the smugness he usually wears as easily as his expensive clothes is missing. "I thought it would help. You were so sad."

"You thought that making out with me and having sex would help me get over killing someone?" I actually stomp my foot on the ground. "You used me to get a good grade, Casper. Which you didn't have to do. I would have been your partner anyhow." I squeeze the keys in my hand so hard they cut into my skin.

"I never said we were exclusive," he repeats.

I fight another urge to punch him. "You did the same thing to Callie, didn't you? Slept with her while you were working with her. For the grade?"

His eyes narrow, and I can tell he's fighting the urge to ask how I know about that. His lips pinch together, supplying me with my answer. "I don't talk about girls like that."

"God, how many are there? Callie dated your best friend," I remind him. "But obviously things like loyalty don't matter to you." I accidentally hit the panic button on my car keys, and the horn starts honking and the headlights flashing.

Casper pushes off the car and waves his hands around. "God. Turn that off." For the first time, he actually seems ruffled.

I snicker at my clumsiness and switch it off, but based on the expression on his face, he is not amused. Good. That makes two of us.

He looks at the house.

"You did say you liked trophies," I say, remembering. "I guess that's what girls are to you?"

There are so many things I want to say out loud. It's liberating to start with him.

Casper lifts a shoulder and stares at the bricks on the driveway. "My dad tells me that this is the time of my life when I need to have fun and keep my options open."

"I don't think he meant that as a permission slip to sleep with every girl who crosses your path." I tell him. "And if he did, he's an ass."

His eyes flash and he opens his mouth, but then he seems to change his mind and closes it.

"You suck. You know that? You totally suck," I tell him and reach for my car door.

"I'm sorry," he says as I climb inside. "I thought we were having a good time."

"You *are* sorry," I tell him. "And as a matter of a fact, it wasn't good for me. Not at all." I slam the door behind me, start the car, and speed away. When I glance in the rearview mirror, he's standing with his hands in his jean pockets, watching me go.

Thank God we got an A-plus on our project.

Sam I am.

• • •

I take the long way home and soothe myself with loud music.

There's a car in our driveway when I pull up. Something about the vehicle bothers me. I park my car on the street and turn off the ignition, looking toward our house for clues.

The blinds are drawn in the living room, and I have no idea who's inside.

I tiptoe in, but Fredrick hears me and starts yapping his high-pitched bark. He wiggles over when he sees me, his butt swinging from side to side, and scratches at my legs, demanding I pick him up and give him a proper greeting.

I hear Dad's voice in the kitchen and a soft female voice. Not Aunt Allie. "Sam?" he calls. "We're in here."

My eyebrows press together.

I put Fredrick down and head to the kitchen. Fredrick follows me. There's a woman at the table. Watching me. My heart stops, but I keep walking. It's Alex's mom. The car in the driveway is the one Chloe was driving when she hit Fredrick.

Mrs. Waverly's eyes fill with tears, and she stands. "Sam," she says, and her voice breaks with emotion. I glance over at Dad for help, but his lips are pressed tight and he says nothing.

She pulls me into her arms. She's clinging to me, but my arms hang by my side. Fredrick growls.

"I'm so sorry," she whispers in my ear.

Dad scoops up Fredrick. His eyes are wide and moist, and he

shakes his head, though it's barely perceptible. Something is up, but I have no idea what it is. He takes Fredrick to the door leading to the basement, opens it, puts Fredrick down, gives him a nudge with his foot, and closes the door.

I shift awkwardly from foot to foot, until Mrs. Waverly lets me go and then look back from Mrs. Waverly to Dad, wondering what the hell is going on. Something heavy is in the air. Something big.

Mrs. Waverly attempts a smile, but it doesn't quite work. Her lips make it halfway up and then droop. Her hands crawl over each other as if there's an invisible itch she can't get rid of.

Dad steps over to her and touches her arm.

"Why don't you sit down?" He turns to me. "You too, Sam."

Frowning and not taking my eyes off Mrs. Waverly, I do as he asks.

She sits too, her head down. "I'm sorry Mr. Waverly isn't here too. He didn't feel up to joining me. He's having a hard time." She exhales and looks up, looks me right in the eye. "I wanted to let you know in person." She leans back slightly and wrings her hands. Looks away. "What happened. Well…it wasn't your fault." Her hands halt.

I turn to my dad, but he nods toward Mrs. Waverly, indicating I should listen. I look back at her.

"The report came in. From the coroner. According to the findings, Alex died from an acute asthma attack—not from coming into contact with peanut butter on his lips or saliva."

I don't say anything. My brain tries to process the information.

"He died from an asthma attack," my dad clarifies quietly.

"Not from me?" The words sound foreign and bounce around in my head. "But…" I've got nothing. "Wow."

I try to fit the new information into my brain. On a faraway level, I realize this will change everything for me. Everything I've thought and felt for the last couple months.

"They ordered an autopsy. Because of the way he died." Tears slide down Mrs. Waverly's cheeks. "It turns out the children didn't disclose everything that went on that night. Zee and Chloe told us tonight." She wipes tears from under her eyes. "Alex was doing drugs. With Casper. And Zee and Chloe knew about it. But they didn't tell us. Not until now."

Her voice breaks, and it validates how weak my victory is. This changes nothing for her. Alex is still gone. My insides ache at the expressions that cross her face. Embarrassment. Anger. But I'm relieved to see the love there too. The lingering and strong love for her son.

"It's not fair," I whisper. "He had so much to live for."

"He was just a kid," my dad says softly. "It was a mistake. God knows we all make them."

Mrs. Waverly gulps back a hiccupping sound, and her head bobs up and down. Up and down. "Yes. I know. He was a good boy. He was."

I shake off a flicker of anger at Alex. For putting himself in danger that night. And for kissing me. But I can't maintain it. He lost. Big time.

"It's not fair," I say.

"No," Mrs. Waverly agrees. "It makes no sense."

Dad takes a box of Kleenex from the top of the fridge and hands them to her. "I may have done the same thing when I was his age," my dad says. My eyes widen, but he shakes his head at me, once. I understand the message.

"Kids try these things. Usually it means nothing. They move on."

Mrs. Waverly pulls out tissues but holds them in her hand. The gratitude on her face is so earnest yet sad that I have to look away. I lower my head. "I did have the peanut butter before I kissed him."

She sniffs. "They said that it only lasts in the saliva so long. You'd brushed your teeth." She stands up. "I'm sorry. You deserve our deepest apologies. I hope you can forgive the horrible accusations that you had to deal with."

"I'm sorry too," I whisper back. "That you lost Alex."

"I have to get back." She clutches the tissues and turns to Dad. "The coroner is going to make the report public. Because of the media exposure and the controversy about the peanut allergy. It caused a lot of panic for parents of kids with allergies."

"A press release will be going out in the morning. I asked them to wait until I spoke with you." She walks out to the hallway and then rotates on her heels. "I would never wish this upon you, Sam, but at the very least, awareness has been raised. It doesn't bring Alex back. But it's something."

She spins and hurries toward the front door, slipping on her shoes and running out the door before Dad can even follow her.

I stare at the empty chair at the kitchen table. "I feel like I should be happy. But how can I be? No one wins. It's kind of anticlimactic."

Dad is standing behind me, watching me. "It removes the onus of guilt from you, Sam. You didn't cause his death. The blame is gone."

He reaches over and pats my shoulder. I wince.

"But so is Alex, Dad. That's the thing. He's still gone."

"He is. But you're not. You're still here." He digs his finger into my shoulder. "You're stiff. How was your swim tonight?"

I stick out my tongue and make a face and brush his hands off me. It's sore. "Terrible."

"I'm proud of you, Sam."

I roll my eyes, and then I put an elbow on the table and rest my chin on my arm. "You really smoked pot in high school?"

"Oh. That." He goes to the cupboard and reaches for a glass.

"You were a *swimmer*," I shout, shocked by his admission.

"It was a girl," Aunt Allie says. We both look over. She's standing at the top of the basement stairs, holding Fredrick, a smile turning up the corners of her mouth. "It's okay if I come up now?"

"I told you to stay up here in the first place," Dad says to her and takes out two more glasses.

"It was a private moment. For family." She bends and puts Fredrick on the ground.

Fredrick hobbles over to me with his broken little leg.

"You are family," Dad says to Aunt Allie. Her eyes fill with tears, and Dad steps over and pulls her in close. "Did you hear? About Alex?"

I scoop up Fredrick, and he attacks my nose and tries to kiss my lips with his little tongue.

Aunt Allie nods and smiles at me. "I'm proud of the way you're honoring Alex's memory, butterfly. But I won't lie. I'm thrilled your name will be cleared in all of this." Dad pulls me in tight, and we all join together and squeeze each other in our first-ever family group hug. Including Fredrick.

When we let go, I pinch my thumb and finger on my free hand and pretend to inhale from a marijuana cigarette. Aunt Allie chokes, and then she laughs and laughs and laughs while Dad pounds on her back.

"It was once, and I got caught and my coach had a fit and threatened to kick me off the team. And I broke up with the girl. And right after that I asked out your mom."

"Well. At least you pulled from your dark past to help another person," I tell him.

He narrows his eyes at me but chuckles as Aunt Allie wipes away a tear. Behind us the phone rings. Dad is closest to it and picks up.

"Hi," Dad says and turns his back to us. Aunt Allie glances at me, and I lift my shoulder. She walks to the fridge and pulls out a jug of cranberry juice.

Dad spins around to face us. "No. It's okay, Rose. I can talk. Sam is good. We just got news actually. It wasn't her fault. The boy had an asthma attack. That's what he died from. Not the peanut butter Sam ate."

Aunt Allie and I stare at him, not even pretending not to eavesdrop. He grins at both of us and points at the phone and mouths. "Rose." And then he puts his mouth back on the receiver. "I think we should make new plans. You can stay with us. You can meet my sister. She's going to be in Tadita for a while."

And then he takes the phone and leaves the kitchen for more privacy.

Aunt Allie shakes her head. But she's smiling. She pours juice into the three glasses on the counter.

Later, I go to my room and sit cross-legged on the bed. I stare at the blank television screen on my wall, remembering the coverage, the glimpses into Alex's life.

I don't turn the TV on. The results from the autopsy won't be on the news yet, but soon.

It's funny, but now it seems almost too bad that it will come out that peanut butter isn't what killed Alex. The debate and increased awareness about deadly food allergies wasn't such a bad thing. Maybe somewhere, some little kid is safer because of my role in the tragedy.

Of course, it's easier to be more generous with my reputation now. Because the burden of guilt has been lifted off me. Maybe it was just meant to be.

Aunt Allie always says that things happen for a reason. Maybe I was meant to help get people thinking about the seriousness of anaphylactic allergies.

I stare at the blank TV, trying to remember Alex, but I never really knew him.

I grab my laptop and turn it on. And I begin to write.

Dear Alex...

chapter twenty-six

Aunt Allie stands in the kitchen, wearing an apron and sticking a pan of something in the oven when I emerge from my room.

"Lemon loaf," she says. "Your dad went off to meet his girlfriend from Orlie."

"He's driving to Orlie now? It's like a three-hour drive."

"No. Apparently Rose was already on her way. She's staying at a hotel tonight because of a reservation she can't cancel. But he's going to bring her here." She reaches behind her and undoes the strings of the apron.

I stare at her and blink. "But we only have one guest room. And you're in it."

"Suck it up, princess," Aunt Allie says and punches numbers into the stove timer. "He's a fully grown man."

"Oh God," I say. "Maybe I liked it better when he hid stuff from us."

She puts an arm around me and takes off the apron and folds it. "You want to do an angel reading while he's gone?"

I gasp. "How'd you know?"

"How'd I know what?" She opens a drawer and slides the apron inside.

"That I wrote a letter to Alex?"

She closes the drawer and puts her hand on her hip. "Actually, I didn't know. But it's amazing, isn't it? I had a feeling you were ready. Things do happen—"

"For a reason," I finish for her.

She hurries downstairs to get her angel cards, and when she returns we sit at the kitchen table and she hands me the deck. "Shuffle them and put them into three piles when it feels right."

I do as she tells me. "Now stack them together."

When I'm done, she takes them from me and flips over the top ones.

"Interesting," she says when she glances at a card with two cherub-looking people. "I always believed you would find your soul mate in this life. Not many do."

I peer at the other cards, wondering what they all mean. She glances behind her and smiles.

"Alex is with us." She tilts her head as if she's listening. "The angels say he's smiling. He's pretending to do something." She smiles. "Revving a toy car?"

My mouth opens.

"The angels say your mom has been watching over you too." She tilts her head. "They say that she sent you a sign. That she's with you. And that she'll let you know when it's time for her to go."

I reach for my necklace, and it warms my fingers. "Why would she have to go?"

Aunt Allie waits for a moment. "To let you live your life. The angels will stay with you. Keep talking to them," she says. "They hear you. They can only reveal what you're ready for. But they're listening. And watching."

I smile. It's nice to know.
I'm glad we finally got to chat formally.

chapter twenty-seven

The next morning while I'm in bed reading, Aunt Allie calls from the living room.

"Chloe is here," she says.

I jump out of bed and hurry to the living room without bothering to fix myself up. Chloe is standing in front of the fireplace with her head down. She looks tiny and fragile, with a huge scarf snaked around her neck, almost hiding her head. A long sweater swallows up most of her upper body, and her thin legs stick out under it.

"Hey," I say, and she looks up. Aunt Allie disappears into the basement.

"Did I wake you?"

"No. I was reading."

"Your aunt is so cool," she says. "She's so good about what happened with Fredrick."

"She is," I agree. We both stare at the doorway she vanished through.

"I owe you an apology," Chloe blurts out.

I shake my head. "No. You don't."

Her lips quiver, and instinctively I move forward, wrap an arm around her, and squeeze.

"The report's out this morning. It'll be all over the news soon. What really happened. That it was an asthma attack. Not the kiss."

I nod and lead her to the couch.

"Can I get you something? Mint tea?"

She shakes her head no. "People are going to find out he smoked pot that night. He'd hate that. He was a good guy, Sam. What he did doesn't change who he was. He was a good guy."

"I know he was," I tell her. I sit close to her.

She picks up one of the decorative pillows Aunt Allie bought for us. It matches the couches. "He told me he was having trouble breathing." She stares off into space. She blinks hard and swallows. "I was going to go check on him. But…" She bends her head. "Instead of going to see him or going to pick up his meds, I was busy. With Casper."

I remember seeing her and Casper wander off together that night. Before Zee took me outside. It's all so sad. So many things, so many tiny changes might have saved him.

"Alex had just found out about Casper and me. He didn't approve." She's crushing the stuffing in the pillow. Twisting it with both hands.

I swallow my anger at Casper. For Chloe. For pretending to like me. Her. For using us. Even if deep down, maybe, just maybe, I know I was using him too.

"Zee was driving himself crazy about you," she tells me. "He's not as confident as he seems, you know. He was going to ask you out, and then everything got so messed up that night."

"I thought you and Zee were together," I tell her.

She lets her death grip on the pillow go, frowns down at it, and then fluffs it up. "Me and Zee? Gross. Why would you think that?"

"Kaitlin told me."

She sticks out her tongue and makes a raspberry sound. "Kaitlin is a bitch. She's been in love with Zee forever." She glances at me and sniffles. "I know he used to hook up with her. But it wasn't serious on his part. And then you joined the swim team. He knew who you were of course, from meets. He broke it off with Kaitlin, but she never gave up. She thinks she's better than everyone else because of her looks and money. What she never got was that Zee doesn't care about stuff like that. He's a jerk for hooking up with her in the first place. He's a guy, I guess. And she was offering. He made mistakes too. But he's over her."

Fredrick comes running into the room then and cough-barks when he sees Chloe. "Oh. Fredrick." She puts the pillow down and bends toward him. "There you are. You did come to see me. You're all right, little fellow?" She pats him, and his little tail waggles at her and he demands to be lifted. "Did you forgive me, little guy? Oh, thank you. You're so handsome."

She moves her mouth away from Fredrick's tongue attack but rubs noses with him. "When I had that accident with him, I was going to see Casper. After we had coffee. He called me. I think it was someone's way of telling me not to go. I haven't been with him since."

I close my eyes. It's such a tangled web.

Fredrick settles down and sits on her lap with his ears pointed up as if he's joined our conversation.

"Oh my God," she says. "You probably haven't heard. It turns out Theresa is pregnant. By Casper."

"Oh my *God*. His *sister*?" I shout.

"Ew," she says, running her hand softly over Fredrick's back. "Theresa's not his sister. They're not related. She's his dad's wife's step-daughter. Theresa's dad died and her mom took off with some guy to Europe. Theresa is close with Casper's stepmom, so she went to stay with the Coopers. Moved in."

"Well, thank God. But pregnant?" I ask. "He was with three girls? How is that even possible?" I reach over and scratch Fredrick behind the ears. "I thought he was a nice guy."

"You know what? I think in Casper's mind, he is a nice guy."

"Why the hell was he sleeping with Theresa?" I ask.

We make an identical face, and Fredrick snorts.

"She brought us muffins once," I say. "When Casper and I were studying."

We stare at each other and then start to laugh. And just as quickly Chloe's laughter fades. "Alex would be furious with him. God, I miss him," she says.

I take a breath. "I know."

Neither one of us talks for a second. Thinking. I take a deep breath. "I've been working with NAAN. It might help…if you joined me."

"Alex didn't die from his peanut allergy," she says.

"No. But he could have. It easily could have been. And there's maybe a reason why it happened the way it did. You know? We can always work with the asthma society too. They go together so often, allergies and asthma. We could coordinate talks at schools."

Chloe strokes Fredrick a little too hard, and he growls at her.

"Sorry, Fredrick," she says. I laugh.

"I saw your mom on TV. Talking about how scary it was to send Alex into a world that thought convenience was more important than his safety."

Chloe nods slowly and pats Fredrick lightly.

"I've got a website started. We can help make kids around here a little safer. I saw a study online that estimated about a hundred and fifty to two hundred people a year die from food allergies."

Fredrick stands and jumps off Chloe's lap. He gives both of us a look of disgust, and I pick him up and put him on the floor so he doesn't have to jump on his leg.

"You've been doing all this for Alex?" Chloe asks.

I lift my shoulder.

"But you don't have to feel guilty anymore," she says. "It wasn't your fault."

"It doesn't matter. Anyhow. I'm thinking T-shirts. Posters. Lots of kids will want to get involved. For Alex."

"But it's not the way he died."

"No. But we can help him be remembered for the way he lived."

Chloe smiles at me. Her eyes shine. "I should go. My mom wants me home." She stands up. "Thank you. For giving me something to look forward to. And my mom. She'll love this."

I stand too. "I wish I could have known him better."

"You will," she says. "I'll help you."

I walk her to the door. When she's gone, I think of my own mom and reach for my necklace. My fingers grasp at air.

It's gone.

chapter twenty-eight

Aunt Allie drops everything and we crawl around every inch of the house on our hands and knees, searching. We comb my room and everywhere I've been. I know for sure I had the necklace on when I went to bed. It never left the house. But as hard as we look, the necklace doesn't show up.

"It's a mystery," Aunt Allie says as she cuts me a thick slice of lemon loaf. "Or maybe it's a sign." She hands me the slice. "Eat up. You need the carbs."

There's a ruckus in the hallway, and we look over as Dad walks in. He's holding Rose by the arm, and the smile on his face could warm an Olympic pool.

"Allie," he calls. "Come here. I'd like you to meet someone."

"Sam," he says. "Rose is back."

• • •

Everyone is on deck, gathered around Clair and the whiteboard. Justin is on my right, and I see his attention shift to something behind us. He grins and then wolf whistles loudly, and we all follow his gaze, including Clair.

A collective group of mouths drop open.

Taylor struts down the pool deck toward us. Not the peppy

bouncing steps we're used to from her. She's morphed into a fashion model, and the swim deck is her runway. She flicks her head to the side. Her hair. It's gone. Well. Not gone. Short. Pixie-cut short. Shorter than mine. Despite that, her swagger makes me feel like a little boy.

She looks frigging amazing.

"What?" she says. "I got a haircut. It worked for Sammy."

"I like it," Clair says, and then she turns back to the white board and finishes outlining the drill.

Taylor sneaks up beside me and leans in close. "Screw my mom. I got tired of being the girl with the long blond hair. I want to be known as a swimmer."

"It's hot."

"See how hot I look when I'm passing you in the water." She winks and lifts her hand for a high five, and I smack her hand hard as she smiles. I smile back.

Zee slides up on the other side of me. I try not to stare at his washboard stomach or make it obvious that I'm getting high on the intoxicating smell that is him. "Is Sergeant picking you up after practice?" he whispers.

"No, I drove." I glance sideways, and my heart swirls when I look in his eyes.

"Can you take me for a drive? Before you go home?"

I nod. Anywhere, I think. But I don't say that out loud.

• • •

We don't speak much as we walk side by side to the car. The night air has frozen the spiky ends of my short hair. I glance over and see ice forming on the ends of his. "You mind if I drive?" he asks.

I shrug and hand him the keys. He pops the doors open and waits while I get inside, then climbs in. "Sarge won't mind?"

"What my dad doesn't know doesn't always hurt him."

"I want to take you somewhere, but my parents rarely let me use their car." He starts up the car. "Don't worry. I drive better than I Parkour." He turns down the radio and cranks up the heat.

He tilts his head and glances at me. "I want to say sorry. For what happened. With Kaitlin. With you getting blamed. And my anger." He sighs. "I wish I could take it all back."

"Not as much as I do," I say as I toss my swim bag in the back.

"But you didn't cause anything." He throws his bag on top of mine and reaches over and pats the top of my hand. "I think I know why you kissed Alex. Because of me." His fingers warm my skin, and a flush spreads through my whole body. "Does that sound jerky?" He takes his hand away and backs the car from the parking spot.

I stare out the front window at the dark parking lot and then the street. He turns away from the main turnoff that leads back to the city and heads toward the highway.

"That night. You and him." He sighs. "I was being a jerk, and Alex knew it. He moved in. I can't really blame him. Stupid drinking."

I glance out my passenger window. Early Christmas lights glisten on some of the houses scattered throughout the fields. I've never been drunk. And I certainly don't know how it's possible that two guys were interested in me.

"We were competitive about lots of things, but never girls. You're the first girl both of us were interested in. But I called dibs." He groans. "Now I really do sound like an asshole. But I meant, I kind of thought you were interested in me too. But I couldn't tell. Not for sure. You're a hard girl to read."

I'm glad of the early darkness so he can't see my cheeks redden.

I watch headlights on the other side of the road. Coming toward us like alien eyes. They light up the inside of the car and then disappear.

"I started doing Parkour the right way." I glance over and he smiles. His teeth kind of glow in the dark. "Well except for a few screw-ups. The true lifestyle, Parkour, it's supposed to be about a guy not looking out for himself, but a guy who looks out for other people too."

"I don't understand."

"It may seem like it's guys doing crazy jumps or risky tricks, but that's all preparation. It's about moving. Efficiently. Quickly. And when you look deeper, you learn it's about developing strength and skill. Training to help other people. It's supposed to be a way of living. Choosing health. Safety. And the body is tested, and it needs to be taken care of. The mind. For other people. It takes discipline. If I'd been doing things right, I would have taken care of Alex that night. I would have gotten his meds. I wouldn't have been drinking. Fooling around. I'm learning more now so I can give something back. I'm not perfect, but I'm working at getting better."

"Whoa. And I thought it was just a bunch of guys jumping around," I joke.

"I'm serious, Sam. I'm going to work hard at it. So if I'm in a position where someone needs my help again, I'll be ready."

I nod. Think of what Chloe and I are working on.

Zee flips on the turn signal, and my heart double dips when I see we're going into a graveyard. He drives for a minute and then parks and turns off the light. "You okay with this?"

I slowly nod, suspecting why we're there.

"I want you to meet my friend," he says.

Tears heat up my eyes, but I blink them away. Zee gets out of the car, and I slide out too. He comes over and takes my hand. He's formal and serious, and we don't speak as we walk, but he holds my hand tight. The night air is cold but it doesn't penetrate our hands.

We don't go far when Zee stops. We're standing in front of a grave with a modest gravestone. There are lots of fresh flowers lying around it. I want to cry so much, but I hold it in as best I can. I want to be brave for both of them.

"Alex," Zee says, and his deep voice shakes on the second syllable. He takes a deep breath. "How's it going, dude?"

He pauses, and I fight the sting of unshed tears and the tickly scratch in the back of my throat.

"I think you remember Samantha." He lifts my hand in the air.

"Hi, Alex," I say solemnly.

He drops our hands down. "I wish you got the chance to know her better. She's pretty awesome. But the thing is, Alex. I kind of like her too." He stops and takes a big breath. "And clearly I am much better looking. And a better date too. Especially now."

I pull my hand away and smack him on the arm.

"Alex and I understand each other," he says but doesn't look at me. He keeps his eyes on the tombstone. He holds a hand up to his ear as if he's listening to something. "Alex agrees."

He smiles but lowers his hand and stares solemnly at the grave. His lips turn down and his eyes soften. Then he rubs his teeth over his bottom lip and blows out though his nose. My heart gets heavy, and sadness clogs up my lungs.

"You're my best friend." Zee wipes under an eye and then takes a deep breath and reaches into his pocket. He pulls out a package. I glance down. It's a Hot Wheels car.

He bends to his knee and leans forward to place the package on a free spot in front of the tombstone. The yellow printing on the bright blue packaging almost glows in the night air, backlit by the lights at the graveyard entrance.

"GM Lean Machine from 1991. Rare," Zee says from where he's kneeling. "Alex was obsessed with finding this car. I searched and searched for it on eBay, and it finally showed up the day the autopsy report came in. It arrived in the mail today."

I can't say anything because if I do, I know I'll cry. Instead I bend my head and swallow back the sadness. Zee stays kneeling for a moment. And then he puts his hands on the ground and pushes himself up. He stands straight and bows his head. "I miss you," he says.

And then in a minute he spins on his heels and takes my hand again. "Okay. Let's go."

We don't speak again as we walk back to the car.

He pops the door for me and we get inside at the same time.

"Thanks for coming. You might think it was weird. But I needed to do it," he says.

"It wasn't weird."

He leans across the console between us. So close I can see stubble on his chin. I wonder if he shaves, and the picture of it makes me giggle inappropriately.

"You're laughing at me?" he asks softly.

"No. I'm just nervous," I admit.

"Me too," he says. And then he leans even closer and kisses me.

And as my head melts in a puddle of dizziness, I finally understand what all the fuss is about.

He pulls back and smiles and reaches into his pocket again. "This one is for you."

He tosses over an industrial size bag of Jelly Bellys. I grin and rip it open with my teeth. "You want some?"

He holds out his hand and I fill it.

• • •

Tadita Times
By Lainoza Hughes

Local Titan swimmers Zee MacLean and Taylor Landy took three gold medals each at last weekend's state swim finals in Seattle. Samantha Waxman also scored gold in the short Freestyle and set a Pacific Northwest swimming record. All three swimmers will be heading to Florida to compete in the USA Swimming National Championship. Coach Clair O'Reilly said MacLean and Waxman have been accepted at Berkeley on full swim scholarships. Landy is planning to attend Washington State.

Upon receiving their medals, Waxman and MacLean dedicated them to Alex Waverly, a promising baseball player who died at 17 years of age earlier in the year from complications due to asthma.

a note from the author

This story is a work of fiction. Which of course means I made it up.

The idea for this story came about because my son suffers from a peanut allergy and also from asthma. Which may sound kind of creepy given what happens to Alex in my story, but I talked to my son when I decided to write this book. We discussed awareness. And the fact that like Alex, he always has to be careful. Always. I want nothing more than for him to be safe. That's why it's so important to carry EpiPens. And inhalers for asthmatics.

In North America, many, many school kids have to deal with deadly food allergies. And yes, I've heard and understand the thought behind the other side of the peanut butter story. Parents who are put off by the inconvenience of supplying nut-free lunches and snacks every day at school. "My kid will only eat PB and J sandwiches," is something I've heard before.

Well. It is an inconvenience. I'm sorry you might need to find something else for your child to eat at school, but I feel fortunate that my son goes to a peanut-free school. I would really like my son to be alive after lunch period. I want him to live a long, long time. And I'm sure no one wants their child to be responsible for someone else's anaphylactic reaction. That's a lot of guilt for a food choice.

A reaction is a worst-case scenario. Yes. It is. But there are some children (and adults) who really are that allergic. Some who can get very sick from breathing the smell or touching the hand of a child who's been eating peanuts. Are we willing to risk it?

And so, the question: can someone with a food allergy die from kissing someone who has eaten that allergen? I don't know. I certainly hope not. But it has to be possible. While writing *Who I Kissed*, I heard a number of stories from people who had experienced anaphylactic shock from second-hand contact with an allergen.

When I recently had my son retested for allergies, his allergist informed me that a vaccine for the peanut allergy is being developed. I don't know how close the vaccine is, but I hope it comes to fruition. I hope that this story never becomes a reality.

acknowledgments

First of all, I have to thank my favorite son, Max, for allowing me to make up a story based on something that he has to deal with on a daily basis: allergies and asthma. Max also introduced me to the fascinating world of competitive swimming and what it's like to be a swim mom. Maxwell is a great beam of light on this earth, and I hope he shines for a long, long time.

And of course, thanks to all the wonderful people at Sourcebooks who helped bring this story to life. My lovely editor, Leah Hultenschmidt, for giving the go-ahead to write the story and helping me to shape it. I love being a part of the Sourcebooks family and thank Dominique Raccah, Todd Stocke, Kay Mitchell, Derry Wilkins, Aubrey Poole, Kristin Zelazko, and Kelly Barrales-Saylor. Also, thanks to Sean Murray and everyone else on the sales team I haven't met, the wonderful cover designers, and the many people behind the scenes who helped bring this book to life. Special thanks also to my agent, Jill Corcoran, for always looking after me and my stories.

I'd also like to thank Todd Melton, Head Coach of the amazing Foothills Stingrays Swim Club in Okotoks, Alberta, for sharing his thoughts and his tangible passion for swimming with me (and my son). For sharing swim lingo and reminding me that going back after a break would feel "like ass." Also, thanks to swim coaches Thomas South (for *1984*) and Emma Hesterman, who make FSSC the best swim club around. And for giving me a few writing ideas too.

Special thanks to Denise Jaden and Jennifer Laugherty for reading this story in the early phases and helping me find my way. Also, thanks to Kate Messner for words of wisdom about journalism ethics. Thanks to Taryn Albright for helping me understand the way the US swim circuit works. Thanks to Laura Hughes and the contribution of her special name, *Lainoza*.

Lastly, thanks to my husband, Larry, who supports my quirky habits and loves our son just as fiercely as I do. And for always remembering to ask if we have the EpiPen packed.

about the author

Janet Gurtler lives in Calgary, Canada, deliciously close to the Canadian Rockies, with her husband, her son, and a chubby Chihuahua named Bruce, who looks suspiciously like Fredrick. Janet loves to hear from readers and can be reached through her website at www.janetgurtler.com. You can also find her on Facebook or follow her on Twitter @janetgurtler.